The Quarry

A Cal Nyx Mystery

Kim Hunt

Spiral Collectives

A Spiral Collective

c/o 56 Sunglo Terrace

Otaki, Wellington 5512

New Zealand

https://medium.com/spiral-collectives

Cover image: © 2022 Biz Hayman

Cover design: © 2023 Biz Hayman Studio

ISBN: 978-0-473-67561-5 (epub)

ISBN: 978-0-473-67560-8 (paperback)

Contents

For Haymo.

This novel is set in Australia.

Always was, always will be, Aboriginal land.

Chapter 1

Dif. Greyridge Quarry.

A WASH OF LIGHT ran through the gaps in the wattled walls. Odd. Never seen a vehicle on the quarry road at night. Through the openings, distant headlights on the highway strobed through the concrete railings of the bridge. *Well, it's not hoons doing doughnuts in the entranceway—no pebble sprays clattering across the chain-link fencing. And lights, shining across my hut, that vehicle's gotta be inside the compound. Someone with a key to the gates.* Dif pulled back the canvas flap of the hide, stared through the poplar trunks.

The sweep of headlights approached the viaduct, veered off right, flaring across the shining river and rock. Dif climbed from the pallet bed, pushed his feet into his boots, crawled from the lean-to and up the flood-bank to the scrub that edged the road.

A silver pickup truck inched up the slope towards the mouth of the crusher chute twenty metres from where he lay. The truck topped the incline then turned and reversed. *Someone familiar with the layout.* The number-plate, DB-04-BB. Dif muttered the numbers over and over to engrave them into his brain. The headlights switched off.

Dif scuttled across the access road and scrabbled up a gravel pile close to the chute to get a better view. With hands splayed across the rubble he dug his feet in to hold his body in position on the unstable surface.

The driver's door slowly opened, the cab-light softly luminescent. Male, heavyset. The man climbed from the cab, scanned once across the surrounds, then walked to the rear and dropped the tailgate. He dragged something heavy to the lip. Dif heard the effort, breath expelled in a drawn-out grunt as the guy manoeuvred a heavy mass. Something whose path across the deck was muffled, wrapped in cloth perhaps. What the fuck, Dif thought.

The man hunched down, hoisting the mass over his shoulder with a guttural grumble as he steadied his legs. Dif recognised the drooping form of a body in a fireman's carry. The man stutter-stepped to the edge of the great machinic maw, bent his knees then hefted the thing into the void. Dif heard the stifled thud as it landed three metres below on the grading grates of the giant hopper. A gasp wedged in his throat. He pressed his lips together so no further sound escaped, then stretched his head and shoulders to catch another view of the man's face when he opened the vehicle's door.

And that was enough to nudge the rocks and stones supporting his weight into a cascading, raucous avalanche back down the slope. Dif yelped as his body tumbled and whumphed onto the road surface. He rolled, looked up. The figure stared down from the edge of the chute, shining a torch. Dif got to his feet and ran for the scrub of the flood-bank as the beam swept back and forth.

'Hey!' the man yelled, sliding down the gravel slope in pursuit.

Dif took off downstream, away from his hide. He spent every day at the river, knew the changes in the watercourse through the rains and the dry. Two hundred metres south he could pick his way across the shallows. He also knew where the dredging machines had scoured out the rocks and left deep, dangerous channels.

The man crashed through the scrub, falling behind. All the tracks along the flood-bank were easy going for Dif, even in the dark. He slipped down among the poplars and lantana, sliding through the mud and roots onto a dry section of the riverbed, then crouched and ran across the rocky flats, took a quick look behind. The torchlight was still making chaotic sweeps from above the scrub margin. He'd be safe on the other side of the waterway. He reached the final channel—the narrow, deep one before the far bank—slipped into the water and paddled. The water was freezing; it never really warmed except back in the shallows where the sun heated the stony beds. Here the current was mild, a backwash of the main flow. Dif crawled up the other side, using tree roots to haul himself free of the water, lay panting in the shadows as he watched the far bank. The torchlight now arced close to his hide, the light breaking through the slats of his walls. Nothing he could do about that. But he was okay for now.

He breathed measured and deep, flopped back onto his elbows as his limbs untightened, watched the other side of the river.

Eventually the man climbed back up the bank and then the incline to the chute. He closed the tailgate on the pickup, climbed into the cab and drove down the slope. The truck paused at the gate. The driver got out, replaced the bolt and padlock, left as he'd come.

An owlet called from the row of gums beyond the stop-bank. Dif breathed slow and deep, prone in the grass. It was still damp from the water-sprayers that plied the road during the day, the dust held tight for now in muddied recesses and ruts. He lifted his chest, rested on his forearms. Tomorrow morning, amidst the din of stone against metal, gigantic trucks would drop cascading walls of pummelled rock over that same chute edge, tons at a time. What to do? He dropped his head down on his arms. Someone's up to no good. Someone's hurt somebody.

Go and see.

No, too dangerous.

Go and see.

He looked around. Sparse traffic up on the bridge, mostly haulage trucks at that hour. The pickup and driver long gone. He crawled back down the bank and re-crossed the river to his hide. His gear strewn on the dirt floor.

'Bastard,' he muttered. Might not have looked much to that prick, but this was his sanctuary. Or had been.

Anything missing? He turned on the spot. Sort it later. He retrieved a rope and small torch from a tin case emptied out from under his stretcher. Found his knife scabbard still on the pallet rail behind where he slept and shoved it down his boot.

He climbed back up the flood-bank and made his way through the quiet surrounds to the chute. As he walked up the rise, his skin twitched, like his clothes were threaded with prickles.

He got to the edge of the shaft, flicked the torch on, ran the beam across the bundle below. It sagged through the metal gratings, thick as railway tracks. Beside him the iron corner-posts of the safety rail jutted vertically. He tied the rope to the base of the nearest one, pulled on it to test its integrity, then put a foot over the edge. With the torch clenched between his teeth, he began his descent.

His boot-soles scrubbed the rough concrete surface of the shaft walls as he tried to slow his descent through the darkness. The amber torch beam swayed over the wrapped lump beneath him. An instinct made him avoid landing there, on top of it. In the corner to his right a foothold of grating. *Don't fall through.* The rope dug into the flesh of his hands and wrists. *Just get down, get back up.*

The tip of his boot scraped across the narrow metal rail. He settled his foot along its length, still holding the rope until his momentum stabilised. The gap between the gratings was about 300 mm, almost wide enough for a skinny bloke like him to slip through sideways. There'd be no getting out if he fell through into the crusher. No one would hear him when the machines and trucks fired up next morning. Nausea ruffled through his guts. He looped the free end of the rope around his waist and tied it off. When he felt secure, he shuffled his feet apart along the beam, putting in some width for balance. Then, still crouched, he turned to face the wrapped mass beside him.

It was sheathed in a blanket. Rope coiled and tied, held the covering in place. *Jeez, these knots.* Using the tip of his knife, he lifted one edge of the cloth and flicked it back, but a second layer of fabric concealed whatever was underneath.

Oh god. Have to use my hands.

The queasiness created more saliva in his mouth. Returning the knife to its scabbard, he spat through the grating, re-gripped the torch between his teeth and took the cloth between two fingers, tentative, as if something there might bite him. The material was wound underneath, the weight of, well, it was a body, he was sure of it, still hoping not - the head perhaps - pinning the folds. He had to lift it.

He slipped one hand under the curve, and cupped the bulge at the top of the neck above the spine. He grasped the material, walking his fingers, gathering the folds, tugging as the cover pulled back, revealing a face in repose.

A woman. Mid-thirties perhaps, mostly unlined, pale. No bruises or cuts. She could've been sleeping.

Dif cradled her head. He was nearly three metres down a concrete sided shaft. He'd struggle to haul himself back out. The woman was dead, he couldn't help her. Well, he couldn't save her life, but the situation was totally bloody off. She'd been dumped. Killed, accidently or with intent. He couldn't get her out, and in a few hours her body would be mashed and macerated beneath tons of rubble. He needed to take something.

Evidence. Some hair, something. He withdrew his knife again. Her hair was shoulder length, pale. He took a hank in his fingers, was about to slice through. Hair's hair—all the same. isn't it? Need follicles, huh.

'Fuck. I'm sorry,' he whispered as he braced against her forehead with the palm of his hand, tugged at a cluster of strands near the crown of her head. He wound the strands of hair into a lock and put them in his breast pocket.

Maybe he should take something else as well—a piece of the blanket, perhaps. He adjusted the torch in his mouth and dislodged the fabric wrapped across her torso. He sawed at a piece with the blade. Beneath the top layer her body was roped as well. Her hands were near her stomach, her left hand clasped. As he withdrew the blanket sample his light shone across the side of her head. Her earlobe was torn. Barely bloodied—happened after she'd died perhaps.

He hesitated. *Well, mate, if you don't look now it might be lost for good.* He felt through her hair, then behind her collar. What would be the chances? He held her head in one palm as he slipped his fingers down between her cold skin and the fabric of her top. The rope bindings prevented him going further down her back. He ran his fingers across beneath the back of her arm and then he felt it, the hook. He withdrew the earring. A silver filigree thing with a dark stone like a teardrop at the bottom. It could be significant. He placed the earring in the blanket swatch, retrieved the lock of hair and put it in the centre, and folded the fabric envelope over. Slid it all into a pocket of his jacket.

'I'm so sorry,' he whispered again while tenderly re-winding the fabric coverings over her face and head. He patted her shoulder, the top of her chest. His hands trembled. 'Do my best,' he promised the dead stranger before he tugged the rope, checked his pocket again and inched back up the line.

At the top, he undid the cord, stood a moment, gazed across to the bridge. No traffic, no tyre and engine noise, just the river's pacifying ripple. The lights at the quarry entrance cast a broad, faint aura over the dust-laden surrounds. In a half-crouch he made his way back down the ramp, got to the bottom and scuttled into the brush above the riverbank.

Chapter 2

Cal. 10 days later.

IT WAS THE STRANGEST message. A text. Three letters. "OTR." Mysterious enough, but the sender was Dif—Dif Stangler. Cal hadn't seen him in several years. If he'd wanted to meet up, he could've been a bit more up front. Phhtt.

Cal tried to call the number, kept getting the mobile provider drop-out.

She pushed the gate open at her Aunt Zin's old Albany Road address and took a deep breath as she cleared the letterbox. Could she go inside the house? Nope, not ready to face that, just go to the sleep out in the yard. She clasped the pile of junk-mail and a flat package from her tailor, walked down the side path to the back courtyard. Skirted a canvas tarpaulin beside the garage, covering timber she'd bought to build new planter boxes for Zin's courtyard. A birthday present that never eventuated. She clamped her teeth, went to the sleep out.

The door creaked. Dry hinges. Fix that later. She tossed her bag on the wooden chair at the end of her bed and tore open the pack of altered shirts. The ranger uniform sleeves were shortened, the caps tighter to fit close over her biceps, the waists tapered from her broad shoulders. She put the new garments on hangers then picked up the mail, flicked aside glossy flyers for crap and more crap. Threw aside window envelopes. One plain and handwritten, addressed to Zin. Guess I'm her proxy now. She recognised Dif's handwriting. Still, a prickle of guilt, opening her aunt's mail. She bit the corner off the cover, thumbed the top apart. A single page of notepaper.

"Hey Aunty Zin, I need some help, need to get hold of Cal. It's kinda urgent. Please ask her to call me.

Hope you're well. Miss you. X X Dif."

So, either it had been sent before Aunt Zin died or Dif didn't know yet.

Cal had already tried to call Dif but the number was dead. She checked the postmark on the envelope but couldn't make it out. On her keyring she pulled out a tiny magnifier that folded sideways into a casing the size of her thumb. Useful for botanical identification at work. She tried again with the postmark. Greyridge. South coast, just beyond the southern boundary of the Royal National Park. A place from their past.

Cal crossed the room, opened a small cupboard and withdrew a cake tin with hot-rod images embossed on the lid. She lay on her bed with the tin on her stomach, pulled out a wad of old photographs and shuffled through them.

Her and Dif out the front of a small engineering workshop, the pair in greasy overalls, a lowered Ford Escort with the bonnet up. Another of a van and trailer, stopped roadside in a barren, bleached landscape,

Cal replacing a flat tyre, gooning for the camera. Dif must've taken the photo. On the way to pick up a project somewhere. Cal leafed through more pictures and paused. A wide-shot, no one in frame. Just hillside, the ocean in the background. Familiar though, North Coast perhaps? Something in the foreground, hard to make out. The colours had faded with time, even inside the tin, out of the light. She wielded the magnifying glass again, saw a four-strand wire fence with a rag tied to the second strand. The faded remnant of shop-cloth, usually poking from a back pocket for wiping tools or hands. It was their code, tied to the wire when one or other of them was at their hideout.

Up the track on the Durrawan headland, their old fort, the den at One Tree Rock. OTR.

Cal sat up. Dif's text earlier—OTR. It was on the North Coast.

Seems odd this is coming up now. Plainly only something I'd understand. Maybe he's left something there. Maybe he's there too. What the hell's going on?

Dif obviously moved around a bit—lotta miles between Durrawan and Greyridge.

The Ford didn't need another run; if anything, it needed a rest. A rock had hit the cooling fins and started a leak. There's your afternoon's work she thought, drain the radiator, pull it out, get it dropped to a specialist. Aluminium welding wasn't her forte, though with enough practice it could probably be added to her repertoire. Not today though. Hire a car, head north and have a sniff around. Hopefully find Dif and see what the hell's going on before returning to work.

She slumped across the bed and stared out the window. Resting her biker boots heel-to-toe, one on top of the other, she watched a heavy front of formless grey cloud sliding like a slow-closing lid across the sky. She closed her eyes.

Fourteen, back in New Zealand, wagging school. She sees Clive Reid's HQ Holden parked on the street, front wheel mounting the curb. Stepfather in name only. Cal scoots down the side of the house, hears the shotgun blast, the scream and second retort seeming louder in the ensuing silence. Makes herself keep going. Crouch-runs around the hydrangea bushes, and looks through the window. His rounded back silhouetted in the hallway, the shottie's butt raised to his shoulder. She races to the laundry, grasps her baseball bat and hurtles through the back door, bat held high. She can smell the burnt air as she swings it, and slams it into his head. Tears the rifle from his grip as he groans on the floor, the bodies of her mother and sister lying beside crimson pools in the room metres away. Cal pumps the action, the spent shell ejects, and the second round is chambered. Clive Reid rolls onto his back, watches in disbelief as she shoulders the butt and pulls the trigger.

That's right. Never underestimate a Nyx.

Authorities were lining up juvvie foster homes when Aunty Zin in Australia stepped up. Cal's flight across the ditch was followed months later when Dif turned up on the lam, Aunty Zin rescuing him as well.

Cal shook herself, stretched, and drove the Ford into Aunty Zin's garage. Let's unbolt this bastard she thought as she began removing fasteners holding the high-performance radiator she'd installed with the Windsor engine. She wrapped the radiator in protective cardboard and tied it securely leaving it near the back door. She cleaned up, locked the doors and walked several blocks along the main road to a large gas station that rented vehicles.

She hired a Mazda SUV then drove home, replaced the gear in her overnight bag with clean T-shirts and jeans, filled a thermos with coffee, packed her radiator in the rear and headed north.

Three weeks away, yet still so keen to leave Zin's place. The clearing out beckoned in vain. It's not the materiality that's daunting, is it? It's the emptiness—the silent abyss of Zinnia Oslo's absence. So much for the weariness of your recent exile. Now you've got a new focus, another journey. And a further justification for leaving the doors shut on the cottage.

She stopped in Ryde to drop off the damaged radiator then set off again, made north for the coast, heading for Durrawan and One Tree Rock.

Chapter 3

Cal.

FORTY MINUTES THROUGH THE northern suburbs, another twenty on the outskirts. Cal drove through the sandstone walls of a cutting, rounded a bend and finally had a view over a natural landscape. On her left the broad waterway of the Hawkesbury River, a great, flat serpent that meandered through the Marramarra National Park and beyond to the west in a dull, murky ribbon. On her right, glimpses of worn rock escarpment, forest clothing the cliffs that bordered the Pacific Ocean as it swept north.

She pulled into a layby and climbed the low white fence at the top of a bank, sat facing the breeze. Small, choppy white-caps approached the broken coastline. She breathed deep, held the rough timber of the fence-capping behind her, and leaned her body forward, eyeing the ochre-coloured rock below. A kelp gull keened and swooped in the updraft. Effortless. Free-falling.

Behind her right shoulder was the old coast road, a twisting stretch hacked and blasted from the wall of rock. One of her favourite drives, the same highway where she and Dif raced each other returning from their pit-crew duties in the old days.

Those images came strongly, carved through the confusion. Dif in trouble, maybe. Well, he was a kind of magnet for shite at times. So was she to be fair. Still, give the guy a break. He didn't ask for the attention he got.

She squinted into the sky as some of the cloud broke beyond an offshore reef. One Tree Rock, she needed to eyeball the place. Couple more hours' drive at least. She stretched, yawned. Went back to the car, glugged some water down her throat, cupped some more in her hands and ran it through her hair. She started the engine and plugged her phone into the charger. Message from Detective Inspector Liz Scobie of Richmond Command back in Sydney.

-Time for me to issue an APB Nyx?

Cal smiled. First things first. She kicked up some gravel and headed north.

For another hour and a half, she drove. The route familiar and not. Same hinterland on her left, ocean to her right, pristine swathes of new motorway, smooth and landscaped. Lots of road-kill, the poor creatures following the same feeding trails they always had. Now bisected by asphalt and killing machines moving at a hundred clicks.

Her stomach squeezed around vacancy. When had she last eaten? Nuts at the servo. Could grab a bite at the next petrol stop. Remembered a little retro café about forty ks on. She could wait, have a proper meal.

Half an hour later Cal slowed for a T-intersection, made a left and then another into the rear car-park of Angie's Café.

She ordered and sat at a small table beside a window. Outside, a trio of geese emerged from under the trailing, willow-like leaves of a peppercorn tree, two chasing one.

Her food arrived. She ate quickly, stretched back and drained her coffee. Grounded and ready.

She paid and was heading out to the hire car when the growl of a lumpy V8 engine yanked a thread of yearning through her. To one side an iridescent blue Fairlane Compact idled to a stop. She felt a jab of envy, thinking what a great trip this would've been in The Beast, her own old '64 Ford. Climbing into the moulded plastic interior of the Mazda rental, she started the engine, deflated by the lack of noise and absent tremor through her seat. No need for GPS, she nosed out to the entrance and resumed her northwards trajectory. Drove for an hour through shorn grassland dotted with giant scything and rolling machines that were putting in long hours, making the most of the dry.

Close to midday, she approached Durrawan and drove through the edges of the industrial area, crossed rail-lines, passed trucking yards, concrete span fabricators, blistered and faded housing. She crossed the river bridge and took the right-hand fork west, out to the coast and peninsula. A treeless region, nothing but scrub less than two metres high, with the odd patch of taller mangroves around the estuaries. The asphalt gave way to dusty yellow track, unchanged since her last visit years ago.

*

Dif wrapped his blankets around his shoulders, his back against the wall, legs drawn up, protecting his body. Through the gaps in the thatching, he could see the hulking crusher chute, its grey mass lit palely in the ambient light.

Have to tell someone, but I can't go to the police, I can't. How many strikes against that idea? The warrants for starters—stupid, stupid stuff, but enough for them to hold me until a court date. Nup, no cells, not again—not ever. DS Tambor and his nasty little tendencies. Cornered with that thug in my face, him and his stale hamburger breath, hands foraging under my T-shirt.

Vagrancy? Sleeping rough in the horse-paddocks. I just wanted to get out of the rain. Guess none of them have ever been homeless.

Break and enter? Security cameras on that yard. Sure, I flogged a few pipes from the rubbish skip, building materials discarded after jobs. Doing you a favour, mate. C'mon, stuff's already paid for by the client — no loss no foul. Whatever. Yeah, and I got in under the fence, I'd hardly call that a break-in. Anyway, cops don't care, especially the pair under Tambor. Dee-Tek-Tiff Sar-Jent Tam-boooor. Nah, he never gives a let-off warning.

Trespass? Dif Do-gooder, or so I thought, idiot me. Tried to cover that hole in an underground tank, horses there in the old orchards could've broken a leg. How's my luck, dragging that metal plate over when the owner cruises past. Course he went to the cops. Yup, dumb, trivial, but enough to cause strife. How am I gonna pay fines? Hello? And NOOO, I don't need the accumulation of petty incidents or police scrutiny, thanks so very much.

Dif grimaced and dug his fingers through his hair, moving his scalp back and forth like he was trying to dislodge dozens of beestings.

Can't do time inside, no way. Drama, all right. Which jail? Male or female? Wrong one and I wouldn't last a week. Be a death sentence, just like Joey got.

Dif swallowed nails as he remembered his friend.

And now there's warrants for my arrest after missing the first court date. Yeh, thanks for that, kinda hard to receive the notice when you've got no address.

No one's going to listen to me. Who am I? Total insignificant. I'm nobody.

Nah. No cops, no DS Tambor.

I'm on my own.

But he had to do something; he couldn't just sit on that knowledge, what he'd seen. The rego number, dammit, he had to follow that up. And quickly. You can't just go to the registry anymore and get an address that way. Authorities have finally tightened that one up after too many dodgy types using the info for ill. What else is there? What's that online thing when you want to buy a vehicle privately? Get to the library. Whatever, he couldn't stay in the hide. Not now that body-dumping creep had found it.

Dif pulled his swag from the tin locker and began gathering his bits and bobs, such as they were.

He left his hut and climbed through the bush-tracks up to the top camp. No plans to disturb anyone but he needed to know there were friendlies nearby. Under a banyan tree he pulled out a small tarp, sat and drew it around his shoulders. Exhausted, and with the beginnings of a plan, he nodded off, his forehead resting on his knees.

*

When Cal had gone as far as she could eastwards, the road became a T-junction following the seaboard. She took the north track, with the peninsula jutting out into the ocean in the distance. Twenty minutes later she came to a small layby off to her right in the scrub. Enough area to turn a vehicle. There were no other cars around, maybe not surprising mid-week. Did that mean Dif wasn't here either?

Cal took her water bottle, locked the car, and started along the goat track to the head of the cape. The ground was reasonably level, though rocky, as she picked her way. Shortly the trail began to ascend, the crumbling sandstone becoming more unstable and dangerous high above the coast. Cal grabbed clumps of tussock, branches and knobbled roots to hang on as she climbed.

After half an hour, she emerged at the point, a cooling breeze off the ocean welcome in the heat. On a bleak little outcrop of tawny-coloured rock, pitted and scoured by the wind, she sat for a moment and allowed the wind to dry the sweat on her skin. The blue of the Pacific Ocean stretched to the horizon, a barely rippled sheet. Below, a thin strip of pale sand was edged with scrub that rose into bushland at the southern extremity. Same to the north. No man-made structures in sight.

Not quite there yet. When she'd caught her breath, she carried on around the northern tip of the point.

On this side of the headland, the rusted remnants of a wire fence threaded through the scrub and tussock. A relic from a farming operation many decades past. Cal paid particular attention as she made her way through the scrappy vegetation. Then she saw it, hanging limp from the second strand of wire, a faded shred of red bandanna, knotted to the line.

Okay. Looks like confirmation I'm not on some fantasy trip.

Through the scrub she could see their old shelter had long since collapsed. A pair of hardwood timbers criss-crossed against the acacia trunks where they'd fallen, but the makeshift brush roof and walls had decomposed. Cal's mouth formed a wry half-smile. Those days of adventure. Unencumbered, buoyant with hope and possibility.

Their special rock was almost lost now that the one sapling that had inspired the moniker was snapped off inches above the ground, its jagged stump bleached greyish white like a piece of broken driftwood. The rock itself, a small dome about beach-ball size, was mostly submerged in the poor soil. And at the back, among the roots of the long dead sapling, was a smaller, flat stone, the cover of their hidey-hole. Cal put her hand over it, like participating in a child's game she was well beyond. Under the rock, she felt something wrapped in plastic. Inside the bag, a small, flat Champion tobacco tin, its rusty surface pitted. She opened the tin. Inside another packet wrapped in foil. Dif had taken every precaution against the elements and insects. Cal opened the folded foil, found an envelope. She stopped and looked around, like this might be of great import.

She lifted the tab of the cover which wasn't stuck down and squinted inside. A few strands of pale hair, knotted in a circlet. A piece of fabric, maybe from a woollen blanket. An earring of worked silver with a dark stone. It didn't look antique or special in any way. No note, no precious thing.

Well, this was apparently of great significance to Dif. She closed the envelope, replaced the foil wrap, the tin lid and the plastic bag. As she slipped the package into her back pocket she wondered why Dif couldn't look after it.

She was in the middle of nowhere. Half-expecting — hoping — her old buddy would appear around the headland. But she was alone, the rising breeze from off the water rushing past her ears in a hissing gust. A trio of oyster-catchers far below skimmed the shore-break, calling back and forth to each other in high-pitched squeals.

She'd followed her nose here and found something that had presumably been left for her. Surely that wasn't it, job done? She rubbed her arms and wrapped them around herself, exposed on the ridge. *C'mon Dif. I need something more.*

One final look around, and she made her way down the headland.

Back at the hire car she had no phone signal and needed to head back into Durrawan to send a message. She started the Mazda and drove away from the coast.

So, what to do right now? Sure, she had the option of going to Greyridge, but that was a helluva hike south before she'd established Dif wasn't in Durrawan. Why had he drawn her to this place? It was safe for getting something to her. Dif had managed that. Now what?

Her phone rang. Scobie.

'Can't make booty calls on work time, Inspector.'

'Where have you disappeared to, Nyx?'

'Chasing up an old mate. North Coast if you must know.'

'Back in town any time soon?'

'Mmm, maybe.'

'Why don't you pop round later? Let me decide if you're still worth the risk.'

'I am worth it and don't pretend you've forgotten.' Cal ended the call as she entered the main street of Durrawan.

It was late afternoon and 3-4 hours drive if she chose to go back to Sydney. *Dif got me here—surely, he'd make himself visible if he could? How much can I do here in Durrawan at night? And his letter came from Greyridge. The package he left might be the sole result of this trip.*

Something for safe-keeping. Guess I'll learn the relevance when and if I track him down.

Been a kinda bleak and lonely few weeks; be good to see Scobie. If I go back to Sydney today, by the time I get there the radiator workshop'll be closed. Be another trip back out to Ryde to get it. Don't fancy that. Stay put, use tomoz morning to poke around Durrawan. Maybe Dif had some other reason for being here. But surely, he would have waited for me to show at OTR? Nah, maybe not. His cryptic letter to Zin could be weeks old. The text he'd sent was only yesterday though.

She rubbed her hands up and down her cheeks as though the sensation might enliven her.

Up the main street in the small coastal town there were two motels. One, The Oasis, was too close to the pub for a light-sleeper not wanting the serenade of brawling drunks. The Blue Lagoon had rooms further from the highway as well as being distant from the bar. Cryptic name though. The parched surrounds featured empty lots covered in a golden fuzz of desiccated yellow weed-stalks. Vacant paddocks behind the suburban yards included more of the same with the occasional wizened acacia holding a lonely vigil. No azure water features.

Cal paid and collected her key, drove to her room, parked and carried her bag inside. She dumped her gear, slumped on the bed and promptly dozed off.

Two hours later she woke, dehydrated and disoriented. She checked her phone: 7.17pm. She rolled off the bed, drank a tall glass of water at the sink and took a shower.

She dressed in clean jeans and a T-shirt, glanced over the info sheet advertising local eateries and phoned an order for a vegetable massaman curry from a Thai place in the main shopping strip. She pulled on her denim jacket and wandered up the road.

Took her time, scuffing along the dusty pavement, gutters scattered with debris and food wrappers. Every second shopfront held a To Lease sign in its window, some of them lopsided and faded they'd been up so long. Fried food, booze and real-estate businesses always holding their own. Several doors along from the Thai takeaway, a realtor. In the window, hanging beside the grid of ads for properties to sell, a large, framed topographical map of the surrounding district. She found Durrawan and followed the thin line denoting the road out to the coast she'd taken earlier. Moving inland, over the narrow strip of arable land, the small patches of green became non-existent mere inches within the sea-border. The map only contained a chunk of the mid-north coast and yet the distances were enormous. She'd driven inland towards New England years ago, meeting Dif and camping on a property somewhere in that hinterland. It certainly didn't show up within the scale of the current map. Her stomach yawped again as she walked the last couple of metres to the takeaway place.

Cal stood aside from the doorway as a balding bloke in low-slung tracky pants exited with white plastic bags stacked with food containers in either hand. He held the door with his elbow for her.

'Thanks, mate,' she muttered.

She paid for her food and hustled back to the motel, stopping only for a six-pack of beer at the bottle-store. Inside her room she shoved the advertising detritus from the small table and opened the containers. The curry was aromatic, full of fresh vegetables and surprisingly good. She scoffed most of it, kicked off her boots, stretched out on the bed and flipped the top off a Peroni with her pocket-knife. She flicked on the TV remote and picked her phone up, wrote a text. Dee owned the Kurrajong property where Cal rented an old shearer's shed. Bordering three national parks, Kurrajong was close to Cal's ranger work areas.

-I'm nearly back in the 'hood. Got something I need to follow up. Hope to touch base soon. Miss you 'n Banjo. Give him a scruffle from me.

She flicked off the text then wrote one to Scobie, saying she was staying for the night and would be in touch.

She nodded off, remembering a long ago conversation with her aunt Zin.

"Dif needs you Cal. He needs some kind of centre."

"He's OK. Got a cast-iron core."

"Be that as it may, he's untethered, wobbling off the rim. Look out for him. No one else will."

Chapter 4

CAL WOKE AT 5.15AM. A pale light bordered the curtains as she sat up and drank water from a glass on the nightstand, still dehydrated from the hike to OTR the previous day. She got up, filled her glass, drank again then cleaned up and got dressed. She threw her gear into her bag, checked the room and left.

A gas-station perched at the apex of the main street where it met the highway entrance. Fill the SUV, grab a long black and a muffin, she'd be good to go.

As she pulled up beside the bowser her phone rang. She turned off the engine and answered.

'Hello. I'd like to speak with Cal Nyx.' The voice of an older man, well enunciated, privately schooled.

'Speaking,' Cal answered. 'Who is this?'

'My name is Morris Forsyth. I'm the lawyer for Zinnia Oslo. I believe you are her niece?'

Cal took a deep breath, her voice lowered. 'That's right.'

'I'm sorry for your loss. It must have been difficult, the suddenness.' He paused. 'I just have a few things to tie up for completion of her affairs. I wonder if you'd mind coming into our offices. At your convenience, of course.'

Through the windscreen an overcast sky. She searched for a flying bird but couldn't see any above the roof of the service station. Her thumb dug into the faux stitching of the rubberised steering wheel. 'Yes, of course. I'm not in Sydney at the moment. Can I give you my email address?'

'Certainly.'

Cal reeled it off.

'I look forward to meeting you. Your aunt was very fond of you.'

How to respond?

'Well, it was mutual.' Now exposed, she became gruff. 'Be in touch then.'

She ended the call, got out, jammed the fuel nozzle into the filler neck. That's right, Nyx. Where were you at the end? Not at the hospital, eh? Nah. You were chasing that lowlife Craig Dolan through the bush up the Hawkesbury. And what are you doing right now? On some other fool's errand up and down the country. What is your problem, Nyx?

She went inside, paid, got a coffee — no appetite for food — and headed south to Sydney.

Three hours later she stopped in Ryde and picked up the repaired radiator, stashed it in the back of the SUV and drove to Petersham.

She parked in the back lane and opened the garage door. Get the Ford back on the road ASAP, sitting idle and wasted like a thoroughbred out to pasture. She lifted the repaired radiator from the rear of the Mazda and angled it in the light. They'd done a nice job. She rested it against the wall inside the door.

Now for Dif's little treasure. If someone broke into the garage, looking to thieve easily pawned gear, the package had to remain undiscovered.

A series of old toolboxes sat in a row under the workbench. Tools were desirable, so not there. Behind the workshop manuals on the higher shelf? Someone might pull them out. Rubbish bin at the end of the bench? Could get chucked out by mistake.

Cal took a roll of black gaffer tape hanging on a 4-inch nail. Ripped off two lengths and criss-crossed them over the package then crawled under the bench and secured the pack between the base of the bench and the front return.

At the sleep-out she changed into overalls; no point showering until after she'd done the Ford. Back in the garage the car was still up on the ramps, its front end raised to give her access to the lower hoses and mounts underneath. With the radiator beside her on the floor, she lay back on the crawler and slid under the front of the car. Pulled the radiator to her, stood it upright and muscled it into position, using two small woodblocks to support it as she got the mounts aligned and threaded the bolts into place. In less than twenty minutes the radiator was sorted and the pipes clamped. She dropped the car off the ramps, rolled it out through the open door, refilled the system with coolant then started the engine. No leaks, but she needed it hot and up to pressure to be sure. She let it run for fifteen minutes while she made a coffee and sat in the courtyard.

Checked again for leaks. Nothing. Sweet. She let the machine cool while she put her tools away and showered.

She checked and topped up the coolant level again before she went out. Satisfied all was well again with her ride, she dropped the insipid SUV back at the service centre and walked the few blocks home. As she came through the rear gate her phone rang.

Unknown number.

'Cal speaking.'

There was a pause of wind-rush noise over broken speech.

'Say again. Who is this?'

More static, then she caught a croaky voice, words still unintelligible.

'Dif? Is that you?'

'Fuck, --line. --range. Try ag--.'

'All right, mate. Be good to know what's going on. You straightened out?'

'-- after me.'

The connection dropped out. Despite Cal only catching the last two words, Dif's tone was heightened and clear.

He sounded tightly strung and scared witless. She hit the call-back button. It went to voicemail with no message set-up. She tried again. Same result.

Cal closed the gate and stood in the shade of the fence. She tapped her phone against her thigh, then walked to the sleep out and unlocked the door. She pulled her photo tin off the shelf and emptied the contents, looking for a likeness of Dif that might resemble his current appearance. *Not that I can be sure of that.* She chose a couple of images, one showing his face front-on and another showing him full-height. They were both taken in the last decade and were the best she could find.

She cleaned up and took a bit of time with her appearance. Her faded jeans were always fresh, if a little threadbare, ditto her T-shirts or cut-off plaid shirts. Her hair was well-cut but styled into an unruly quiff. She checked her hands again. Working on cars meant there were oil stains that never quite disappeared, no matter how much degreasing goop and nail-brushing she did. Still, she gave them another go, wiped her hands, slung on her denim jacket and left.

As Cal turned into the street that fronted Zin's house, she passed by the park on the corner. Something caught her eye from the small rotunda, like the flashing flame of a cigarette lighter. Probably some kids having a quiet joint in there. She chuckled. She and Dif used to do the same before they went home to Zin's place. Dunno why we worried. Not as though Zin would've been overly uptight about it.

What to tell Scobie since visiting OTR? If something sinister had gone down, something that had sent Dif on the run, then it was potentially criminal in nature. But if Dif hadn't fronted the police, would she be betraying him by confiding in Scobie? I trust Scobie. Doesn't mean it's my call to decide whether Dif might. Tricky. Scobie's an ally and could possibly help, but it's not clear what risk I could be taking with Dif. Keep schtum on the full picture for now — or at least the pieces of the picture that I know, minimal as they are.

It was more than three weeks since she'd seen Scobie. She drove to the nearby suburb, still within the Inner West and parked in the back lane. On the balcony of Scobie's Alexandria apartment, one of the pale curtains ballooned in the open doorway. Cal unlocked the back gate and climbed the stairs in double-bounds. The door opened as she got to the top.

Scobie stood with one hand languid on her cocked hip. Her gaze direct, a small smile lifting one side of her mouth. Cal stepped towards her and slipped an arm around her waist, pulling Scobie into her. They kissed as Cal backed Scobie down the short hallway. They made it as far as the living room couch... the floor-rug... the couch again.

Later, Cal held a Peroni while Scobie had a glass of wine beside her as they sat cross-legged on the floor in Scobie's living room.

'So, fruitful trip up north?' Scobie asked.

'Kinda. More damson plum than Bowen mango.'

Scobie blinked, smirked.

'Mate of mine got in touch, then disappeared. Felt I owed a bit of effort to follow it up.'

'Lucky mate.'

Cal looked towards the ceiling. 'More family really.'

Scobie paused before speaking, her voice gentle. 'Family?' she asked.

Cal looked at her. 'Yeh. Sorta foster-brother. Aunty Zin took Dif in not long after me. We were thick as.'

'You've never mentioned him.'

Cal looked away. 'We kinda ... drifted apart.'

Scobie gave a small nod, remained silent.

'Last I knew he was living rough down south. I'm gonna check a few places out.'

'Why were you up north then?'

Cal hesitated. 'He sent me there.' It sounded lame. 'I'll explain another time. But he wrote a note to Zin and it came from down south. He doesn't know she's dead.'

Scobie nodded.

Cal got up, stood behind Scobie, bit the back of her neck. The warm, citrus and vetiver Scobie scent. The woman's pheromones were like gelignite. Cal opened her jaws, bit harder. 'C'mon.'

Scobie made a small, involuntary, guttural moan. 'Won't be distracted, Nyx.'

Next morning Cal woke early, realised where she was and rolled closer to Scobie. Not yet ready to rouse herself. Weak light filtered through the large north-facing windows, and she dozed with her arm around Scobie's waist.

She woke again when her phone rang. Could hear Scobie in the shower as she picked up. Unknown number.

'Cal speaking.'

'Oh. It's Myra Neufeld. Your aunt gave me this number. I live next door.'

'Yes, of course, Myra. What's up?' Zin's long-time neighbour had never rung her before.

'I'm so sorry to bother you. But Zinnia's side window is smashed, by the path. I don't know when it happened. I sleep on the other side at my place. I hope no one has broken in. But I don't think it was the wind.' The woman's voice tremulous.

'I'd better check it out. Can pop round now. Lucky you caught me; I'm heading off down the coast. Don't worry Myra, I'll sort it. You keeping well?'

'I'm fine, Cal. Aside from missing Zinnia. I'm sure you do too. She was a lovely neighbour.'

'Yup. A lot to miss.' Didn't mention she'd been unable to enter the house thus far. 'Thanks for letting me know, Myra. I'll do what I can meantime.'

Cal got dressed, knocked on the bathroom door and called to Scobie, 'Neighbour of Zin's says a window is smashed. Gonna check it out. Call you later.'

'Okay, hun.'

Cal warmed the Ford up outside Scobie's apartment then drove from Alexandria over to Petersham. She parked out the front as she wasn't staying long. From the street, the window frame hung ajar from the side of the house. Cal walked slowly along the side access-way, noting shards of glass on the concrete. Probably more inside. And was someone in there still? What damage would greet her? *You have to go in.*

Maybe Dif was responsible? But he knew where the spare keys were hidden. And surely he would've let Cal know if he was in Petersham. Nah, couldn't be Dif.

She walked to the back courtyard, unlocked the garage and sorted through a stack of timber offcuts resting on brackets against the back wall. A section of ply looked promising. She grabbed her driver-drill, a box of long square-drive screws and a pencil before returning to the outside window. She held the ply up to the frame. Bit wide but the length was fine to cover the damage. Marked her cut with a pencil, went back to the garage, where she trimmed the excess with a quick sweep of her circular saw. Clutching a small set of aluminium steps under her arm, she hooked the claw of a hammer over the waistband of her jeans and returned outside with the timber. She climbed the small ladder, used the hammer to knock out all the loose and jagged shards of glass still embedded in the edge of the frame. Positioned the piece of plywood over the timber mount.

A voice called. 'You don't let the grass grow.'

Cal twisted around. Myra Neufeld craned her neck above the side fence.

'Hi, Myra. Just a temporary fix. I'll re-glaze it when I've got more time.' Cal held the ply, drove the first screw into the frame, then another. Turned back to her neighbour now she could drop her arms.

'Have you been inside? Anything missing? Any damage?' Myra asked.

'Bit of a hurry Myra. I'll check it next time. Reckon whoever did it is long gone.'

Cal drove in four more screws, two on each side. The roof eaves were deep enough that the window was weatherproof. She climbed down from the ladder.

'Thanks for getting in touch, Myra. Let's have a cuppa when I'm back. Sorry, gotta be somewhere.'

'Okay, Cal. That'd be nice. I'd like that.'

Cal took her tools back to the garage as a pall of guilt draped her shoulders. *What is your fucking problem? You're not that bothered about intruders, are ya? Least you can see them, have a go at them if necessary.*

Fact is, the idea that a burglary or damage might have occurred is secondary. Zin's house, her property, even now she's dead, just highlights your negligence. Not at the hospital when you could've been Nyx. Your choice. Live with it.

She locked the shed, got in the Ford and accelerated out of Petersham, scattering dust and rubber in her wake.

Chapter 5

Dif.

BEFORE IT WAS LIGHT, Dif boiled water on his camp-stove and made tea. He pulled his cleanest shirt from his swag, slicked his hair back with water and put a small notebook and pencil in his pocket. The walk to the township of Greyridge was about three kilometres.

As he was leaving, he heard the rumble and rattle of several early quarry trucks driving down the hill from the highway. From the hillside where he'd spent the night he looked below towards his old camp by the river. The ramp of the crusher chute emerged in the pre-dawn, its dull, rust-pocked sides towering over the gravel mountain below. He turned away, put his hands in his pockets and strode out along the narrow bush track, damp grasses slapping at his boots. His knuckled fists pushed against the random nails and grit in the bottom of his pockets.

Ten minutes later, he emerged from behind screening trees beside the main road, his body stooped against a veil of drizzle, grey jacket billowing. He followed the edge of the road for several dozen metres then turned onto the road up the headland and into town. He passed the old orchards and horse paddocks where he'd covered the hole in the underground tank. Hope that mare is okay he thought swiping at the tiny drops of moisture that swirled in the air, gathering on his skin, his shoulders, his eyelashes.

He made one stop before the library. Crouching in the lighted doorway of a gift-shop, he pulled out his notebook and pencil, wrote a message, tore out the page and folded it. He crossed the street in the semi-darkness and approached the police station, which wasn't yet open. He shoved the note under the front door and scooted away.

When Dif arrived at the library, his shoulder-length hair hung in drippy strands behind his ears. He held the front door open for an elderly woman with a walker, its seat ajar like a baby bird's mouth, gaping with books. Dif smiled, his stained teeth and grime-streaked cheeks receiving a nod and smile in return. He walked to the computers at the rear of the library and waited. Without utility bills or a legitimate address he couldn't get a library card. Someone had to finish their own search with time still in credit. A young boy in school uniform, shoeless, hoisted his backpack and abandoned his seat. Dif took over, and tried an internet search using the rego number he'd memorised.

A bit of minor information about the vehicle specs, odometer readings. There was no way for him to access the owner's address. Probably to do with privacy laws. The owner had to be selling the vehicle and Dif would need that name and a driver's licence number. No ownership history from the transport agency, unless he was an authorised business entity. He wasn't.

But he might know someone who was.

Before he left he made one more online search. Should be safe on a public computer he thought as he typed in Crimestoppers. He read the instructions for making an online tip. Two bullet points halted him; personal details and contact details.

'No way,' he muttered. I thought it was anonymous. They must be out of their minds.

He followed further prompts without actually filling in any information. Huh. So, it's optional to put that personal info to be passed onto police. Not doing it. And I'm not using my phone, even if I had credit. How can you trust them?

The session timed out and he left the library.

*

Cal headed directly out of town, south on the B33, planning to hit the A1 at Heathcote. Greyridge was north of Wollongong. Maybe have a poke around there before venturing into the community services offices located in the larger town to the south. Greyridge was the place postmarked on Dif's letter to Zin so he must've been there for some reason. Surely, he hadn't simply passed through the place? Probably lived there in some format for more than a day or so.

Now that Cal had her photos of Dif other rough sleepers in Greyridge or Wollongong might be able to offer clues as to his whereabouts or places he'd stayed.

It took over an hour to get beyond the endless stop-start of traffic lights beyond the Inner West. The old Ford was a machine geared with long-legs and it liked to stretch. As soon as Cal hit the freeway south, she floored the throttle and let the engine breathe. She thought of early days with Dif, her introduction to engineering, school days in New Zealand.

Cal had nudged Dif. 'Get ready for some competition.'

'He let you in?'

'Once a week, elective class.' The tutor an old guy from Sheffield.

'That's a start.'

'Think my copper work blew him away,' Cal said.

'Coolios. Come and help me on the weekend. I'm dropping a Cortina motor in the Prefect.'

'Good practice. Gonna wedge a Transit engine into a lowered Anglia. Just saving my pennies.'

The highway swept along the high escarpment just inland of the coast. The forest there was mostly low scrub, still recovering after the last lot of bushfires.

Twenty minutes later Cal peeled off the highway towards Greyridge, an old settlement on a plateau above an estuary and wetland.

She drove under a rail bridge and parked on a scraped-out moonscape that looked like an army ordnance detonation site. Random mounds of concrete slab sprouting cockroach legs of rusted reinforcing littered the flat areas. Truckloads of rock spoil and blasted chunks of construction waste joined the composition. Domestic discards including swollen and peeling particle-board furniture, black plastic rubbish bags and garden waste decorated the margins where dumpers were less likely to get their vehicles bogged. A free-for-all option for those who couldn't or wouldn't pay at the local refuse site up the coast.

Cal parked, grabbed a water bottle and negotiated her way through the piles towards the undulating tracks that disappeared through the mountainous tailing knolls, now covered in scrub and weeds. This was where Dif had raced in motocross events years before. Cal used to go along and help with the incessant repairs required over an afternoon's events. Not quite the fearless rider that Dif was, Cal could at least follow instructions and hand over the correct spanner.

The walking track climbed, following an old chain-link fence that eventually ran down the hill to the wetland.

Cal stood at the top of the hill and viewed the old quarry. Still a working entity sited near the northern bank of the river, but down across the marshland and coast there were changes. A series of humpies were dotted amongst the scrub beside a lagoon just off the side of the beach. Rough sleepers, maybe? Further back, less than five hundred metres away on higher ground, was a cul-de-sac of massive new houses.

Along from the lagoon and beach above the opposite shore of the estuary was the older part of the settlement. It covered the northern headland, closer to the beach but protected from the quarry noise and traffic by the river valley. It all looked much the same. The wetland below her was criss-crossed with tracks like those through a terraced rice-paddy. They ran to either side of the wetland and up the hills, above or below the surface depending on how much standing water filled the marshes.

Cal remained on the hillside, turning back the way she'd come and re-crossed the dumpsite into a copse of native fig trees that ran along a low ridge. The tree branches spread and hung low, almost touching the ground in places. It was like entering a cavern, a dark, open space encircled by the drooping outer branches of the fig trees. Beneath the canopy, a pair of old plastic chairs had been placed at a large wooden cable spool set on its flat side like a table. Beside one of the tree trunks a bundled blue tarp was stashed as if someone had tidied their camp before leaving. There was no rubbish or food waste lying around. It was like she was encroaching on someone's home.

Beyond the fig trees she veered out of the track onto another that travelled down to the wetland but on the opposite bank. The main quarry site was slightly inland from there. The grind and clatter of the machinery carried on the wind. Huge moveable conveyor belts carried crushed rock up a tower where curtains of gravel fell into giant mounds. Gigantic yellow haul-trucks carried dredged gravel from the old river flats or climbed the tracks up the lower escarpments where rock was shattered free from the walls with explosives and delivered down to the crushers. The noise was horrendous close by. The drivers must have soundproof cabs.

Cal walked back to the dumpsite where she'd parked and whipped out her phone for a quick search of social service agencies in Wollongong. She found a couple of foodbank and referral centres run by church groups and drove south to check them out.

Fifteen minutes later she left Squires Way and headed inland from the streets of garish apartment blocks sheathed in reflective glass above the coast. Within three blocks the picturesque frontages had become boarded-up or vacant windows, makeshift fencing across empty lots and shattered, rubbish-filled kerbsides. The 'Helping Hand' Christian support was a single front with a recessed alcove and doorway. A guy in bib-and-brace overalls cleaned the front window with a squeegee in one hand and a tea-towel in the other. He turned and smiled at Cal's greeting, his four front upper teeth missing.

Inside was a long, narrow room without partitions. At the front of the room a low, chipped veneer counter held piles of curling printouts. Behind the counter was a desk and computer, but no sign of life. Midway down the room a cluster of mismatched, empty armchairs were formed in a circle. Beyond them were trestle tables stacked with boxed and canned foodstuffs. Several women were chatting and filling cloth bags and cardboard boxes with packages of food. Behind them a rear door stood open.

'Good morning.' A bright voice.

Cal turned back to the counter where a woman had appeared from hiding. 'Power plug came out. All good now. Makes a change from the overload-switch tripping.' She had curly brown hair and stratospheric eyebrows.

Cal smiled. 'Wondered if you could help. Old friend of mine, might've been sleeping rough round here.' She slid her photos of Dif across the counter.

The woman—Marjorie, according to her name-badge — peered closely at the images. Her smile receded; she shook her head. 'He's missing? Yes?' Her eyes went up to Cal's.

Cal nodded.

'Not familiar to me. I'll just ask the other girls.' She took the pictures and walked to the far end of the room. Cal watched the shaking heads, the glances her way. Marjorie came back. 'I'm so sorry. Can't help.' She handed the images to Cal.

'Anywhere else I should ask round here? Other services like yours?'

'We're the only foodbank, dear. The rough sleepers usually do the rounds of all the help services. Even if they're just passing through. We'd be one of their first stops. Have you tried the Vinnies Van?' She smiled gently.

Cal shook her head.

'They do dinners five nights.' She reached under the counter, passed Cal a flyer with a time schedule. The van moved around several stops in the early evening during the week. Wollongong, Albion Park, Bellambi.

'Okay. Thanks.' Cal kept the flyer and left. Worth a try.

So, a basic service like the foodbank wasn't familiar with Dif. Was it possible he'd been staying with someone down there, not living rough at all? Was it possible Dif was only there for some specific purpose? And if so, how did that run him into trouble? Or had he come south because of the trouble, whatever it was? Early days, keep an open mind. Talk to the folks on the Vinnies Van. She could do that tonight. Then back to Greyridge, start sniffing around there again and try and catch some local rough sleepers. Night-time or early morning; hopefully she could find them in their doss spots at the quarry and estuary. Ask some questions, do what she'd done there in the Gong, see if it led anywhere.

She'd missed a call from Scobie while she was on the headland. No service out there. Scobie hadn't left a message.

Cal tried to call back but it went to voicemail.

Then her phone rang. Dee. Cal pulled over, knowing it must be important.

'Dee, what is it?'

'Sorry, Cal. I thought you'd want to know. It's Banjo. He ripped his side open on something when he was out gallivanting in the paddocks. May have been a broken wire in the long grass. I've had to stitch him up. Hoping there won't be infection. I've got him under sedation in the surgery.'

'Jesus. Poor bugger. Sorry you're dealing with it on your own, Dee. You okay?'

'Yeh. Kinda weird working on your own animal. Just had to put it out of my head. Simone, one of the vet nurses, came in to help me. She's so sweet. That spread the load.' One of the horse-mad local teens, Cal figured. They sometimes helped Dee with feeding out and meds when she was stuck elsewhere on a job. Cal had done it as well on occasion.

'Well, he's got the best of care for sure. Give him a gentle squeeze from me. I'll get there when I can. Soon. I'll let you know. Lotsa love.'

Cal drove into the Wollongong city centre, parked then walked to the Vinnie's Van at the railway station. She waited on the steps of an adjacent building, not wanting to interrupt the busy staff, or the hungry folk who'd turned up for a meal.

She enjoyed the warmth of the stone steps, now out of the harsh light but slowly releasing the heat stored within during the day. What if she didn't see Dif again? What if something terrible had happened? Don't even go there. But it was a possibility. Zin had been her last blood relative. Had she left it too late to reconnect with Dif?

The queue at the van had dribbled away. Some were leaving with their food while others sat on nearby benches and ate.

Cal sidled up to a pair on a bench. The man looked about seventy, in tracky dacks and a torn flannel shirt. His skin was dark and grimy with an oily sheen. A pair of grazes had scabbed on his left cheek. The woman with him was younger with lank, stringy hair. Below her eyes hung demi-moons of bruised flesh that made her look inordinately tired, but her eyes were bright and shiny.

'Good grub?' Cal said.

The pair both smiled.

Cal held out the picture of Dif. 'Old buddy of mine. Got in touch with me but I've not been able to find him. Might have been staying near Greyridge. Familiar to you?'

'Diffo,' the old guy said straight away, holding the photo in a palsied tremor.

The woman leaned in and nodded confirmation.

Cal waited, eyebrows raised.

'Know the estuary at Kaiung?' The old guy used the shortened name for the river. His eyes were cloudy and thickly opaque. Could he actually see her or was simply speaking in her direction? But he had positively identified Dif, and she hadn't mentioned Dif's name.

'Yeh, I know it,' Cal said.

'Other side. Not where the camp is. Other side near the quarry.'

'Good fella. Helps people.' The woman pulled out a tobacco packet and retrieved a thin cheroot that had been lit before and extinguished.

'Seen him lately?' Cal asked, her eyes going from one to the other.

'Nah, actually.' The old bloke looked to the woman beside him.

'Must be coupla weeks now. He'd be here, ay Jim?' The woman looked to the old bloke.

'Mostly stayed up there. But we'd see him at least one night at the van. Bit of a hike coming down to the Gong. He'd get supplies and head back.'

'Social coming here.' The woman lifted her head towards the van where the two staff were packing up. 'We all have a yarn, catch up. Diffo was a regular. Not every night or nothin', but weekly—ay, Jim?'

'You know anyone who might know where Dif would've gone? Anyone at Greyridge I could ask?' Cal said.

The pair answered simultaneously: 'Truby.'

'E's bin there longer'n anyone. Got a camp down below the toffs,' Jim said.

Cal asked, 'The new subdivision?'

'Yeh. Trube's like the captain of the camp. Not the boss or nothing. But he knows stuff. People go to him first,' the woman said.

'There all the time, is he? If I wanna talk to him?'

'Pretty much,' Jim said.

'Did you notice any change in Dif before you last saw him?'

Jim pouted in contemplation.

The woman frowned a little. 'I thought 'e was a bit ... mmm, ragged looking.'

Jim nodded in confirmation.

The woman continued, 'It's hard to look tiptop when you're sleeping rough. But Diffo always went to trouble.'

'Wasn't quite himself last I saw. 'Ard to put ma finger on why,' Jim said.

'Know whatcha mean. Something rattled 'im,' the woman said.

Cal frowned. 'Can I leave you my number, in case you see Dif? You mind getting in touch?'

'Giv'us a couple dollars for the phone, ay. No one's got mobis.' Jim held his hand out.

Cal wrote her number on an old petrol receipt and handed Jim a tenner. 'Thanks for your help, 'preciate it,' she said.

As Cal walked away her phone buzzed. Scobie.

'Hey, how's tricks?'

'I've been better, to tell you the truth. You have a minute to talk?'

Cal could hear the lack of levity in Scobie's voice. She stopped what she was doing. 'Of course. Fire away.'

'I've got to go to Melbourne. There are problems with Mads' new bub. Imogen's in an incubator and Mads wants to stay with her, of course. Joe can't take time away from work. Ginny's only three. My mum has her hands full with Dad...' Scobie was breathless.

'Hey, I'm so sorry to hear all that. Anything I can help with?'

'Thanks, Cal. Don't know how this is going to pan out but I need get down there. While it's acute anyway.'

'Anything I can do, just ask. Take care.'

'I'll be in touch.' Scobie ended the call.

Chapter 6

AFTER DIF'S FRUSTRATING ONLINE search he left the library and walked along the main street in Greyridge until the shops petered out. At an intersection with a side road a double storey wooden building stood on the corner. Having seen better days, its careworn livery belied its heritage, pre-freeway inland. Like a nostalgic diorama the petrol bowsers no longer pumped fuel, but the forecourt and service bays still served a purpose. Around the side of the building the retired owner, Ely Wolgers, worked on his own pet projects and entertained similarly time-rich comrades. Dif wandered through an open side-gate and found Ely with another elderly man hunched over the engine bay of a '34 Ford coupe. A third bloke leaned out from the driver's seat.

'Try it again?' the driver called.

Ely tipped petrol into the open carburettor throat from a soft-drink bottle and gave a thumbs-up as he leaned back. The starter motor burred and the engine fired, coughed and sent flames from the open throttle body.

'Ely,' Dif called.

Both men at the engine bay turned. Ely clapped Dif on the shoulder.

'Just the fella I need.'

'Oh, yeh?' Dif pouted.

Ely handed the bottle to the other man, then guided Dif towards the workshop. 'Tiny welding job. Can't let you go 'til you've seen it. You're an elusive fella.'

On a cleared bench, a series of machined alloy linkages were laid out.

'Not my strength, Dif. Can you do it?'

'Course. I actually need a favour, Ely. Do you a swap?'

'Anything.' Ely made an expansive gesture with his arms, stretching the faded plaid of his shirt.

'You still have access to DMV?'

Ely drew back a little. 'I'm registered, yes. Helps with buying and selling. Checking stuff's legit. They've changed the name again. Transport NSW or something now. Can't keep up.'

'Look up an address for me? I've got the rego.' Dif's voice was scratchy.

'Okay, mate. All kosher, is it?'

Dif puffed air from his nose. 'Yeh, mate. Promise.' He wrote down the number, handed it to Ely and walked over to the MIG welding kit. He took off his coat, fingered his hair behind his ears. Muttered to himself. 'Shielding gas, argon. Check.' Adjusted the settings on the machine. 'Direct current. Check. Reverse polarity settings. Check.' He lifted the hand-piece and flipped down the mask.

Fifteen minutes later with the name and address he needed, Dif crossed the road and walked to the other end of the main street, stood beyond the shops on the road south and stuck his thumb out.

Brent Coswell, the pickup owner, lived at 47 Emu Crescent, Stockton. About a thirty-minute drive inland but a ways off for Dif without wheels. Most of the traffic would be heading to Wollongong down the coast, not inland. Still, he had to get onto things. Hopefully the police would soon start their own inquiry. *Still. Not waiting around for those idiots.*

It took forty-five minutes to get his first lift. A truck driver with a container-load of white-ware heading for the Gong picked Dif up and dropped him twenty ks later at the turnoff inland to Stockton.

Dif waited another thirty minutes for a Stockton ride. A pair of plumbers in a pickup pulled over and he climbed in the small doorway behind the cab. He shared the seat with a red-heeler and a mass of torn and spat-out burger wrappers.

Twenty minutes later they dropped Dif beside a strip-mall in Stockton.

*

Detective Sergeant Lyle Tambor saw a familiar figure disappearing down the dim street as he turned up at the station and parked around the back.

'Fuckin freak,' he muttered fingering the keypad and entering the rear door. He flicked on lights and walked past the bathrooms and holding cell to the side offices and front desk, flipped the computer on, left his coffee there, and used the keypad to open the staff door. He went through to the public entrance doors and unlocked them and set the auto switch. On the floor beneath the doors, a folded note. Nice start. What would this one be? Death threat from the family of someone he'd nicked. Embittered neighbour dobbing in the next doors? He went back to the desk, pulled nitrile gloves from a box, returned to the front entrance and picked up the note and read it.

"I saw a body dumped at the Greyridge Quarry. In the big gravel hopper top of the ramp by the entrance. I got the rego number of the ute. DB-04-BB. Please follow this up.

Signed, a concerned citizen."

Must've been that Stangler he saw on the street earlier. Who else would see something in the quarry at night? What a fuckin joke. She/he calling itself a citizen. Drug-fucked fantasist, wasting our time. He screwed the note in his fist, was about to toss it in the bin, then he shoved it in his pocket. He went to his office, grabbed his coffee and fags and went out the back door.

Under an old magnolia tree, he lit a ciggy and drew hard as he watched smoke drift up through the branches. Was this what Vic Lasprilla had been hinting at? He withdrew the note from his pocket, flattened the paper on his arm as he remembered the recent conversation with the entitled prat. That and the extra fat envelope Vic had left for Tambor inside the newspaper.

'Anything odd happens in the next fortnight, don't dig too deep, huh?'

Maybe the freak did actually see something. Lasprilla was more ruthless than Tambor had realised. Keeping this under his hat could be worth a bit, and then some. Stangler wasn't a problem; he had the odd-ball's measure. And now he had some weighty dirt on that silver-tail Lasprilla. Life was on the upswing.

Tambor memorised the rego number, then struck his lighter, touched the flame to the paper and held the corner until it became an insubstantial tracery of grey.

Chapter 7

CAL DROVE BACK UP the coast. She stopped at a supermarket and stocked up on torch batteries and some snack foods before she returned to the Greyridge camp area. Rough sleepers didn't necessarily hang around their camps all day, but come dusk, especially as it got colder, they would certainly be wanting to hunker down. It was almost full moon, but if it became overcast later, Cal didn't want to be negotiating unfamiliar tracks in darkness.

In her urban digs, on her way to bed at night, she often stood at a window staring at the moon and night sky with a longing that drew on her with a pull as ancient and tensile as spider-web. When she lived away from artificial light-sources she developed a different kind of vision. Moving through scrub and forest using moonlight was magical, primal perhaps. She had to do it occasionally on nocturnal work projects and found the experience unique, precious and probably alien to many city-dwellers.

The camp site was on a small plateau beyond a brackish lagoon that emptied into the ocean only during flood-times. Rather than negotiating the hill track from the top and having the flooded marsh to deal with at the bottom, something she might have attempted in daylight, Cal parked instead near the estuary on a small coastal road. She made her way along a bumpy track that wound through the rocks above the high tide line. Dog-walkers and surfers used it to access the water. Once on the sand it was a lot safer and easier to approach the camp.

As the sun set behind the escarpment, Cal could hear dusk birdsong, but no cricket or frog noise — winter was truly setting in. A deep-orange glow tinged the treeline above, but the lower foreground was becoming dark. She smelt campfire smoke, some scrub-wood, some driftwood, burning salts in the timber with that stale, acrid tinge. She walked the edge of the lagoon and followed a side-track that curled through the low scrub, could see firelight and hear voices as she got nearer.

She called the bushman's greeting as a polite heads-up of her approach. 'Coo-eee.' A whoop at the end, to make it gentle.

The voices stopped.

Several structures made of wooden pallets and tarps formed a semi-circular compound. Three men sat on upturned milk crates beside a fire.

'Sorry to disturb you guys. Looking for a friend of mine. Some fellas at the Vinnies Van said to ask for Truby.' She didn't approach further.

A tall, black-bearded guy with a faded Mexican blanket across his shoulders stood. 'Who's askin?' Not unfriendly.

'Cal Nyx. I'm looking for an old mate, Dif Stangler. He got in touch, but I haven't been able to get back in contact. Seems he was down this way though.'

The tall guy stepped forward. Cal offered her hand, and he took it.

'Truby,' he said. 'You're a mate, are ya?'

'Kinda family. His note sounded a bit desperate. I went up north looking for him. Now I'm down here. Spoke to Jim and a woman at the Vinnie's Van. They said Dif definitely stayed at Greyridge but they hadn't seen him lately.'

Truby lifted his chin in acknowledgement. The other two by the fire, both older looking, remained silent, watched.

Cal continued, 'I had a wander up top. There was a camp under the banyans...'

'Cobb's place,' one of the other men said. He wore a battered and stained felt hat. His beard was grey, plaited into a single strand.

'Yeh, Cobb's place. Not up fer grabs,' the other sitting bloke said. He was beardless but unshaven. His age indeterminate but his face had the ruddy bloom of alcoholism, his skin dark and taut with bloating, his nose thick and misshapen with old fractures.

Cal held her hands up, smiled.

Truby spoke again. 'Dif's camp was on the other side of the river, up near the quarry. You'll have to go right around, cross the bridge.'

'Okay. Any of you fellas seen him lately?'

''E got the willies 'bout somethin'. Took off,' Plaited Beard said.

'Think 'e mighta been back on the dak 'n the piss,' Broken Nose said.

Truby blinked and gave a small nod. 'Reckon something got to 'im.'

'Or someone,' Plaited Beard said.

'Any idea what?' Cal said.

They shook their heads.

'Any of you have phones?'

The three laughed.

'Storey's got one.' Broken Nose hooked a thumb at the guy beside him. 'No credit but.' He laughed with a grating croak.

Storey pulled an ancient Nokia from his pocket. 'Wi-Fi at the library. WhatsApp's free. Nowhere to charge it out 'ere.' He waved his phone at the sky and the three of them broke into guffaws.

Cal smiled, shook her head. 'Can I leave my number? Just in case. You might hear something from someone else.' She scribbled on another bill receipt. 'On the off-chance.' She handed the note to Storey. 'Thanks. I'll be off then. Enjoy your evening fellas.'

'He stayed at the caravan park once when he was crook,' Storey said.

Cal stopped, turned back. 'The one at Bidgee?'

'Only one north of the Gong. Nex' one's down Nowra.'

'Thanks, guys.'

The sky was clear out over the ocean, but a bank of cloud had accumulated against the escarpment. She made her way back to where she'd left the Ford. Decided to leave her recce of Dif's old digs until the morning, leaned on the roof of the car and called Dee.

'How's the boy?'

'He's stable for now. Tough old coot that he is.'

'Yeh. Guess he's survived worse.' The accident that had brought him into Dee's care in the first place, a mangled foreleg that had to be amputated. 'And how are you holding up? You've got a bit extra on your plate at the mo.'

'Yeh, I'm just busy. It's probably a good thing. Be lovely to see you and catch up.' Cal could hear the weariness in Dee's voice, slow and lacking energy. Dee continued. 'No pressure. Sounds like you've got your hands full too. Take care Cal. I'll keep you posted so don't worry about him too much.'

'Okay, mate. I wanna see you both. I'll get there soon. Just a couple more things down here to check.'

Too bad she didn't have her work truck; could've slept under the canopy in the rear. You're on leave she reminded herself. Don't need to look too presentable; not like you're representing your service. She decided to sleep there in the car. She retrieved a plaid blanket from the boot, climbed in and rolled her seat back almost horizontal. Cracked her front windows an inch for fresh air and lay back. Maybe it was talking to those rough sleepers, maybe she was just feeling a bit adventurous. She still had the luxury of protection from the elements; it wasn't like she was doing it tough. Tomorrow morning she'd check Dif's camp and the campground. She closed her eyes, embraced by the sound of the ocean heaving into the rocks below.

Chapter 8

CAL WOKE BEFORE SUN-UP, wandered to a public loo block across the point and splashed icy water over her face and hair. She headed back to the car, drove up towards the escarpment and through the cluster of Greyridge shops, stopped for a takeaway coffee and took the northbound road which crossed the Kaiung River. On the other side she drove down to the older part of Greyridge, a washed-out suburb on the headland.

The road to the quarry came off a car-park terminus near the shore. The access was open during the day for the trucks that served road crews and construction sites. At night a tall gate was padlocked, preventing entry up that side of the river.

She parked in one of the bays near the beach. No shading trees but it was cool, a south-east breeze coming in from the ocean. She walked towards the quarry.

Inside the main gate the road split; one road went to the actual excavation and crusher site and barred entry except for authorised users. The other was a public access to the bush trails on that side of the river. Dusty signs warned of heavy machinery operating. According to Truby and co at the camp the previous night, the strip of scrubland between the quarry access and the river was where Dif had his camp. The bush strip was less than ten metres wide but quite dense in places so there were few breaches except where determined clearings had been made to access the water. Tangled lantana wove through the native acacias and pretty much obliterated everything.

Cal walked several hundred metres along the outer edge of the bush before she realised, she must have gone too far. A pair of water dragons basked in the morning sun on a twisted metal railing that protruded from the scrub. Be going into their partial hibernation any day now she reckoned. She turned to go back, this time searching more closely. A water truck drove past on the main road above, spraying to keep the dust down. Cal peered into the criss-crossed branches beside her, looking for signs of Dif's camp, and was almost back where she began when she found it.

The scrub in front was intact, a green wall. Two rusting tin cans at ground level among the weeds gave it away. Like the flats used on a stage, the entrance to Dif's site was hidden behind two parallel layers of vegetation and she had to ease sideways between them. Could smell the broken lantana stems as she edged through the entry and into the tiny clearing beyond, completely invisible from outside.

The site had been trashed. Dif wouldn't have left it that way. She toed through the empty tin cans and fire ash. Righted an old wooden beer-crate with a folded coffee sack for cushioning and sat down, staring at the humble surrounds. Some might have seen it as dereliction. She sensed something else. Like a kid's fort, organic, instinctual, when a child went into the woods or the far reaches of a garden and built their own shelter or hideaway. Play that was about survival.

Anything of value there had already been gone through, maybe by others who lived rough nearby.

A couple of wood pallets formed sidewalls and roof. The front facing the river was open. The back, facing the trail, was hidden with camo tarps and brush and the undisturbed vegetation behind it. A half pallet formed a bed shelf, but the bedding was gone. Underneath a metal locker had been emptied, the contents scattered on the dirt floor. Beside the open front a small metal barrel had been cut-out and formed into a fireplace.

Cal scuffed her boot through the litter on the ground. Picked up an empty envelope addressed to Dif at an old Sydney address. The handwriting on the front was Aunt Zin's. A tremor of sadness, then a jab of anger that Dif would have left something like that behind. Was it not precious to him? A single photo was trodden into the dust and grit on the ground. Cal crouched, took the picture in her fingers, shook and blew the surface clean. Familiar. Another trip up the north coast. She put the envelope and photo on the bedframe.

Her phone buzzed in her pocket and she balked, stood up. A text from Scobie.

-Any joy?

Cal gave the screen a lopsided smile, thumbed a message back.

-Update you soon.

She sat back on the bed frame. *Dif got in touch out of the blue, said he needed help. Still, pretty opaque. Don't even know if I'm pointing myself in the right direction.* She leaned back on her elbows, stared through the open front. *Have to keep going, have to get some answers.* A lull in the passing trucks, quiet. The lap of water against the banks.

She closed her eyes. The water, her breath.

Slow. Right. Down.

Opened her eyes, scanned the surrounds, closer focus, inside, not outside. Along the pallets, up the sides, across the saplings that supported the roof tarp. Cal squinted beneath the tarp edge overhanging the horizontal front pole by a few inches, shading the inside. She could make out an interruption of the smooth, mottled timber surface. Got up and ran her hand across the de-barked exterior, felt with her fingertips. Something carved into the wood. She lifted the front edge of the tarp to get more light in, focussed her eyes.

"CN + DS → WW"

CN. Cal Nyx. DS. Dif Stangler. WW? *When did I last see Dif? C'mon, think!*

Cal reached up and held the cross-pole in her hands, let her weight drop as she hung there, something she often did from the top of a door.

"WW".

She swung back and forth, the pole taking her weight as she closed her eyes. The smooth timber squeaked under the grip of her palms.

'Fuck me.'

She dropped from the pole, turned and picked up the envelope and photo, studied the image more closely. A stretch of highway, and on the right-hand side of the road would be the distant mangroves towards the Durrawan coast where she'd recently been. But the picture was north and west of there, heading inland. Dif was in the driver's seat and the bonnet was up. Cal might have taken the picture.

Suddenly she remembered the map she'd seen recently. Where was it? Durrawan, in that realtor's window, the place inland they'd visited long ago. She and Dif were visiting a friend at her isolated cabin—Suzette, a hippie woman. Dif with a longer layover there to detox. The cabin and farmlet had a name, Wyld Wood. "WW."

Everything in the hut, apparently discarded, was a message for her. Cal was sure of it. She looked at the address on the envelope. It was a Petersham boarding house Dif had moved to, a women's squat. Before transition. It kept Dif nearby to Zin and Cal but took some of his drama away. Then he'd gone to Wyld Wood to clean up. Cal had driven him there. Everything was a sign only Cal or Zin could know or understand. And Dif obviously wasn't aware that Zin had died.

Traffic crossed the distant bridge up the valley in a steady thrum. Massive yellow trucks bounced along the opposite track, back and forth between the quarry face and the crushing chutes. To the east the river-mouth. To the northeast the peninsula, Greyridge. A freight train roared and clattered across the valley bridge, sending pulsating waves of muscular noise across the water. Dif's lullaby.

Cal took a photo of the carved message, pocketed the envelope and photo and climbed the slope back to the top of the stop-bank. Looked like she'd be heading north again.

Chapter 9

THERE WAS NO POINT Cal staying on at Greyridge. Dif had obviously scarpered, but he wanted her to find him. It was late morning. A couple of hours back to Sydney, then she could head north. If she pushed it she could be back near Durrawan early in the evening. She had to keep moving. There was no telling how long it was since Dif had left Greyridge, or how long he'd wait for her at Wyld Wood—if indeed he was still even there.

Cal got back to the Ford then remembered the comment about Dif staying at the Bidgee caravan park when he was crook. That place was on her way to Sydney if she took the coast road instead of the freeway. But the things Dif had left indicated he was probably at Wyld Wood. Was there any point following up another lead down here? It might give her a fix on dates, a timeline for Dif's movements. Maybe too much of an opportunity to waste, especially with the mileage she was putting in up and down the New South Wales coast.

She fired up the Ford, reversed and dumped the clutch, laying a not insignificant patch of rubber as the car accelerated up the incline. It reminded her of how Dif had acquired his nickname, shattering the gear centres out of three differentials in one weekend. Fourteen years old, no licence, showing off in one of his early modifications, an over-powered engine with standard Hillman driveshaft and rear in a Minx. Cal worked at a wrecker's yard, and got Dif mobile again with a replacement axle-centre. Dif blew that one, and the next, before finally figuring out how to lay a patch without totalling the rear end. Ha!

She grabbed another coffee in Greyridge and headed through several small communities on the undulating coast road before landing in Bidgee.

The main street ran parallel with the seaboard, had a high side and a low side. Houses on the high side were grit blasted, their windows caked in salt. Front lawns tawny with dead grass and weeds, occasional trees, bent and shorn to the pattern of the prevailing wind. Lower down, the houses without ocean views fared slightly better with the survival of the odd coastal banksia or stunted black-wood tree. The side-road to the caravan park terminated at a fork, one a gated track leading to the apex of the headland and a transmission tower, the other welcoming visitors and holidaymakers to Lazy-Dayz Caravan Park. A cartoon dog in striped shorts holding a Pina Colada underlined the conviviality.

Cal drove in and parked outside the office. A pair of red flax from her old homeland, planted either side of the doorway, a little droopy in the midday sun. She could smell the gum from the base of the leaves, a summer smell, from her childhood. As she waited inside for a staffer, she eyed a laser-cut plastic desk plaque which announced, Manager: Jonas McHardie. He emerged from a string of clacking beads hanging in the doorway. Wearing thongs and shorts with a washed out short-sleeved shirt, he was medium height, balding, solid going to fat.

'G'day. Friend of mine might have stayed here recently. He's gone missing. Wondered if you could check and give me the date he booked in?' Cal proffered the photo. 'Dif Stangler.'

Jonas McHardie bunched his lips. 'You gonna pay the damage bill for 'im?' He spread his hands on the counter. His lower jaw pushed slightly forward.

Cal raised her eyebrows. 'Oh. Sorry to hear that.'

Jonas McHardie's eyes narrowed, the muscles in his cheeks tightened. Then he blinked.

Cal pulled her shoulders back a little further, straightened her spine. 'Can I see it for myself? I've come down from Sydney.'

'Not happy. Peak season, lost revenue on top of the damage.'

'Seriously. When I find him we can sort this. Insurance cover you?'

'Not the point, is it?' He reached for keys behind him on a rack. 'Compound at the back fence. Old Vagabond with a blue stripe. Be quick, eh. Don't let the kids in there.' He handed over a toggle with a green plastic tag, two keys.

Cal nodded. 'Was Dif ever a resident here?'

'No. Never seen him before that one time.'

Cal went to the car, drove slowly along the winding driveway past permanent caravans with annex attachments, decks, small garden strips. Then a long kitchen and shower block, a shaded children's play-area, and towards the rear of the park, behind the main ablutions block, a two-bay garage with a ride-on mower under a lean-to. Beside that, a large fenced-off cage held half a dozen caravans side-by-side. Two wide gates formed most of the front wall, allowing a vehicle to hook-up and pull the vans in or out. There was barely room between them to slide in and open a door. She parked and stared for a moment. What had set Dif off?

The Vagabond was an old twelve-footer at one end. She got out, tried one of the keys in the gate's padlock, tugged it through the hasp. Did a careful side-on manoeuvre past the front of the drawbar to the door of the caravan. Stood a moment, took a deep breath then used the other key and pulled the door. It stuck. She yanked harder. The door caught in the frame then came back, nearly dropping into her shoulder. The top hinge was broken through.

The overheated air from inside was ripe with bitter odours of fire and ammonia. She peered in. Gauzy curtains went across the back window, the garish top-curtains in splotchy daubs of blue and red and tan, pulled back by stud clips. The interior was light-filled. Another vestigial smell, petroleum based. Lighter fluid? Was Dif sniffing that stuff?

The faded vinyl flooring showed a lengthy melted patch in front of scorching patterns on the kitchen cupboards.

The Formica top of the cooker area was also charred and blistered. The wardrobe doors were both shattered, the thin ply and veneer covering hung in gaping, jagged holes where a fist or boot had smashed into the panels.

A series of cupboards that ran like foot-lockers around under the seating squabs at one end had suffered similar damage, all six of them. She scanned again across the damage, especially where the blaze had occurred. The back of her brain was irritated by something but she couldn't draw it forwards. She took a final look around then closed the place up.

Back in the office, she put the keys on the counter. Kept her hand there. 'Who found it empty?'

Jonas McHardie reached for the keys. Cal didn't move her hand.

He stared at her, seemed to be considering something. 'Kids kicked a ball over the fence. Door was ajar. They told their parents.'

'But you'd never seen Dif round here before?'

'Nope.'

Cal took her hand away from the keys. 'Can you just give me that date and I'll be out of your hair?'

McHardie ran a finger along the desk ledger, eyes down. His finger stopped on the last entry of the page. 'May 19th.'

'Thanks for your time.' She turned and went towards the door.

Jonas McHardie replaced the keys on their hook. 'Be waiting for the cheque,' he said.

Cal arrived at Petersham after midday. She wanted to check things before she drove north again. She parked outside the rear entrance, tested the roller door on the garage, went to the gate and twisted the lock. She walked to the garage side door, dragged it open, the bottom scraping across the accumulated dust and grit. Looked okay. Went to the sleepout, tossed her bag on the floor, made herself a coffee and called Scobie before she got on the road. Sitting on a chair outside the door she filled Scobie in on her discoveries and her intention to head north again.

'You have a phone number for Suzette?' Scobie said.

'Nah. Too long ago. Don't think I ever actually had her number anyway. We visited in those days. Remember?'

Scobie laughed. 'You have her address?'

'I'll be finding the place from memory. Middle of nowhere. Can't have changed that much.'

'What about a surname?'

'Nah. I don't know the surnames of a lotta peeps I knew back then. It's a bloody hassle when you wanna visit them in hospital.' Cal drained her coffee. 'How's your sis and the bub?'

'Mm, Imogen's stable for now. Mads is a bit of a wreck.'

'You must feel powerless. Just gotta leave it in the hands of the experts, ay?'

'That's it.'

'Well, keep in touch and look after yourself. I'll let you know if I find anything up here.'

Cal finished her coffee and looked across the yard. Should water the pots before she left. And check that broken window. She put her cup down by the sleepout doorway, looked at the backdoor of Zin's cottage. Walked towards the three steps, paused, picked up the hose, turned on the tap, and watered the pots on the edge of the landing. She gazed at the screen, crusty with dust and cobwebs. Zin would've whisked those to the winds. She turned the tap off.

She walked down the side path of the cottage and reached up to make sure the board she'd screwed over the missing pane was still secure. Was startled to find the plywood had been loosened. Someone had jammed something under the screws and levered the board back from the frame, then re-seated the ply-embedded screws back into the widened frame holes. So, it wasn't just the original break-in, someone had come back, or someone else had taken advantage of the now vulnerable access point.

She couldn't keep ignoring this. Couldn't keep avoiding entering Zin's space. Especially if there'd been a further forced entry. Place could've been cleaned out by now. Why didn't she just bloody deal with it before?

She walked around to the back door, unclipped her keychain, pulled the screen-door, unlocked the back door and pushed it open. Her previous unease at entering her dead aunt's space, first time since she'd died, was now layered with an additional apprehension. Would the place be trashed? Was someone still inside?

The air was still and stale. She stepped into the alcove beside the laundry and walked into the kitchen. It smelt of Zin, despite her absence. Coffee and lemon polish and Babe cologne. She went to the bench, reached over the sink and opened a pair of wooden sash windows. On the benchtop next to the kettle, Cal's Ford mug, an old present her aunt had found in an op-shop. Cal could see something inside the mug. Leaned over. A pile of gold foil-wrapped chocolates in a stack, like doubloons. Cal picked up the mug, clasped it to her chest as she slid down to the floor, her back against the cupboards. She buried her face in her knees and began to sob.

Some minutes later, Cal drew herself together and splashed water on her face at the sink. She went no further than the kitchen, turned back and locked the door. She climbed into the driver's seat of the blue Ford and made a call to her Parks Service boss, Ben Herring, before she took off.

'Fisho. Howzit? Brace yourself.'

'Always in that mode when you call. What's up?'

'Any drama if I extend my leave? And sorry for the short notice.'

She heard his keyboard clicks.

'Pushing it.' His tone was friendly.

'Yup.'

'Y'know you've got plenty up your sleeve. Thing is the sickies we've had. Still, nothing too dire that can't wait. I've got the crew on urgent and essential at the mo anyway. How long you wanting?'

Cal gritted her teeth. ''Nother week?'

'All done.'

'Thanks, Fisho.'

'See ya then.'

Cal started the car, checked gauges and headed west for Kurrajong, a significant but necessary diversion before going up the north coast.

An hour and a half later she pulled into the winding driveway of Dee's smallholding. Wound down her window and called to the Jerusalem donkeys, Bindy and Blue, who trotted over to the fence.

Cal got out, leaned on the fence, breathed into their nostrils and rubbed their noses, one with each hand. 'Missed you fellas.' Leaned in, smelled their warm hides. 'Bring you something on my way out.'

She continued up the drive, parked outside the old shearers' quarters and stretched before walking over to Dee's cottage.

Went around the back to where Dee had a small outbuilding that served as an emergency surgery and recovery space. She knocked lightly and went in, called for Dee. No reply. Went inside and checked the two small backrooms. Cages were empty. Went back outside and up the back steps onto the porch, called again, knocked, walked inside as Dee came up the hallway, holding a finger to her lips.

'Hey, stranger,' Dee said as they hugged.

'You need a haircut—been so long since I saw ya. Where is he?'

Dee dropped her head to the side, indicating the front room at the other end of the hall.

Cal stopped herself from sprinting, went through the doorway and crossed the room to the large, flat wicker basket. Banjo had his head and shoulders in a patch of sunlight that streamed through one of the front windows. His eyes were open. A large bandage covered a shaved wound on his side. Cal lay down, put an arm gently around the red dog, buried her face beside his. He smelt like warm straw, with the backdrop of astringent disinfectant.

'My darling woofy,' she whispered into his soft ear. He nuzzled and licked her face, not with his usual vigour but she appreciated the gesture. Lay with him for a few minutes, stroking his back gently, well away from his sore side.

'Let you rest now. Love you, buddy.' She kissed him and got up.

'Cuppa, mate?' Dee said.

'Reckon.' Cal looked back, wiping her cheeks. Banjo's eyes were closed.

Cal filled Dee in on her recent travels, mysterious though they remained.

'You're a magnet for strife, Cal.' Dee said it light-heartedly.

'Not me. My mates.' Cal topped up their mugs.

'Whatevs. Sounds somewhat sinister. I wish you had some help.'

'If I can find Dif I'll have it. Joined at the hip back in the day. Been a while but hopefully we can pick up where we left off, sort this shite.'

'People on the margins live dangerous lives. I hope he's okay.'

Chapter 10

IN HER CONVERTED FARM shed, Cal packed several pairs of clean jeans, T-shirts and denim shirts into an overnight bag. She walked back to Dee's cottage and entered quietly via the back door. Dee had made herself a sandwich, was eating at the counter.

Cal spoke in a near whisper. 'I don't wanna disturb him again.' She nodded her head towards the front room up the hall. 'Just give him a big smooch from me when he wakes.'

'Course.'

'I'll be in touch.'

'Me too, if there's any change.'

Cal gave her a quick hug and sneaked back out. She stopped at the hayshed and grabbed a couple of apples and carrots to sweeten Bindy and Blue on the way down the drive. Beyond the hayshed, the sun glinted from the side of a disused grain silo. Cal and Dee were working at fitting it out for a B&B. Not much progress lately.

Three and a half hours later Cal passed the Durrawan turnoff to the coast. She continued north for fifteen minutes then headed inland on a secondary road that passed through grey pastureland sparsely dotted with dingy-looking sheep. It was warmer up here than down in Sydney and the South Coast. Still dry too.

Aware that she might be nearing where Dif was hiding out, she checked her rear-view mirror to make sure no one was behind her. The enigmatic messages from Dif seemed to call for a level of caution. The road climbed a little through some remnant forest, shady and tunneled beneath great gum trees. Out the other side the dry returned. Cal found the route familiar and basically unchanged. She checked her mirror again then turned left onto the unmarked track and minutes later arrived at the cottage.

Cal got out of the car, half-expecting—hoping—to finally lay eyes on Dif. Suzette stood on the wooden veranda, then came down the steps as Cal turned off the engine. Suzette was a petite dynamo, a wiry little woman with long, unkempt hair hanging loose around her shoulders. It was more than a decade since Cal had seen her. They were both now in their mid-thirties, still utterly recognisable but subtly changed.

Cal got out, leaned down, hugged Suzette. 'Long time.'

'Yeh. For real.'

They stood back.

'Come inside. Lot to catch up on.'

Cal followed her up the steps. The wooden cottage was faded and worn on the outside, rustic.

Inside was dark, cool, the air moving through a hallway from front to back with screen doors halting the insects.

Cal followed Suzette to the rear kitchen, peering into open doorways ready to greet Dif.

'Cuppa?' Suzette asked, filling a kettle at the sink.

'Where is he?' Cal asked, unable to wait through further pleasantries.

Suzette shook her head. 'He took off last night.'

'No!' Cal slapped her thigh. 'Fuck me, I'm on a bloody goose chase.' She slumped back against the edge of a solid timber table. 'Jesus. I can't believe it.'

'I'm sorry. I only discovered him gone this morning. There was no way I could get in touch.'

Cal folded her arms. She felt like punching or kicking something. 'What's going on? What do you know?'

'Left a note on the table.' Suzette pulled a small piece of paper from her pocket, unfolded it, handed it to Cal.

"Sorry, gotta go. Thanks for your help. I won't forget it. X Dif."

Suzette pulled cups from the cupboard. 'Tea or coffee?'

'Tea, thanks. Think I need to calm myself down.'

'You eaten?' Suzette asked.

'I'm okay, thanks.'

'Just some bikkies then.' Suzette put two vintage biscuit tins on the table, got the milk, sat down with Cal. 'He turned up about a week ago. Literally, walked up the drive. What's that? Two kilometres from the turnoff? He'd hitched to there. I recognised him, of course, but gee, he's so thin.'

She swung the teapot around and around. 'You like it strong?'

'Yeh.' Cal raised her eyebrows and smiled, ready to listen.

'He was desperate to get inside, out of sight. I mean, look at us here. It's the boonies. But he wanted to get indoors. He was so freaked out. Fully nervous. Traumatised even.'

Suzette poured Cal's tea, opened both tins. Cal saw the Choc Mint Slices, delved in. Waited for Suzette to go on.

'He'd seen something, Cal. He wouldn't tell me what. Said it would put me in danger. I mean, I know it all sounds ridiculous, and it was obvious Dif has been back on something. But his fear was real. Know what I mean?'

Cal nodded, solemn, waited until Suzette was done.

'He was living rough down south and he saw something bad and whoever did the something knows they were seen. That's as much sense as I could get. He came here because it's unknown.' She shrugged and Cal acknowledged it with a nod. 'He wants help with something, and he was waiting for you. Meantime he'd been doing like an informal detox here, I s'pose. He said he'd tried to get a message to you. I guess he just got nervy again. He took off.' She blew out a big sigh.

'Fuck me.' Cal shook her head. She explained the text and note from Dif and the searching she'd done at Durrawan and Greyridge, how she'd figured out to come to Wyld Wood. She left out the bit about the hair in the envelope. 'I can't believe I've gotten here and bloody missed him. Now where's he gone? Truly. I can't keep driving up and down the friggin' coast.'

Cal took a swig of tea. 'But what he told you kinda makes some sense of his erratic behaviour. Whatever he saw must've been serious. Did he leave anything in the room?'

'Not that I noticed,' Suzette said.

'So, all week he's not mentioned any other plans ... places?' Cal opened her hands, shrugged.

Suzette closed her eyes, shook her head.

'Mind if I look in the bedroom?' Cal said.

'On the left.' Suzette looked up the hall, sad, resigned.

Cal peered in the doorway. A single bed with an old-fashioned metal frame and head rails. Quilts and crocheted covers neatly pulled up. If Dif had left in a hurry, he'd left things tidy for his host. Suzette had come to the doorway beside Cal.

'Did he have anything when he arrived? A backpack? Bedroll?'

'He had a little swag.'

Cal walked into the room. On the left, a small timber dresser, three drawers. Under the window, a desk and chair. 'This was Ginny's room?'

'Mm-hmm.'

'Where's she now?' Cal felt a jab of guilt, so pre-occupied with her search for Dif she'd not even asked after Suzette's daughter.

'Melbourne, studying.'

Cal turned, smiled. 'She was a little strappling last I saw. You must be so proud.' Cal remembered the shy, thin girl who looked more like her father. 'Okay if I just have a look?'

'No problem. I've gotta feed the horses. Come out the back and join me when you're done.'

'Will do.'

Cal crossed the room and turned around, saw behind the door a free-standing wardrobe. She opened the doors. Girls' dresses, blouses. She felt like an intruder, closed the doors. Defeated, she sat on the end of the bed. She'd done a lot of miles the last few days, and still Dif eluded her. Wanted her help, but Cal had failed to reach him. Dif had left very specific messages for Cal, first to Durrawan and OTR, and then the carving in his hut that had led Cal to Wyld Wood. She'd only just missed him, but the system had worked until now. If Dif had taken the time to leave a note for Suzette, surely, he would have left something for Cal? And what had scared him off again?

Cal leaned towards the bedhead, lifted the pillow, ran her hand underneath. Nothing. Crouched and looked under the bed. Nothing. Lifted the mattress. Slatted base. No joy there.

'Fuck.'

Cal sighed. Swung her arms. Went to the window, squinted at the intensity of the white light outside, the differentiation of objects made more difficult, hazy in the monochromatic, faded surrounds. Brought her focus in to the cracked-timber windowsill. A small vase with everlasting daisies sprouting from its mouth, warm oranges and yellows. Two horse figurines, a mare and a foal. The side curtain wafted back in a puff of breeze. And in the corner of the windowsill was a tiny toy truck, smaller than two joints of Cal's finger. Dull, bare metal, devoid of paint, all chipped away in smash-up games.

She puffed a short breath from her nose. She knew it wasn't Ginny's toy because she recognised it. It was Dif's. She reached out, looking in the miniature pickup tray. Empty. Turned it over. Like something a carrier pigeon might dispatch, a minuscule slip of paper was rolled and inserted into a gap beside the narrow front wheels. Cal smiled and went outside to the Ford.

In the boot she had a toolbox, and on the top tray alongside her feeler gauges and points file was a pair of tweezers. She grabbed the edge of the note and pulled it out, flattened it on the toolbox lid. No words, just a sketch. A profile like a hangman's game of an open-sided shed with a loft platform. Cal knew immediately what and where it was. She and Dif had camped there in the past. When Suzette had her rare get-togethers, friends either stayed indoors, in tents, or in the shed, depending on how feral or adventurous they were.

The shed wasn't visible from the house as it sat behind a patch of bush off to one side. Should Cal tell Suzette? Had Dif not told her once again because he wanted to keep her out of danger? So now, how did Cal get to Dif without alerting Suzette?

Cal crossed the dusty yard to a feed-shed, stable and fenced yards.

Suzette topped up a water trough as a grey mare and a bay gelding watched her with benign interest.

'You get many visitors here?' Cal said.

'Not really. I kinda like it that way.'

Cal nodded approvingly. 'Anyone drop by yesterday, before Dif took off?'

Suzette turned to Cal, a small, concerned crease at the bridge of her nose. 'No. It's rare. Maybe an occasional neighbour—damaged fences or needing help. Other visitors ring first. What's going on, Cal? Should I be worried for my own safety? What's Dif gotten into?'

'Just trying to figure why he wouldn't wait for me. It's fine, Suzette. Obviously Dif's toey about something. I just thought if someone had visited and Dif's laying low or running from something, it might have set him off. Just frustrating.' Cal banged her boot-heel into the dust. 'I'm gonna stretch my legs. Been cooped up in that car for days. You mind? Just gotta figure what to do next.'

'Course not. You're welcome to stay if you need. Have a meal. Catch up. Whatever you need, Cal.'

Cal gave her a hug. 'You're a honey.'

Cal filled her water bottle at an outside tap. It was warm but it still thirst-quenching. She had to work at not breaking into a run in her desperation to reach Dif, knowing finally he was so close. She felt duplicitous, conflicted at lying to Suzette. But she didn't want to panic the woman more than necessary. She reminded herself that she'd made sure she wasn't followed to Wyld Wood and Dif had no doubt done the same. They were just being careful. Suzette wasn't in danger.

Cal wandered around the side of the house and veered into the patch of small gums that protected the dwelling from the worst of the afternoon sun's glare. She kept her eyes down on the track and margins, looking for red-belly or tiger snakes that might be basking in the winter sun. It was quiet and still in the grove, and patches of dappled shade cooled the air some. Cal hurried on, emerging from the bush, and right where she visualised it in her mind, there was the hut, its tall, open front and sides grey and silvered from weathering.

Chapter 11

Cal hesitated at the clearing in front of the open-sided hut, peering into the shadows under the loft platform.

'Dif?' Cal called. 'It's me, Cal.'

She took a step closer, then another.

'It's me, mate.'

Finally Dif stepped out from the dark. Cal rushed over, took her old friend in her arms.

'You loony fuckin nutter. What's goin' on?' Cal stepped back.

They were much the same height, Dif maybe an inch taller but stooped, thin. His long hair, usually raked into a tall quiff, was flat and hanging around his pale cheeks. He made a wan smile that brought a flicker of light to his sad brown eyes.

'Lot going on my friend.' His voice hushed. 'We should keep this from Suzette. Come with me.'

Cal followed Dif behind the hut and up a small incline of twiggy scrub and exposed rocks. At the apex Dif crouched down and indicated Cal should do the same.

'Thanks for coming. I knew you would. I knew I could rely on you.'

'What's going on, mate?'

Dif looked around. 'I'm gonna fill you in. Just keep an eye out, okay? We can see the track in from here. If we keep down, we'll be out of sight.'

Cal observed Dif as he spoke. He seemed lucid, though also anxious and paranoid. His eyes darted all over the surrounds, not fixing on Cal's face, though this appeared due to nervousness rather than anything like dishonesty, and Dif had always been stand-up in the past so there was no reason for that to change.

Dif spoke quietly and continued his vigil of the surrounding landscape. Cal watched too as she listened, leaning back on her elbows to keep her body low. Dif told her about the night at the quarry, the woman's body dumped in the chute, his fear of going to police in person, the outstanding warrants and his attempts to find the vehicle he'd seen that night at the chute.

'So, you got a rego number, got an address, followed it up, but whoever was driving the pickup wasn't who you saw that night at the quarry, right?'

Dif nodded.

'And it's not possible whoever you saw borrowed the pickup?'

'I think the plates were stolen. I think the guy I traced it to, Brent Coswell in Stockton, wasn't involved at all. Same vehicle, but swapped plates. The only way we could confirm that is if we checked an engine number and see if it matched. Silver Triton pickup—how many tradies are driving them?'

'Or just ask the owner you traced if his plates were ever stolen.'

'I guess,' Dif agreed.

'Gimme that rego number. I'll see what I can find out. So, what was going on at Bidgee, the caravan park? Why did you end up there?'

'When he found my hut that night I had to leave. He'd have known it was only roughies out there. I couldn't stay. I went to Bidgee to just figure things out.'

'Bloke there said you trashed his caravan?' Cal opened her hands, waited.

'I was wasted. I think I must've accidently started a fire. I can't remember.' Dif wouldn't look at her, his shame evident. 'I had a coughing fit and threw water on it. I just took off.'

'So, the envelope. The hair. Came from the body?' Cal asked.

'I couldn't get her out of that chute. I took it for evidence. It was all I could think of. I left it for you, for safe-keeping.'

'And you've never considered telling the cops what you saw, or even leaving an anonymous tip?'

Dif looked up. 'I did leave a message. Before I left Greyridge.' His voice had risen. 'I did what I could. I was a basket-case, Cal. I couldn't think straight, I hadn't slept, I was freaked out. I couldn't use that Crimestoppers thing cos I had no credit. I did the next best thing. I slipped a note under the door at the cop station. It was early morning, before opening. I had to take off. I did what I could, Cal.' His voice cracked with emotion. 'Anyway, I checked that Crimestoppers site when I was at the library. It gives the option of leaving personal details. I just don't trust that I wouldn't be traced. I'd already left the note at the cop-shop.' He faded off, sighed. 'They would've known it had to have come from someone sleeping rough there, to have seen what I did. They don't take us seriously. They think we're all crazies, ghosts. I just hoped someone other than Tambor would find it.'

Both his hands had gone to his head, his fingertips rubbing back and forth across his scalp. 'I've been checking the papers. When I have credit I check the newsfeeds on my phone. I thought the cops would've found her by now. But there's been nothing. Tambor must've had something to do with it.'

'Who's Tambor?'

'The head-honcho there, DS Tambor. He's got it in for us.' Dif looked up and around, like he expected this character to jump from behind a tree. 'He's destroyed camps, come in the night and tossed people.'

Dif's unease was so apparent Cal wondered if she was missing something.

'You saw the new subdivision?' Dif looked at Cal who nodded. 'Well, that's Koori land. That's why Truby started the camp there by the estuary. It's for his people. Doesn't look good having Land Rights flags flying down there, interrupting the view of the coast. Tambor must be in cahoots with the developers. So, he makes these night-time visits to all the camps. He arrived one night with a water truck and hosed everyone off. He's a real charmer.

Dif's top lip curled. 'I couldn't risk going to the cops in person. It's not just the warrants or the fear that they would've held me in the cells. I'd be toast inside. You know that Cal.' Dif's voice crackled. 'Laws about which jails trannies go to are just policies. They don't guarantee anything. You end up in the wrong prison, it's a death sentence.' Dif swung his head, ducked, looked around.

Cal nodded. 'Yeh, I know, mate.'

'Or you end up in solitary for your own safety. Permanently. Who can survive that mentally intact? I know I couldn't.'

'You don't need to explain.' Cal let out a long breath. 'I'm seeing someone, a cop. Scobie might be able to help.'

Dif stood immediately, backed away. 'No! Fuck no, Cal.' His eyes bulged like golf balls. 'Are you not hearing me?'

'Calm down, mate. Sit down.' Cal patted the ground.

'No. I won't calm down. Jesus, Cal. I want to trust you, but you're not getting it.'

'I'm not doing anything we haven't agreed on first. Cool it. We gotta work something out though.'

Dif remained at a distance but crouched down on his haunches.

'No cops, Cal. I mean it.'

Cal had never seen him so wound-up, angry, terrified. 'What is it?'

Dif wheezed the air from his body in a short burst, his top lip pulled tight across his teeth. 'Tambor's a sick puppy. After one of his clearance sessions at the camps one night he pulled me in on vagrancy. That's their go-to when there's nothing else.' Dif's gaze moved away from Cal's face. 'He drove away from the camp, parked up, got me in the front of the squad car. Conversion therapy.' Dif spat on the ground.

'Jesus.'

'Another time he took me to the station. No CCTV in the staff bathroom. He gave me a real good hiding. I pissed blood for days. That's why I moved to the other side of the river. It wasn't far enough. He never found my camp there, but it wasn't safe for me to be out and about in Greyridge. Anytime, anywhere, I never knew when he was going to just grab me off the street. I had nowhere to go, no money. I felt trapped.'

'I'm so sorry, mate.' Cal put her hand on his shoulder. 'Aren't there other cops there, at Greyridge? Are they all like that?'

'He's senior. There're only a couple of other constables—standard small-town stuff. He's a law unto himself, a cowboy and a low-life.'

'Okay. I get ya, and I promise, no cops. You think whoever dumped the body knows who you are?'

'He came after me. He found my hide. He could've asked anyone and found out who I was, who lived there.

I didn't stick around to find out.' Dif shook his head, a resigned downward cast to his mouth.

'Well, he'll be desperate if he killed that woman and was concealing it. Can't have been an accident.' Cal paused. 'Mate, we can't do this on our own. This prick can't get away with it—the authorities need to know.' She held a hand up before Dif could argue. 'I'm not saying or doing anything without your approval, but we need to figure this out.'

She held Dif's gaze until she blinked. 'Fuck me I need a coffee. What are we gonna do meantime? Where can we stay? It's too nerve-wracking here. I don't feel good lying to Suzette or putting her in any danger. Any ideas?'

'You should be off the radar. You think there's any way that low-life could've gotten onto you?' Dif said.

'Unless he was watching when I went to your Kaiung hut? And then followed me to the hidey-hole at OTR in Durrawan. But I didn't see any vehicles out there. Or at the quarry.'

'And you reckon you weren't followed here.'

Cal shook her head. 'And I went to Scobie's before here.'

Dif stiffened again. 'What did you tell her?'

'Missing friend. That's all. Chill, man.'

'We could get on the road, just keep moving around while we sort this. I need to keep moving. I feel like a target when I'm stationary.'

'Yup. Or hole up somewhere else we can't be found. Kinda feels like we need to keep in range of online access and stuff. Like I said before, we can't do this on our own. We need to keep safe, plan, and get some help. How much gear you got? Just your swag?'

Dif nodded. 'All I need. Just some food supplies would be good.'

'What about Durrawan? No one knows about that. We could camp in the National Park or on the coast. I can drive close to town if we need to message anyone. Keep my phone off the rest of the time.' Cal raised her eyebrows.

Dif nodded approval. 'Sounds good.'

'Okay. I'm gonna say my goodbyes to Suzette and make a quick exit so we don't need to worry about her. Can you cross the paddocks to beyond that curve?' Cal pointed to where the drive was out of Suzette's vision from the house. 'I'll pick you up there in about twenty minutes. Okay?'

Cal scooted back to the house, found Suzette in the small feed shed beside the post-and-rail compound. The pair of horses were now eating from a wide-mouthed bucket of chaff.

'Such a lovely peaceful spot. Sorry we've brought these disruptions,' Cal said.

Suzette straightened up, hung a lunging rope on a wooden peg. 'Not at all. Wish I knew what was going on. I'm sure you must too.'

'I'm gonna push on. Gotta find Dif and sort things out. Sorry to blow in and blow out like this.' Cal shrugged awkwardly, uncomfortable with the subterfuge of her meeting with Dif.

'Hey, it was nice to see you both. Weird circumstances, but still.'

'Just gonna grab my bag and I'll be gone. I'll leave my number on the table. Thanks again, Suzette.' She gave the other woman a hug.

'Take care. Let me know how it goes with Dif,' Suzette said quietly.

'Sure thing.'

Two hundred and fifty metres along the track curved around the base of a small incline, knobbed with rocks and a trio of thin saplings. Once beyond that Cal's vehicle wasn't visible from Suzette's place. Cal scanned ahead for Dif. Admittedly there wasn't much cover, but Dif could've laid low then waved at Cal's approach. She slowed to a stop, looked left across the parched, bare paddocks to the spot where she and Dif had spoken earlier. She ran her gaze back and forth across the landscape of stubbled grass remnants and stones. No sign of Dif.

She turned the engine off. Waited another ten minutes. Still no sign of Dif.

She felt exposed just sitting there.

'Fuck me fuckin' sideways.' She slapped the steering wheel. 'What now?'

She waited another five minutes. Nothing.

'You're a fuckin asshole, Dif. What the actual fuck?'

Cal got out. Slammed her door, then regretted it because the hinge pins were already worn, and she'd likely bent the catch now. She went over to the 6-strand wire fence, squeezed the top two wires together in her fist, stepped over and strode towards where she and Dif had chatted less than half an hour before. She panted a little as she scrabbled up the hillock in the heat. Her breathing was shallow, her anger clamping her insides. She momentarily considered Dif might have succumbed to a snake-bite and then she felt fluttery in her chest, partly anxiety, partly guilt. She got to the top of the mound, looked all around. Could see the route she and Dif had taken up from the approach behind the cottage, then remembered to crouch down again, in case Suzette spotted her and wondered what the hell was going on. Cal crawled around the small, flat apex, looking for signs of Dif's escape.

If the flat was a clock-face, and Cal's car was parked at nine o'clock and Suzette's house was at five o'clock, Cal saw recent scuffs and tracks down the one o'clock position. Looked like Dif had taken off towards the bush that bordered the main road. If he hadn't gotten there yet and thumbed a ride, he could wait until he saw Cal leave and hitch away then.

Cal kicked uselessly at stones then made her way back to the car. She got in, closed the door gently this time. It sagged more now, a gap at the ill-fitting bottom where the road dust could come in. Nice. She drove slowly to the main road intersection, paused, then planted boot and fish-tailed a massive cloud of gravel and dust for Dif's benefit if he was indeed watching.

She swore and grizzled to herself for five kilometres. When she had exhausted that she considered the logic of what had transpired.

Shouldna mentioned Scobie. Ya fucked up Nyx.

Chapter 12

DIF DIDN'T WAIT. SKIRTING the brush at the roadside he made inland, westwards, certain Cal would return either to the coast or south to Sydney. If he'd felt alone before, what was he now? Bereft. Enough already. Forget all that. He hitched his swag. Fifteen ks he reckoned to Red Flat. A tiny settlement back in the day, probably unchanged. Two businesses on opposite sides of the road, a general store and a pub. Below the pub, a roughly grassed field ran above the river. That would give him a water source. Farmers and transport trucks if he wanted to skedaddle. Undaunted by the lengthy walk, he followed the road from within the scrub until he was certain Cal was well gone from Suzette's place. Then he left the scrub and made his way along the roadside where the going was easier. Two to three hours he reckoned.

It was still afternoon when he arrived in Red Flat. Protected from the western sun by the roadside gums, he welcomed the sheltering shade. Same couldn't be said for his lower extremities. His feet swam in his old boots, the threadbare socks sliding inside no matter how tightly he pulled the laces. His soles were rippled raw with blisters;

he'd compensated by altering his gait onto the outer edges of his feet. Consequently, the muscles and tendons of his thighs and calves were pulled in unfamiliar directions and painfully fatigued.

The place looked much as he remembered. Half a dozen grimy pick-ups parked on the gravel forecourt of the pub, two with dog boxes on the trays eased into the meagre shade offered by a pair of old blackbutt gums. Across the road, the general store, its entrance protected by a narrow veranda.

Dif crabbed along to the shop and crossed the pale decking, the boards worn smooth and warped with deep, dust-filled cracks. Inside he grabbed several tins of beans and a handful of snack bars, kept his head down, mumbled his thanks to the pinched woman behind the counter. Back outside he hobbled across the road and around the side of the pub as a sort of ruse if anyone took any notice. The sound of Cold Chisel's "Flame Trees" drifted from inside like it was still the mid-eighties. Dif limped down to the river to make camp. One night only, should be safe he told himself.

An old trestle bridge passed high over the waterway a hundred metres south of the pub. He made his way beyond the shadowed support structure to a stand of blue gums and sandpaper figs. The ground beneath was dry and sandy. Dumping his swag, he pulled an old shirt from within and with his empty water bottle swinging from a belt loop he wobbled to the water's edge, slumped down, untied his boots, and drew them from his feet.

The material of his socks had welded to his flayed soles. Taking a breath, he doused his feet, still sock clad, into the stinging water and held them there, hissing between his teeth at the pain.

When he'd acclimated to the cooling water, he peeled off his socks, wincing as pieces of his soles came with them. He rinsed the socks and wrung them out, tossing them over his shoulders. His feet were a mess of wrinkled and torn skin and patches of pink, weeping flesh. Using his teeth, he tore the sleeves from the flannel shirt and wrapped his sorry flippers, then bobbled back to his campsite on his heels. He gathered small sticks and grass clumped among the rocks and brush from previous floodings and made a fire where he set his socks to dry. Using a pocket-knife, he punched into a can of beans and wrenched the blade around the rim cutting away half a circle of the lid before placing it on a rock at the fire's edge.

With his swag unrolled, he crouched, crossed his legs, dropped his head, and closed his eyes.

Cal had found him. She had responded to his weirdo message, even after all the space and absences between. And he had run. *She was your last chance. Feel safe now?*

What if she'd been followed, despite her assurances? What if the bloke from the quarry had watched the south coast hut, seen Cal, stalked her to Suzette's place and was just waiting for his moment like now, now I'm alone?

Dif squirmed where he sat, opened his eyes, scanned the darkness. He fought similarly themed ideas all night, his body occasionally succumbing to exhaustion.

At one point he woke, strained his ears as he sought what had disturbed him. Saw an orb of light through tree trunks beyond the pub. He scrabbled for his belongings, his body taut with terror, remembering the torchlight sweeping the riverbank and quarry. *He's come for me.*

As he pulled his swag into a roll he looked again, realised it was the moon through the trees. Sat clutching his gear to his chest, relief and despair taking their turns through his weary system.

*

There was no point Cal hanging around. Dif wasn't eager for her company. That much was clear. She might as well head south to Greyridge and follow up what she could there. That's where everything had gone down. If Dif had to lie low, she could still represent his interests. Following anyone's track would begin down south. She had a vehicle description and rego, and a couple of other tips. They were a start. No time to waste. What if she made an anonymous call to Crimestoppers herself even if Dif wasn't keen? Couldn't hurt.

She needed a coffee.

Driving back to Durrawan, she stopped at a servo and bought a long black and a savoury scone. She parked away from the bowsers and considered her next move. It was late afternoon. Scobie was still in Melbourne. How much was she going to divulge? If she told Scobie about a body being dumped, Scobie would be obliged to pass that information on. She couldn't ignore it, even if she was on family leave. Could the police be involved in any way and Dif still remain safe? Dif had made it clear where he stood. No cops. He seemed to think Tambor would know it was him, however the tip-off came. Something dirty about that cop. Okay, no call to Crimestoppers then.

Nevertheless, it was tempting to ask Scobie to check what local cops had made of that possibly stolen rego plate that Dif had mentioned. Cal knew Scobie couldn't do that without registering a case file number with the request. Plus, Scobie wasn't at work anyway. Still, it was frustrating knowing that access to those searches and case info was a few simple keystrokes for a copper.

Whatever, she decided she should be judicious with what she let on to Scobie until she had a clearer picture.

She wrote a text.

-Hope Mads and Imogen are doing ok. I'm back in Durrawan. Dif's scarpered. I'll probs head to South Coast. Feel like a frickin yo-yo. Take care xx

Cal finished her coffee, fired up the Ford and left the service station, heading for the highway south. The land beside the road was arid. Pale yellow grass stubble, withered grey weed stalks, stony beige ground. In the distance, occasional remnants of forest, a haze of drab grey-green.

Inland, the deserts bore the ochre and reds of iron ore, colours that highlighted their surrounds. Where she was, only the mangrove estuaries near the coast had access to ample moisture.

She ran her mind back over the things she'd seen on her previous trip down south. Something there was niggling at her. It wasn't about Dif's hut at Greyridge. And it wasn't about the quarry or the chute or what Dif had told her he'd seen. Her mind moved to Bidgee, the caravan park. She shook her head as if that might re-mesh some cogs. She gazed up through the broad windscreen. The sky was dull, heavy and low to the east. Rain coming in beyond the coast. The landscape sure needed it. The brutal cycle, fire and water. Elemental.

Fire. That was it. Her brain had latched onto the thing, the itch.

Dif said he'd started a small blaze in the caravan, but he couldn't remember doing it. Cal assumed it was because he was out of it. What if he had been out of it but didn't start the fire? She'd smelt lighter fluid in the closed space and thought Dif must have been sniffing the stuff. What if there was another explanation? What if someone else had tried to set the van alight? With Dif still inside? She needed to take another look at that place, and she'd have to do it on the sly. The manager there wasn't thrilled by the mention of Dif at her last visit. If she ploughed on now without stopping in Sydney, she'd have the cover of darkness to work in at Bidgee.

Chapter 13

CAL DROVE ANOTHER TWO hours, approached outer Sydney on the Pacific Highway then headed for the south coast taking the A1, avoiding the city proper. She stopped for takeaways at Engadine, did some stretches in the parking area then continued the Princes Highway south. So much sitting and driving. She was feeling the absence of physical activity that her work usually entailed. It made her sluggish and agitated all at once. An uncomfortable mix.

An hour and a half later she took an off-ramp from the freeway to the old coast road and wound down the escarpment through the small settlements that dotted the strips of land beside the ocean. The sky was clear over the coast and the full moon loomed large, casting its beacon across the water like an ethereal, gilded pathway. Cal enjoyed the show but knew it wouldn't aid the subterfuge she intended.

It was 9.30pm. Still too early to nosy around the caravan yard. She drove directly to a car-park and public beach access a little north of the holiday park, wound her seat back, dropped the windows and closed her eyes, calming her mind before her next mission.

An hour later she got out of the car and wandered through the empty children's play area. She worked her legs on the swings, something she hadn't done since childhood. Then she ran around and around a twirly flat roundabout, holding onto a metal rail. To her surprise she found it exhilarating and fun. A long rope hung from a tall pole nearby. She took a few swings on that, her body stretching and pulling down through her arms and shoulders. After ten minutes in the playground her blood was moving fast through her veins, her pulse was up, her lungs cleared. She was ready for action.

When she got back to the car, she had a message from a new number.

-PS. At quarry, back window of Triton, behind driver's seat, sticker, shield-shaped, like those alarm security warnings. D.

Dif had gotten hold of a phone. Cal snorted and shook her head as she thumbed a response.

-WTAF? You don't think an explanation is in order?

She sent it. Then thumbed a follow-up.

-Mate. Trying to help. You piss off. Gimme some fuckin credit.

Hit Send with a thump of her thumb like she wanted to slap Dif in the side of the head.

Nice work Cal. Spray and walk away. He's scared, remember. You callous nong.

Drove another 5 ks.

'Fuck's sake.'

Thumbed another text to Dif.

-Sorry mate. Keep in touch. Don't wanna do this on my own.

She drove the short distance to the Bidgee Holiday Park and left the Ford in a side-street that ran close to the rear of the park, about four hundred metres from the front entrance. She pocketed a torch and her phone and threw a thick denim jacket over her shoulder and dodged into scrubland behind the holiday park, following a tall, chain-link fence to the locked-off storage yard for unused or damaged caravans awaiting repair. There was an existing track; kids probably played there. She certainly would have.

At the back of the storage yard she stopped and listened. The fenced yard stood beside the service sheds which were unused at night. Cal could see lighted vans and trailers across the open grass areas and through the shrubberies. *Be quick 'n' slick Nyx.*

She tossed her jacket over the barbed strand on the top of the two-metre chain-link, then dug the narrow toe of her cowboy boot into the diamond shaped holes and hauled herself up. At the top she adjusted the sleeves of her jacket to cover as much of the spiked row as possible, stretched one leg, then the other over the top. Clinging to the wire with her fingers, her weight dragged, her fingers went numb as she flailed for a toe-hold. She got herself over and down the other side, sliding into the gap between the rears of two caravans. She couldn't pull her jacket down now—the barbs had embedded in the fabric. *Fuck me dead. Had that one for years. It'll look good if I can untangle it but.*

She crouched and caught her breath as she glanced across her surrounds. Already she could smell the scorched plastics and timbers from inside the caravan where Dif had stayed. A shrubbery on her left masked the light of the nearest trailer at least twenty metres away. The curtains were pulled and alternating lights indicated someone watching a screen inside. If she was quiet that one shouldn't be a problem. Adjacent to the storage yard, the work-sheds were locked and dark. The amenities block and kitchens were well beyond and all quiet.

Cal crept forward to the caravan door. This time she was prepared when she tugged it and the top fell away from the frame. She scuttled inside and pulled the door to behind her. Now her inspection would be less cursory. The main window of the van, facing into the park, had its curtains hooked back. She'd need to keep the torchlight pinpointed and low, but she was most interested in the other end of the space anyway.

She duck-walked towards the kitchen area, turned on her torch and ran the beam over the bottom of the cupboards and floor. Distinct charred patterns ran across the laminate. Not in smoky drifts as she might have imagined, but in distinct narrow streams. One of the lower cupboard doors hung open, its inner catch melted, ineffective. Inside the shelving was totally charred through, and she could see beyond to the ground below, outside. Above the charring, a sink, its threaded metal outlet going nowhere, no pipe or hose. But she couldn't see the melted remnants of the hose she expected. The worst of the burning seemed to be inside this cupboard, not in the kitchen area on the outside.

Then another thought struck her. The kitchen burner ran off gas. There should've been a gas hose to a gas bottle located outside the van. Why hadn't that exploded? She looked inside the hole again. Found the small, stainless braided inlet for the gas burner that ran out through the floor towards the back of the caravan. Intact. Was that simply good fortune? She kept the torch on, took a couple of photos on her phone. Closed the cupboard door, took some pictures of the scorch patterning there.

She was about to creep back to the door when she heard a vehicle on the road outside, a diesel engine idling. She switched the torch off, kept her head down, waited, and held her breath. The gate out front of the yard was locked. No reason for anyone to come in, she hoped. Nowhere for her to go if they did. The vehicle moved slowly but kept going, and the sound receded.

Cal slipped outside, jammed the door shut and shimmied to the rear. Just a couple more things to check. At the back she dropped onto her side and peered underneath, flicking her torch on. The flooring was burnt on the outside. She pushed herself under, her feet scrabbling on the gravel surface as she shone her light upwards. Directly above her and above the scorched shelves was the sink outlet. Theoretically, the outlet pipe should've dropped down there. And didn't flames move upwards? Why was the floor burnt on the outside?

She shone the torch across the ground. Nothing. Then across the base and frame of the van. And there it was, the green outlet pipe, wedged between two bits of steel framing at the wall and floor joint by the wheel well. She reached for it, pulled it over, and checked the ends. No burning or melting. It had been removed before the fire. Cal pulled her phone out, took a picture of the pipe, and crawled back out.

Before she climbed the fence she established one more thing. At the rear of the van a metal cage held the gas bottle. Cal clasped and turned the outlet valve. It was definitely open. She lifted the bottle. Light as. Empty. *Double check*. Closed the valve off. Opened it again with her ear close. No hiss inside the hose. No smell. Empty. Dif had woken and escaped a badly set fire. The empty gas bottle had also saved his life.

As Cal returned over the fence, she clung on near the top and worked the barbs from her denim jacket, eventually unjagged with additional hard-core distress treatment. She dropped down and got back to the car close to midnight.

She drank some water, pondering as she sat in the driver's seat. She knew fire was a tricky element to understand and she was no expert. But it seemed that the caravan fire had been lit from both inside and outside. That someone had pulled off the outlet pipe and squirted accelerant in from under the trailer, shot stuff up inside the cupboards. The streaks inside the caravan seemed to indicate either Dif or someone else had squirted accelerant inside. Even if that was Dif, in blackout rage or whatever, surely that couldn't explain what Cal had seen outside and underneath the van. So, had someone been both inside and outside, while Dif was oblivious? Stoned or comatose. Helpless.

And, but for the fact the gas bottle was empty and Dif had woken and escaped, he would've been blown into orbit.

It was deliberate and calculated and it was meant to be fatal. Seemed to confirm that Dif was a target. Someone knew who he was and where he was. And what he had seen at the quarry wasn't fantasy. Whoever had dumped the body and gone after Dif wasn't mucking about. She felt queasy for that last angry text she'd sent to him. Remembered her promise to him.

She couldn't pass anything much on to Scobie.

It was late but she texted her anyway.

-You awake?

-Mmm hmm.

-Can I call you?

-Affirmative.

Cal rang, filled Scobie in on what she'd found without giving her all the background she'd been piecing together.

'That's attempted murder if it checks out. Arson is serious. You're dealing with someone desperate and vicious. What on earth was Dif mixed up in?'

'Trying to figure it out.'

'Where are you heading now?' Scobie's tone, raised with urgency.

'Might check out that Triton.'

'Well, be careful.'

'Okay. Miss you, DI. Miss those vigorous interrogations.'

'I mean it Cal. Keep on your toes.'

'Okay. Will do.'

Dammit. Managed to land more worry on her plate now. Nice one Nyx. Negotiated that really fuckin well.

Cal was growing weary of sleeping in the car. One more night, she told herself. Too bad she'd made herself so unwelcome at the caravan park. The manager wanted compensation for Dif's damage. He wouldn't give a tinker's cuss for what Cal had found. He was holding Dif responsible.

She thought about how she'd had to get in over that fence. Whoever had come to target Dif might have done the same. Maybe she should check that area out some more, in daylight. Then she realised the burnt caravan was in the storage yard because the manager or caretaker had moved it there. It wasn't parked in the holding area when Dif was staying in it. *Shit. It could've been anywhere.* Which meant whoever had tampered with it and set the fire could've accessed it via a different point. Maybe there would be CCTV coverage. Maybe someone had seen something.

The manager was certain Dif created the fire. He wouldn't have bothered asking any of the other residents if they'd seen anything. Dif had taken off, convincing McHardAss of his guilt. Case closed as far as he was concerned. Cal needed to find out where that van had been parked prior to the fire. She also needed a different approach now McHardAss was so prickly with her. Something else to follow up.

She covered her shoulders with her jacket and rug, closed her eyes. After tonight, home or motels—no more car seats.

Cal woke up in the Ford, stiff and groggy. Before she even opened her eyes, she began thinking about the silver Triton. It was a, what do they call it, material sighting and it pointed towards the person who'd driven that night to the quarry. She hadn't much to show for her time down south, though what she'd found at the caravan was suspicious. Either way, it gave her another nudge towards bringing Scobie into the circle. Scobie could follow up tips with colleagues even if it wasn't within her jurisdiction. Meantime, Cal needed to come up with anything she could. Waiting around wasn't an option for her or for Dif. The sooner she latched onto solid evidence the sooner more help could be directed Dif's way.

She was banking on the idea that the Triton driver lived on the south coast. Her searching so far found two Mitsubishi dealerships that might have supplied a vehicle. One in south Wollongong and the other in Kirrawee on the southern edge of Sydney. How could she come up with a ploy to get the information she needed?

Names and addresses of buyers. What have I got? Bribery? Hacking? Nah.

C'mon. Time's a wastin.

Dif had said that he thought the killer had been to his hut and somehow knew who he was. That letter from Zin was there, it identified Dif. Did the killer already know who Dif was, or had he asked around? And if he had, that meant someone other than Dif could possibly identify this person. The rough sleepers at Greyridge were a community of sorts. If someone wanted to find Dif or his camp or if he'd moved on, the killer would have had to ask there. Unless they already knew him. That was unlikely or they wouldn't have dumped a body so close to his hut. She needed to go back to the lower camp, have another word. She washed at the toilet block and set off along the coast for Greyridge.

Chapter 14

CAL PICKED UP A takeaway coffee before leaving Greyridge, gulped impatiently and burnt her mouth. Drove with a numb tongue, parked on the headland and walked the track along the rocky shoreline, around the estuary to the camp.

A cooling onshore breeze riffled over the waves. A gentle creek drained from the escarpment above filled the tea-stained lagoon, near the high-tide line. The camp was located on a bend beyond the blast of the seaward gusts, a small clearing with a central fireplace marked by stones and surrounded by the makeshift shelters.

Cal approached slowly and saw two men doing repairs to a roof with some short offcuts of corrugated iron. She recognised the pair as Truby and Storey from her first visit and called out as she neared.

'Sorry to bother you fellas again. Brought you some baccy.' She tossed three packets of tobacco to them as they knelt on the rippled iron.

'Nice one,' Truby said. 'You find Dif?'

'No joy yet. He's giving me the run-around.' She laughed, then became more sombre. 'He's got the wind up him from something he saw at the quarry so he's lying low. But he did manage to get some info to me. I'm following up. Dif took off nearly two weeks ago. Looks like someone got his name, knew about his camp. Who would've dobbed him?'

Straightaway she realised what she'd said. 'Not you fellas. But anyone new around here or the other camp up top? Someone who doesn't know the protocol or might give a person away for payment? You fellas had anyone come here asking about him?' Cal changed the weight through her legs. 'Aside from me? I'm kosher.' She laughed again and hoped they instinctively picked up on her decency, though she'd no right to expect it.

The two men looked at each other. Truby spoke.

'We asked around after you came last time. Cobb said a bloke went to the top camp up by the tailings.'

Cal visualised the first site she'd visited at the apex of the hill where Dif had raced years before. She'd walked through the camp under the banyan trees.

'He was askin' about the hut near the quarry and who lived there.'

'Did Cobb describe him?'

'Big bloke. Not as big as me. Solid,' Truby said.

'Did Cobb tell him anything?'

'Didn't like 'im. Kept schtum.'

'Anyone else up there he could've got info from?' Cal asked.

'There was newbies near the concrete flat. Not regulars, travellers. He mighta gone there first. Common knowledge where the camps are to dossers, people need to know what's what. Should be able to tell the difference between brethren and straight-street though, bad form. They're not so welcome up there now, been told to move on.'

Cal nodded.

'Would they have known Dif might have gone to Bidgee? Would they have said?'

Storey shrugged. 'Possible. People go there for a time-out if they've saved their dole. Hard livin' like this for some.'

'Don't s'pose Cobb saw a vehicle or anything?' Cal heard the desperation in her tone.

Truby and Storey looked at each other, smiled.

'Maroon Range Rover. Sports model. Said the bloke parked back up the track and walked in. Cobb followed, saw 'im leave. 'E told us, case you came back,' Storey said.

Cal closed her fists and struck the air in triumph.

'Cobb said it had racks—y'know.' He raised his hands above his head, curved his hands inwards, ran them back and forward above his head.

'Gotcha. Really appreciate it. Please thank him from me.' Cal smiled as she turned to leave.

'I woulda called but 'ad no signal.' Storey broke into a throaty laugh, waved his ancient Nokia beside his head.

'Better get that roof sorted. Rain's coming.' Cal winked as she left.

Well, that was interesting, she thought. No mention of a silver Triton pickup. Did the person who dumped the body have more than one vehicle? Had they gotten rid of the pickup? The physical description wasn't exactly detailed. But it was similar to the person Dif had described.

Gotta find those other roughies and see if they'd got a closer look. See what they'd told him. Nah. Given the bum's rush for breaking the code, Truby said. Dobbing Dif in like that. Wonder if that dude paid them off?

Still, gotta 'nother lead. Maroon Range Rover with the Sports options. Couldn't be many down the coast. Surely? Cost a bomb.

So, how to find it?

Cal walked back along the coastal track to where the Ford was parked in a small layby above the rocky promontory. She sat in the car and considered how best to use her time.

She did a quick search on late-model Range Rovers to get a clear image of the styling updates. The SUVs had a lower stance than standard model and a different grille. The sports bonnet also had a carbon-fibre bonnet insert. The roof-racks Cobb had mentioned would make it a bit easier to distinguish as well. How many of those were likely around? All those options added to the cost. Specialist servicing as well. Owner of something like that would be paying through the nose for a simple oil change. She did another regional search and found a sales service centre—Monaco Prestige Eurocars in Bowral. The image showed a BMW F80 and an Audi TT up on a hoist. Cal imagined the ka-ching for any work on those and was glad she could do so much of her own maintenance.

So, the guy Cobb spoke to wasn't driving a silver Triton but he fitted Dif's general description. Maybe he'd stored the Triton. Maybe it was never his to begin with and he'd borrowed it. That would endear him to whoever he'd borrowed it from, if it ever came out. Risky though, involving someone else. Maybe he had it up for sale or had already sold it. If the killer thought he only had Dif to deal with, he'd probably offload the pickup. People used online platforms for that. Cal brought up the Gumtree site on her phone and searched for late model silver Tritons on the south coast. She got two hits: one in Kiama and one in Shellharbour. Both still for sale.

How was she going to tackle it?

She could pose as a potential buyer, though she wasn't exactly comfortable with the idea. Pretty suss and wasting people's time. Well, what was the alternative? What if one of these people had been at the quarry that night? She had to do it.

She looked through the windscreen and watched the curve of waves running into the coast as she rang the first Triton ad in Shellharbour. She'd seen experienced wave-riders walk directly out across the rock escarpment, launching themselves straight over the reef where the breakers smashed into the sandstone crags. Others, less adventurous, walked the track along to the sand beach and made their laborious battle through the shore-break, out and around to the point where the waves peaked.

A woman answered Cal's call. They arranged for Cal to see the car within the hour. She had time to sit and let her mind wander a while before she had to leave. A lazy drift just being near the ocean. It always calmed her.

A late-model Lexus pulled up beside Cal's Ford. The chick slid out and unloaded a thruster surfboard from the roof-racks, placing it carefully on the grass beyond the asphalt. She returned to the Lexus, opened the boot, dragged out a wetsuit and began to undress between the two vehicles. The woman was slightly built, athletic, and had a bathing suit on under her hoodie and jeans. Cal looked away, put her hand beside her face so the woman might feel she had some privacy. A minute or so later the woman walked to her board, the top half of her wetsuit still down around her waist. She had long, black dreadlocks and a massive tattoo around her middle that rounded her back and rose to her shoulders, a squid and a shark enmeshed in battle. The woman was focussed on what she was doing, unknotting her board leash. Then she stretched and tugged the neoprene wetsuit along her limbs, looked up and saw Cal watching, smiled. Cal smiled back.

The woman picked up her board and ran towards the shore. Cal sighed, started the Ford, and backed out. As she edged past the Lexus she saw an emblem on the lower corner of the rear window. "Bidgee Boardriders" with a graphic of perfect waves and that headland further north on the coast. The sticker was shaped like a shield.

Chapter 15

CAL STOPPED THE CAR and stared at the emblem. Remembered what Dif had said in his text.

'Holy fuck,' she muttered. The owner of the pickup was a local board-rider? That might narrow things down. She snuck out her phone, sneakily zoomed in and snapped off a shot of the emblem.

She drove for twenty minutes, past Port Kembla and Lake Illawarra, and pulled up at a property several streets back from the coast. The pickup was on the driveway, the concrete wet from a hose down. Cal got out, walked over to the vehicle and took a vague look at the tailgate while homing in on the licence plate for a surreptitious check on the screw heads. Couldn't tell if the screws had recently been removed because they were still relatively new and untarnished. Older screws might've shown obvious tool marks if corroded. Never mind. It was worth a try.

A woman emerged from a path beside the house.

'Found us okay then?'

'Yup. All good. Mind if I just look over it?'

'Absolutely. We've sold the boat so don't really need it anymore. Used to put the kids' surf-ski on the back.'

Cal raised her eyebrows with effort, her smile more a grimace. Hated the noise those machines made at the beach. Dreamed of empty coastlines.

She feigned interest in the vehicle, overriding the guilt that she had no intention of buying the thing. Walked around the front, checked the tyres for uneven wear, made her way to the driver's side.

'Okay if I look inside?' she said, hand poised on the door.

'Of course, of course.' The woman encouraged her with an open-handed gesture.

Cal leaned into the pristine interior, took the opportunity to glance across the rear cab window. No sticker or evidence of a recently removed one. She emerged, wiped her hands down her thighs.

'Okay. Got a couple more to see. I've got your number.'

'Don't want to see the engine or take it for a drive? It's not a problem.'

'Nah. I'll take it for a run if I come back. Just have to eliminate a few more options. Thanks for your time.' Cal dipped her shoulder and walked off with her hands in her back pockets.

Got back to the Ford. One down, one to go. She rang the Kiama number. No answer. Left a message.

Her phone rang. Scobie.

'Hey, Scoobie-Doo.'

'Jesus, Cal. Don't call me that.'

'What's happening, DI?'

'Imogen is stabilising. I want to give another thirty-six hours here before I leave. I'm hoping to be back in Sydney by the weekend. Just don't want to go too soon. Maybe you could pick me up from the airport?'

'Love to. Give me a heads-up when you know your flight. Got some stuff brewing here. Don't wanna get caught out.'

'I'm not going to ask.'

'Good idea.'

Her phone rang again. The Kiama Triton number.

'Gotta take this call, sorry,' Cal told Scobie.

'Sure. Talk later.' Scobie rang off.

Cal thumbed in the other call, made her greeting.

A male replied. 'Sorry I couldn't get back to you sooner. You're after a Triton, huh? When would you like to take a look?'

'I could come now if it suits you?'

'Sure. I'm at work. I can pop out to the car park.' He gave Cal the address in south Wollongong. 'Just come round the back.'

'Great. See you shortly.'

She drove south, taking the freeway, then peeled off into an older section of the small city. The streets were featureless, flat, devoid of trees or vegetation other than weeds that grew through broken concrete, around the damp bases of old warehouses and along the fence-lines of disused yards. The address was fronted by a strip of faded storefronts, half of them with To Lease signs inside the grimy windows. She turned left down a laneway to a cul-de-sac of light industrial businesses. She passed an open doorway with a parked forklift, emptied wooden pallets stacked on their ends against an outside wall. Opposite that, another dark workspace had a vehicle on a hoist inside and a wire-haired dog on a long lead wagging its downcast tail in a slow rhythm from the shadows of the workshop.

A high chain-link fence marked the boundary to an adjacent business beside a laneway. Cal parked beside a concrete wall in the lane and texted the Triton owner. Further down the dead-end alley she saw the pickup. She got out and wandered over for a quick look before the owner came out. Squatting by the number plate she saw the screws looked undisturbed. She stood and went to the rear window of the cab. It looked smooth and unblemished. She angled her neck towards her shoulder, for a more acute sightline, ran her fingers over the surface. Smooth as.

'Don't worry. She's clean as a whistle. Been looked after.'

The hearty tone came from stocky bloke in a short-sleeved shirt. He'd emerged from a small joinery two doors along from the end building. He wore cargo-shorts and running shoes, his big toe punched through the tip of the right one. He pressed the key fob and opened the unlocked driver's side door, sweeping his arm like a maître-d'. 'Try it out.'

Cal played along, sat in the seat, held the steering wheel, reached for slider controls, looked in the side-mirrors. 'How many ks?'

'Twenty-seven thou, give or take. Barely run in.' He chuckled.

'Why you selling it?' Cal looked up at him.

He leaned on the roof over her, the sun radiating from behind his head, a blinding halo. 'Missus wants an SUV. What can ya do?'

Cal made to get out. He didn't move.

She crossed her left arm to the right side of the wheel and made to haul herself through the doorway.

'S'cuse me, mate.' She could've run her boot-heel down his shin if required.

'Course. Want me to start 'er up?'

'Nah. S'okay. Got another to see first. I'll be in touch. Thanks.'

Cal walked away.

Dodgy bloke, similar build to what Dif described. No ridges, no sign of a recently removed sticker. Could've done a good job of scraping it off and cleaning it though.

What to do next? She needed to follow up her theory about the caravan park. Find out where was Dif's caravan was parked when the fire happened. Maybe there'd be some CCTV footage from inside the grounds. And the Bidgee Boardriders sticker. It must be a club so presumably there'd be a membership list somewhere. How to get at that? Another hurdle. She was feeling useless.

C'mon Nyx. You might need to ask for help. Fuck off. Not like you don't have clever mates. Don't wanna be a pest. Fuck's sake Cal. Just ask.

Yeh, maybe later.

She did an online search of the Bidgee Boardriders club. They had a shared clubroom at the local Lifesavers, which was unusual, she thought. Weren't board-riders and surf-lifesavers traditional foes? Like, the SLS were the goodie-goodies? Maybe they had to put that stuff aside in a small community where there weren't huge resources for separate amenities. Looked like the Bidgee Boardriders had a big membership too, several hundred. The shield emblem formed part of the website banner. She got the sense there was an elitism, local honour in having possession of one of the membership markers displayed. Only registered members could get one. How could she get hold of that list? *Shoulda majored in technology instead of biology, Nyx.* Take too long to wheedle her way in and join up. She needed help. Scobie's mob could do it, but she couldn't ask favours there. The DI was pretty tied up anyway. Who else?

And what if she could do if she even got the list? Hundreds of names, for sure. Seriously, was she gonna check every single one? *Fuck's sake Cal. Snap to it. Follow whatever crumbs you can find. Who knows what might surface? Just fucking get on with it. Eyeball that list, you might connect a name or address, something familiar.*

She had so little, she had to keep digging. And she *really* needed help.

Cal left the southern suburbs of Wollongong and headed back up north towards Bidgee on the old coast road. The sky was overcast but the cloud cover wasn't dense, rain seemed unlikely. Light traffic meant she reached the Bidgee caravan park in less than twenty minutes. She parked outside beyond the entrance and considered how to approach things. She didn't really want another run-in with McHardAss. In the distance she could hear a mower—not a little two-stroke, a bigger ride-on.

She got out of her car and walked towards the entrance to the campground, keeping in the shadow of the small trees planted on the nature strip. She investigated the entrance and beyond where the noise was coming from and could see the machine through gaps in the hedging in front of the ablution block. She waited for a better look at the driver when he turned the machine by the road edge. He was a wiry fellow, looked older than the manager. Could she make her way over and speak with him without the manager seeing her from the office? Hopefully being on foot would help. She skirted the reception area and kept wide of the sightline from that building as she walked towards the ablutions block and hedging. She waited for the mower guy to finish his sweep and face her way so she could get his attention, put her hand up in a friendly wave.

The guy got off the ride-on mower and shut the engine down. He pulled off his earmuffs.

'Sorry to interrupt you, mate,' Cal said.

'No worries. Had enough of the racket anyway. These things only shut out so much.' He waved the ear-pods as he moved away from the machine to the shade of an overhanging bottlebrush tree, put a hand on his hip.

'You may be able to help me with something.' Cal pointed to the rear lockup yard where the unused caravans were kept, including the one Dif had stayed in. 'Mate of mine was in that Vagabond. Where did it used to be parked?'

'Bit of damage in that one. Take a bit of work to get her right. Was on that concrete pad along from the office, hedge beside it. N'other one there now. Good spot, close to the showers.'

Cal nodded. 'Mate was lucky to get out.'

'He was. Could've been nasty. Silly bugger, smoking in bed.'

'Not a smoker mate. That's the thing. Bit odd really.'

'Hmm. Boss said the guy was a nutter, mucking around with lighter fuel.' The guy looked away from Cal. 'Sorry, y'know. Your mate.'

'Yeh. Kinda mysterious ...' She let it hang. 'You have contractors maintaining the vans?'

The mower guy pulled his chin back. 'Nothing wrong with that caravan. They're parked up, not doing road miles. Bugger all maintenance required. 'Cept when some knob goes troppo.'

'Fair enough. Just doesn't add up though. For me, knowing my mate.'

The caretaker pointed, using his third finger; the first two digits were missing at the bottom knuckle.

'There's something on that pole opposite the office.' A CCTV fixture that emerged from above a shrub border beside the driveway. Cal had already noted it on her way in but wondered if there was anything more.

'Only one I know of. Manager probably gave it a once over after the fire. He didn't mention seeing anything or anyone. You're right though. Bit of a mystery.' He tapped his earmuffs against his thigh.

'I gotta get on.'

Cal compressed her lips, gave a small nod.

'Thanks for your time.' She turned and headed towards the office, walking slowly, looked up towards the surveillance camera, kept going towards the exit.

She got to the car and withdrew a notebook from the centre console. Drew a small sketch—the layout of the park sites, the probable CCTV pole and sightlines, the proximity of other vans, the ablution block sightlines, and any possible unsighted access from the main road beyond. The Vagabond may well have been close to the manager's office and near to the ablutions block. But late at night it was unlikely people would've been using the showers or kitchens, so someone not wishing to be seen would have little to bother them from that quarter. The CCTV camera focussed on the office and the driveway in front of it. If someone entered the area from outside, there was plenty of cover to do so, and to get around and under

Dif's van—especially if the occupant was on a bender and nearly comatose.

Cal doubted that whoever had attempted to torch the van had driven into the complex; they would've come on foot. So, unless they lived nearby, they probably drove and parked in a nearby street. She pulled up a map on her phone and scanned the area for possible CCTV cameras. The main coastal road, aside from the freeway inland, would likely have some cameras up near the main shopping centre, but there were numerous side streets to the shore area. She thought about her previous trip to Bidgee when she'd climbed the back fence into the holiday park. She'd entered via a side street near the Play Area. *You'd hope every kids' playground would have CCTV now. Make life difficult for the paedo quotient.*

Her phone pinged a text. It was from Dif.

-Not keen on getting near Tambor territory. Do what I can from afar. Can that work?

Cal texted back.

-Guess so. Keep your head down.

She left the holiday park and cruised slowly back along Ocean Drive, the main coastal thoroughfare that snaked like an ancient trail along the headland. It ran close to the shore all the length of the coast except where it was too precipitous or flood-prone.

The children's play area and car-park were several hundred metres north. She turned in, her eyes focussed through the top of her windscreen, checking all the concrete and timber light-posts and power-poles for cameras. Her headlights swept across the shadowed play equipment and lit the stolid toilet block and changing sheds. On the front corner of the building, the familiar orb of a CCTV cover jutted below the eaves. It had a clear view across to the road and car-park where Cal currently sat. She did a three-point turn, checking again as she drove out.

At the apex of the northern end where she'd driven in, another camera was fixed high on a power-pole at the junction with the entrance road. That one would capture passing traffic on the main road. If someone had entered the holiday park to torch the van Dif had stayed in, it could possibly be recorded, and maybe not so hard to find if they'd come late at night. There'd be little traffic down there. The other possibility was someone had gotten in the same way Cal had, over the back fence. Either that or they were already inside the holiday park, another reso.

CCTV was one thing. Having access to it was another. She'd reached her limits with online searching. Both the public cameras and the Bidgee Boardriders register required skills she didn't possess. Ditto the Triton rego number. Scobie was no help because she was stuck in Melbourne and Cal would be pushing the envelope to ask favours of a non-existent police investigation. Even if it was, Cal's requests wouldn't be kosher. The sooner she got them on-board and with Dif's consent, the better. She began to feel shaken. Here she was with all these tiny pieces of possibly linked information, but nothing that gelled. She had to up the ante.

Cal thumbed through her contacts then hit a number. It was picked up after two rings.

'Pascal's Bits and Bytes.'

'Pirate, you numpty pretender. It's Cal.'

'Ah, the bug-catcher. How goes it in the world of segmented body parts?'

'You need to get away from your screens, mate. And it's botanicals I do as much as faunals, yeh?'

'Both far from my purview. So, why you calling?'

'You still restoring that Galaxie?'

'Lifelong project. But you might see a little progress. Why?'

'Got a pair of original tail-lights and trim. Need a favour. Maybe we could do a swap.'

'I'm still here.'

'Prefer not to elaborate over the phone. Where you hangin' these days?'

'Undercliff.'

'At your mum's?' Cal tried to tone down her incredulity.

Silence at the other end. Then: 'Sydney rents, mate. Get real.'

'Can I drop round? I'll text first.'

'Bring the lenses.'

Chapter 16

WHEN CAL GOT BACK to Sydney, she drove first to Zin's place in Petersham and parked outside the garage door in the rear lane. Inside the garage she retrieved the Galaxie tail-lights from a cardboard box on a shelf. She folded a sheath of bubble-wrap around them and put them in a smaller box. Then she checked the package she'd taped under the bench. Nice and snug still. She carried the box for Pirate outside and put in the boot of the Ford.

She should check the place again, the broken window. But all she wanted to do was leave ASAP. She'd made it as far as the kitchen last time. No further. Still hadn't been down the hallway. *What's the matter with you?*

There'd been an intruder, someone who may still even be inside. *That's not what scares you though Nyx, is it?*

She crossed the yard, slowly climbed the steps and unlocked the back door. Zin's old bedroom was at the front of the house. A hallway ran up the length of the semi and the rooms ran off it. Cal walked through the kitchen and approached the other end of the cottage. The door to her aunt's old room stood ajar. Cal entered. It smelt of the scent Zin wore and clove cigarettes. Smoked them at night as some kind of misguided relief from nicotine and tar for her lungs. Even when she found out the clove fags were just as harmful as regular cigarettes, she kept up her evening routine.

Dust motes floated through the light from the stained-glass panels in the tops of the sash windows.

Cal walked out and checked the other bedroom, the one she and Dif had shared for a time until Cal started using the sleepout.

The second bedroom contained two single beds. The bed nearest the door had no bedding on it, which was odd as Zin had always kept them made up for visitors. Cal stepped into the room and around the base of the first bed. There on the floor was the bedding—not dumped, like Zin had been going to take it out for washing, but arranged on the floor as if it had been slept in. Near the pillow were two pieces of partly crushed gold foil like the chocolate wrappers from the kitchen.

'What the fuck?'

Cal went down the hallway to the back door, checked the inside lock. It wasn't deadlocked. She always deadlocked it since she was out of town so much. *Did I forget to last time? Guess I was kinda messy that day.*

Someone crashing here. Jesus fuck.

It felt sacrilegious.

Yeh, cos if you were actually here occasionally, it might provide somewhat of a disincentive to break-ins.

But she had so much in front of her, Dif's predicament took precedence. It just wasn't feasible for her to remain in Petersham. Sorting it would have to wait.

Cal left things inside much as she'd found them, deadlocked the back door, and left.

She drove to Undercliff in less than ten minutes and parked outside the stark, brick bungalow with a closely mown lawn and solitary palm tree in the yard. People don't know what to do with a garden space, she thought. Plant some trees and you could have birdlife in there. She walked around the back and down to the basement that Pirate had converted to a bedsit and small workspace. Cal knocked on the west-facing door, weathered from its exposure to the afternoon sun. Chunks of desiccated putty were missing from the edges of the opaque, central window and the green-painted woodwork was streaked with long cracks of silvering timber.

'Down the back,' a voice called from behind her.

Cal retreated down the steps and scanned the back garden, saw a hand gloved in elbow length leather, waving from beside a dilapidated trellis. She wandered towards the figure who stretched a pair of secateurs through a cascade of barbed and twisted canes.

Pirate wore aged paisley-patterned harem pants. Her soft, jowly face beamed beneath a bounce of shaggy hair as she dropped a handful of small, orange orbs into a basket on the ground. Her left eye-patch was positioned over the top of her glasses. 'Rose hip syrup. Second best treat of autumn.'

'What's the first?'

'Cooler weather, natch.'

'Nice to see you outside, you old diesel,' Cal said.

'Run three k every afternoon.' Pirate gestured for Cal to return up the path.

'Yeh, right,' Cal scoffed.

Two widescreens on a long desk showed web-pages Pirate had been tweaking. Above them a wall-mounted screen displayed a re-run of the Monaco F1 Grand Prix. Cal recalled the spare room in Stanmore that once housed an early main-frame Pirate had constructed. Compact design had come a long way since those days.

Cal stood beside a chair whose seat was lumped with a cloth bag spilling yarns and crocheted crystal bags. Pirate lifted them gently onto the floor. Cal handed over the cardboard box.

'Have a pew.' Pirate delved into the box as Cal studied the tiny, laced bags now on a table. She shook her head.

'Ohhh.' Pirate lifted out the first tail-light. 'Nice. No fading.'

'Or crazing. They're mint.'

'Sweet. What do you need?' She looked at Cal, bunched her lips.

'Can you get a list from a club register? Bidgee Boardriders. I need names and addresses. Just looking for one in particular.'

Pirate raised her eyebrows. 'Name?'

'I'll know it when I see it.' Cal shrugged. 'Look, I won't do anything iffy with it. You'll just have to trust me. But I need that list.'

'Wanna wait?'

'Sure. Great.'

Cal looked up at the F1 race onscreen. 'My wheat-from-chaff test question at the race-track: "Some say Mick Schumacher got a leg-up through the family oligarchy."'

'Those in the affirmative would be train-spotting drongoes. Nowhere to hide at 300k. Genetics, mate,' Pirate mumbled.

'Totally.'

After mere minutes, Pirate turned to her. 'Just printing it out now. That all you need?'

'Um, can you get into Transport NSW?'

'You have a rego number?'

Cal gave her the number Dif had taken the night at the quarry and Pirate jotted it on a notepad.

'This one takes a bit more back-door work. What are you after?'

'Engine and frame numbers.'

'Can I text the info to you later?'

'Absolutely.'

'Anything else?'

'Jeez, pushing my luck here, aren't I?'

'You don't ask, you don't get. What is it?'

Cal got up from her seat. On her phone she brought up a map of the playground near the caravan park in Bidgee.

'Well, if you're up for it, is there any way you can get into a Local Council's Parks CCTV footage? Or do they outsource it to private security firms?'

'I can get into anything you like. What are you after?'

Cal leaned over towards Pirate as the printer whirred and sent forth pages of names and addresses. 'There's a play-area here.' She zoomed in on her phone screen. 'And a camera on the corner of this building. I reckon it captures the car-park. And this one —' she scrolled across the map '— gets the passing traffic here.' She pointed to the intersection of the road to the caravan park. 'I'm looking for vehicles late that night, probably after 9.30pm. Doable?' She leaned down and wrote May 19th on a pad next to Pirate's keyboard, the date McHardie gave her from the caravan ledger. She also jotted "silver Mitsi Triton pickup & maroon Range Rover."

'Might take a bit longer. Have to access better systems and go through endless footage once I do. Can you leave it with me?'

'No probs.' Cal grabbed the sheaf of printed information. 'Really appreciate it.' She waved and went towards the door. 'Sun's out. Want some air mate? Leave it open?'

Pirate nodded. 'Yeh. The vitamin D should reach me in here, eh?'

Cal hurried back to the car. There were half a dozen pages of names and addresses. She was desperate to examine them properly, carefully. She needed a coffee. There was a small café on the corner of a nearby park.

Armed with a long black takeaway she sat on a bench under some trees overlooking the river. The water was a murky grey and smelt of anaerobic decay. She figured most of the light industry of the surrounding suburbs were dumping all sorts of toxic crap into their storm-water runoffs. Nevertheless, scruffy looking ibis pecked and pranced along the muddy margins.

Cal gulped her coffee and did a cursory scan of the Bidgee Boardriders' list. Nothing jumped out at her on a first look. Unsurprising since she didn't actually have any names yet to go on. But the link to this club could be crucial, she needed to familiarise herself in case she sourced a name elsewhere. *So little to go on*. She felt desperate, anxious. *Follow all prospects.* Maybe her path had been skewed; the emblem Dif had glimpsed that night could have been anything. But the shape he'd described fitted what she'd seen on the surfer woman's Lexus. *Keep reading, embed the names in your mind.* In the absence of other options, she had to find a way to link a person or vehicle to a name or address on that list.

What else could she check out while she was in town? Her only other lead was the Range Rover that Cobb had seen and the guy asking after Dif. The links to the quarry and the body were all local. It didn't gel that someone from elsewhere had dropped a body in a unfamiliar setting. Following that logic, the driver of the Range Rover was also local. So, chances were, they'd have their vehicle serviced at the nearest specialist. Bowral.

Cal couldn't access their records and she'd already asked a lot of Pirate. She needed to be more creative. What she had in mind required attributes and skills she didn't possess.

Chapter 17

CAL PULLED UP THE contacts list on her phone and made a call. After half a dozen rings it went to the message service.

'Mina. Cal here. Need your help with something. Can you call me back? Catch ya.'

Cal was desperate to get something moving. She didn't know how or where Dif was. A possible murderer was currently walking free and might be chasing after him and Cal was running out of options. She didn't want to ask her boss for more time off, and so far she'd gotten nowhere.

Cal's phone burred. Mina returning her call.

'Hey, chick. How's tricks?' Cal said.

'The better for hearing from you. Where are you these days?'

'Roving and raving. Same old.' Cal snorted. 'Got a bit of a proposal. How are you fixed for time this week?'

'Always fit you in, hun.'

Cal blushed. 'Can't tell you the ins and outs on the phone. Can I see you, run it by you first?'

'Sure. You in town tonight? I'll be done by 8.30.'

'Cool. Where shall we meet? Whatever's easy for you.'

'How 'bout Tosh's?'

'Newtown, right?'

'Yeh, South King Street. Left-hand side. See you before 9.'

'Thanks Mina.'

Cal parked in a back street and walked to the bar. She ordered a Peroni and sat with an eye on the doorway. She'd lived in and around the area for more than a decade and seen the inevitable gentrification. It certainly wasn't as diverse as it used to be. Fewer old people, less students, hardly any working-class folks.

Mina arrived wearing a zippy little faux-leather jacket with fake-fur lining and looked immaculate despite having just changed gear after leading her barre class. She carried a large gear bag. Cal was bemused by the layered, warm-down clothing in expensive colours. Was that a wrap or a skirt?

'G'day, gorgeous girl,' Cal greeted her old friend.

Mina's hand went around Cal's back, rested on her belt. Curvaceous and as tall as Cal, she wore her chestnut hair twisted into a topknot. Her dark eyes seemingly had a quick slick of eyeliner, but she wore no other make-up. Cal wondered what other mysterious lady business she'd done to look so good.

'What can I get you, lovely?' Cal grinned.

'After my day, a gin and lemon, thanks.'

'Gotcha.' Cal waved over the barwoman, made the order.

'So, I'm keen as. What's the gig?'

Cal laughed. She loved that they didn't need to fill in the intervening time gaps. 'Okay. Bit of a challenge—for me, anyway. You'll do it on your ear, I've no doubt.' Cal lowered her voice. 'It's not strictly above-board.'

Mina leaned in, her enthusiasm raised another notch.

'I need you to pose as a potential prestige car buyer.'

Mina threw her head back and guffawed. 'Ha. Playing out a fantasy. Piece of cake.'

'It's kind of particular. Down in the Southern Highlands I'm trying to trace a specific vehicle. I know they don't currently stock a Range Rover Sports, but I reckon if you go in and express interest in one and say you'd like a test drive they could ask the owner of this one, sweeten the deal with a discounted service or something — especially if you order a car through them and they think they'll be getting a commission.'

'I like it.' Mina sipped her drink, eyes wide open as she waited for Cal to go on.

'It'll require a bit of performing from you. I want him distracted—the business owner. I don't need to tell you what's required in that department.'

'Indeed.'

'Thing is, I want to be nearby to see where this vehicle goes and who's driving. So, once you're done I wanna follow the rooster who owns it. The less you know about all that the better. But if this vehicle can be drawn out and

I can get a fix on it it'll be a huge help to me. Whaddaya reckon?' Cal took a long draw on her beer as she waited for Mina's response.

'I love it. Haven't had a show like this in a while. I'm totally up for it.'

'You're a good egg, Mina.' They clinked glasses. 'Okay. I wanna get onto it ASAP. I'll have to tee up a car for you, something spectacular. When are you free to do it?'

'Most of the classes I'm giving are at night at the mo. I can free up a day for you, so long as it's not too early.' She winked.

'Great. I'll get onto a car and confirm with you. Next day or so. Cool?'

'Totes.'

'You okay to ring this guy in advance and see if you can organise a test drive? Cos he'll have to get in touch with the owner.' Cal lifted from her seat, pulled out her wallet and handed Mina a folded note. 'Sales Manager. George Antoniou. You feel okay about swingin' it?'

'For sure. I'll get myself psyched before I call. Nothing ventured, huh?' She put the note in her handbag. 'And I'll work on my look.' She touched her hair, knotted in a high twist. 'This'll be more Anna Wintour in her front row seat at the Paris catwalk for starters. Pitch-perfect blow-dry, status lady lob.' She grinned.

Cal had no idea what Mina was referring to but nodded anyway. 'Course. You'll nail it. I'll try and sort a car tomorrow morning and I'll ring you to let you know what I've got. That way you can sound legit about looking for a new purchase. Just wait till then before you call him. Don't need to overplay it. Don't want anyone getting antsy.'

'Perfect.'

When Cal dropped Mina home it was after 10pm. She was wired, and still had someone to see about a car at the foot of the Blue Mountains. She'd drive out to Kurrajong, get onto it first thing in the morning.

She got home in less than an hour and a half, wishing the traffic was always that light. As she cruised up the driveway Dee's cottage was in darkness. Woman always had an early start. Cal parked beside the old shearers' quarters, gently closed her door. Banjo would know she was home, and hopefully not feel the need to give a warning bark. She went inside and threw her gear beside the bed, lay on top of the covers.

Next morning a familiar bump on the door roused her. Banjo.

Cal hid behind the door as she pulled it open. A purple ball dropped and rolled through the gap.

She heard Banjo's nose puffing air as he entered the room and peered around the door, looking straight at her.

'Can't fool you, can I?' She leaned down and kissed his head. 'You all better now, fella?'

Banjo licked her face, his singular front paw leaving the ground in a playful mini-leap.

'C'mon, then. Quick one.' Cal went outside with the dog and hurled the ball from the veranda. Banjo's rear paws scrabbled for grip as he accelerated after it, off the steps, across the gravel drive and grass verges, skidding to a crouch at the pole-fencing, where he deftly retrieved the toy from under the bottom rail. The donkeys nibbled greens, unperturbed.

After a few more throws Cal considered the over-exertion probably wasn't ideal for healing stitches. She peeked towards Dee's cottage, hoped Dee hadn't seen her potentially undoing the surgical work.

'C'mon, mate, best not overdo it.' She swung her head to bring him back onto the veranda before she went inside to make coffee.

Banjo sprawled on the deck at her feet in a shaft of morning sunlight.

'Things to do, places to be, buddy.' She couldn't meet his eyes. 'Make it up to you when your stitches are sorted.' She ruffled the thick fur at his neck, tipped her coffee dregs into the rose border and went inside to grab her keys and gear.

First things first, sort a car for Mina. She drove to Bentley nearby on the river flats, an area of old working-class suburbia and industrial parks near the waterway. She cruised by a trio of self-storage lockup areas then turned down a rough track beside a scaffolding supplier and a paint factory.

The track was lined by a series of low, broad, corro-sided buildings with roller-door frontages, their side and rear yards in varying states of orderliness. Beyond them, a long stretch of land provided a sort of buffer before the back fences of the suburban yards several hundred metres across the intervening wasteland. Occasionally run over by a tractor-drawn mower, the chopped-back weeds and grass provided cover for semi-feral chickens dumped there by owners who had lost interest.

Cal had befriended some of the engineers in two of the back workshops. They were all car nuts.

She followed a pocked side-track between two sheds to a yard of machine carcasses. Someone had cut a couple of 44-gallon oil-drums lengthways, filled them with soil and canna lilies beside one of the towering sheds. A noble attempt, but the leafless stalks did little to soften the bleak surrounds. Opposite the floral beautification a cavernous barn-like structure stood with an open doorway double the width of a large truck.

A patchwork terrier emerged from behind a primer-coated 4WD parked in a lake of muddy water. The small dog made half-hearted warning barks as Cal approached but didn't come any closer.

Inside the building, a wheel-less bus body rested on massive wooden chocks. Across the space, beside an open side-door, a small white-haired man in grey coveralls. Gnarled hands gripped a portable grinder, no safety glasses or ear-muffs to be seen. He looked like a character from a 1960s British gangster pic, long pale hair swept up and over in a slick bouffant, thick lips forming a narrow pout as he wound down a threaded screw on a large press. Cal walked into the man's sight-line before he fired up the machine. The dog still yapped a warning from the far doorway.

'Mac.' Cal lifted her chin in greeting.

The man paused, put the grinder on the edge of the press. 'Do for ya, Cal?'

'Need some help.'

'Aw, yeh.'

'You still detailing limos?' Cal raised her eyebrows.

'S'ma little earner, mate.' Mac swung his head down the side of the building. Cal knew people lived in a partitioned-off back section of the shed they were in. But further behind that was another large construction like a small aircraft hangar. They were so far back from the main road and totally obscured by factories and sheds, the only people who knew of the existence of them were those who lived or worked there, or select visitors and associates.

'Nearly smoko, ay? C'mon. This repair is giving me the shits. Idiot patched up the chassis rot with Bondo.'

'That'll be effective in a smash.'

Mac led Cal out the side door to a narrow yard. In a small three-sided bay, piles of winter wood lay under a sheet of corro, timber off-cuts and log-ends cut into short lengths. Alongside that stood a rust-streaked shipping container with a small bench and chairs rigged up for a tearoom near the doorway. At one end of the bench was Mac's office—an old desktop computer and curling desk-pad strewn with torn-off cardboard serial-numbers and oily smears. Mac filled the kettle, lit a fag and pushed aside the open packet of shortbread fingers.

Cal explained the top layer of how and why she wanted to set-up a Range Rover test-drive to find a particular owner. She omitted the background of Dif's situation. 'Late model, full sports options. Burgundy colour. Can't be many like that in one area, huh?'

'How ya like ya tea?' Mac spoke around his ciggy.

'White and one, thanks, mate. So, I'm thinking if I borrow one of your choice rides, it'll help sell Mina as a potential buyer. She's trustworthy and a good driver. Her dad used to rally.'

Mac nodded, stirred the teas, put a mug in front of Cal. 'Let's see what I've got booked out. When you thinking you'll need it?'

'Soon as. Mid-week is good. Might work best for you too?'

Mac sat at the desk and squiggled the mouse, brushing crumbs onto the floor, until an image of a supercharged Holden pickup filled the screen. Cal leaned on the door-jamb.

Mac hit an icon and typed in a password, looked over his shoulder at Cal. 'What are ya after? Anything particular?'

Cal picked up her tea, peered at the screen. 'Probs something more posh than rock'n'roll.'

'Got a cream Caddy might fit the bill.' Mac checked the online bookings for his limo hires.

'Still got the Merc coupe?' Cal asked.

'Won't be leaving the stable for a while. Bit of a soft spot.' Mac brought up the image of a silver Mercedes C207 coupe. The car was sleek and sporty yet still refined looking.

'I reckon that would fit the bill. Is it available?'

'Yup. It's got unmarked rego plates too. Keep you under the radar.'

That was a plus. Cal didn't want attention drawn to the car being an executive hire.

'Sweet. Only need it for a half-day.'

'What you up to anyway?' Mac drained his tea. Asbestos mouth.

'Following up something dodgy a mate saw. Long story.'

Mac pulled his head backwards. His neck was stringy and grimy, looked too small for his noggin. 'What kinda dodgy?'

'Rather not say for now. Best you don't know. Your car won't be in any danger, mate. Nothing like that. I just need to keep all my enquiries on the down low till things settle. Fill you in then. Okay?'

Mac pouted. 'No skin off my nose. Go fer broke.' He stood. 'Wanna take it now?'

'Oh. Yeh sure. Gotta make a quick call.' Cal stepped outside to check in with Mina.

'I'll get back to this mongrel job then. Keys are on the board there.' Mac nodded towards a series of hooks on a timber offcut screwed to the side of the desk out of sight from the doorway. 'It's parked out back. You know the drill.' Mac waved as he returned to the grinder in the shed.

Yeh, Cal knew the procedure. Fill it with fuel before returning it, pay for mileage and don't crash it.

Now she was set. Just needed Mina to sweet-talk the test ride down south and they'd be good to go. Piece of cake.

She rang her. 'Hey, chick. We're on, if you can confirm that test drive. Then you can cruise out here to Kurrajong in the morning, I can take my Ford while you drive the other down to Bowral. Otherwise, whatever day as soon as.'

'I'll get onto it now. What's my ride?'

'Merc coupe. C207.'

'Yippee. I'll text as soon as I know.'

Three hours later Cal's phone bipped. Mina.

'How'd you go, girl?'

'We're all set. Midday tomorrow. He must've put some pressure on the guy. Don't know what he promised him, but we're all teed up. The guy's going away later in the week so we lucked out.'

'Far out. You good to get out here mid-morning?'

'Lock it in. Sorting my outfit tonight.'

Chapter 18

Mina's wardrobe didn't run to the understated look required for the scam. After giving her barre class she took an uber to her sister's apartment. Christina, an accountant, lived in Annandale.

Mina exited the lift and knocked on her sister's entrance across the hall. She held up a bottle of Pinot Gris as Christina opened the door.

'Nice one,' Christina said as they hugged. The older sister was similar in height to Mina but a little shorter through the middle and longer-limbed. Her shoulder-length hair was reddish-blonde, but they shared a resemblance through the eyes and chin.

'Don't want to keep you long, Chi-chi. Know it's a school night,' Mina chirped.

Christina grabbed a pair of wineglasses from a cupboard over the speckled granite bench and put them in front of her sister.

'How's your week so far, hun?' Mina poured wine and handed a glass to her older sister.

Christina closed her eyes in a long blink. 'Same old. Love my job. Boss is a narcissistic prat.'

Mina didn't push. 'Okay. Show me what you've got, sweetie. Cheers.' They clinked glasses.

Christina ushered her sister into the bedroom where she'd laid out several sets of shoes, skirts and handbags.

Mina lifted one of the shoes, something she would've described as clumpy. But she kept that to herself. 'Darling, I'm used to balancing my heels on one finger. Maybe something less block, more kitten.'

Christina sipped her wine. 'What are you up to anyway?'

Mina held up a pencil skirt. 'This is the business.' She stroked the fine fabric with an open palm. 'I'll team it with my never-fail cashmere.' She looked to Christina who'd tilted her eyebrows, not to be fobbed off.

'Um, sort of an audition. Different skill-set than what my usual jobs require. Just calls for a variation on my wardrobe, hun.' Mina held the skirt to her hips, dropped her head to one shoulder as she checked the mirror.

'Sounds mysterious, Min.'

'I'll fill you in later.' She checked inside the waistband. 'Helmut Lang. Sweetie, he might be a narcissist, but that boss of yours sure pays well.' She raised her glass to Christina. 'Sorted.'

Mina arrived at Kurrajong next morning in her Golf Turbo. A hyper-excited Banjo ran in circles beside her door.

When Mina got out Cal wolf-whistled. 'Look at you. Salesman won't be able to hear a word you're saying.'

Mina struck a pose and giggled. 'Let's do this thing.' She appraised the Merc in a glance. 'Wow, Cal. Swisho. Might not give it back.'

Cal beamed. 'We can cruise down, then do a bit of getting in and out and stop-starting so you feel more casual with it.'

'Sounds good.' Mina climbed in behind the wheel, adjusted her seat and the mirrors. 'Even smells luxurious. I could get used to this, Cal.' She primped her hair in the vanity mirror.

'You deserve it.' Cal smiled. 'Really appreciate your help.'

'How d'you want to play this?'

'You follow me down? I'll stop about five ks away, let you know we're close. I'll keep driving past the place — you'll see it on your left. You go in and do your thing. I'll go through Bowral and park on the southern exit near the Botanic Gardens. If he's from the coast, as I suspect, he'll have to go that way back. You text when you're done, and I'll pick him up when he passes. That's the plan anyway.'

'T'riff.'

Cal pulled out in the Ford, Mina followed in the Merc and they headed for the A9 south. Cal drew away and Mina let some distance play out between them before she gave the Merc its legs. When she put her foot down her body pushed back into the seat as the twin-turbo 4.7 litre engine opened up. Mina whooped, feeling like she was in a movie as she flicked through the 6-speed, the roadside blurring beside her.

When Cal waved Mina off to do her thing, Mina checked her make-up one more time, took a deep breath and cruised towards the target down the road.

Antoniou the salesman had told Mina on the phone he'd lent the Range Rover owner his personal vehicle and sent him off for coffee.

Mina slowed and eased to the far end of the forecourt, then swept left, parking outside the showroom with her driver's door facing the front window so Antoniou could get an eyeful as she got out. She hoped he wasn't gay.

She saw the maroon vehicle parked nearby. Before she got to walk inside, George Antoniou appeared through the double glass doors. He was tall and trim with recently barbered hair and tanned skin. His dark trousers and pale blue shirt were crisp and well-tailored. Ditto the sports jacket.

He held out his hand to her, shook with both. 'George Antoniou. Perfect timing. Can I get you a coffee before we head off?'

'Mina Gianetti. Lovely to meet you, and thank you for setting this up. So good of you.' Mina radiated. 'No need for coffee, thanks. I'm on a bit of a tight turnaround. Not to be rude.'

'Of course. No problem.' Antoniou led her towards the Range Rover. 'Bit of a change from your Merc.'

'I love the Merc but the kids ski. Both sports mad. It's just not practical, sadly.'

Mina had noticed when she first pulled up that the Range Rover number plates had been obscured by dealer plates attached over the top. No doubt a privacy and security measure for their premium clients. She didn't want to bring attention to the fact she'd noticed, but was disappointed. It was a nugget of info she'd wanted to give Cal.

She peered below the tailgate bottom edge. 'No scuffing on the bumper top. Not a golfer then.' Mina winked at Antoniou who gave a small shake of the head but was giving nothing away regarding the owner. He pressed the tailgate button on the smart-key and the rear door lifted open.

'Plenty of room for my tack. Great. Boot on the Merc is a bit pinched. Let's go for a spin.'

Mina slid into the driver's seat as Antoniou climbed in on the passenger's side.

'It's so good of your friend to do this. I can't tell you how grateful I am.' Mina kept her tone low.

'It's all good. I'll do him a deal on his next service so we're sweet. Spreading the love.' Antoniou chuckled. Mina saw his eyes drop to her exposed knee.

She adjusted the rear-view mirror. 'So, Commandshift? I do miss a manual.'

'Yes, they're becoming a rarity. Not a purist's manual but a nod in the direction.'

'Takes all the fun out of driving.' Mina eased onto the main road and turned for the highway, put her foot down.

On the outskirts of Bowral, Cal waited. The guy driving the Range Rover was probably based on the coast. Everything had happened in that region. Even if there were two people involved, surely they shared the same area.

It wouldn't do to appear from behind the Range Rover anywhere near the dealership. Better to pick him up as he passed through the town and headed southwest. In a carpark beside the Southern Highlands Botanic Gardens, she held on for Mina's call. Risk was that the driver would take M31 heading southwest for the Hume Highway, and she'd lose him. But based on what she'd gathered so far, her bet was on Kangaloon Road towards the sea. Also possible he might stop in the town for something and wouldn't come her way immediately. Just had to hold her nerve and wait. A lot of time, energy and favours at stake.

Cal gnawed the side of her thumbnail, scratched her head. She looked in her mirrors, monitored her breathing. Payoff could be big if this worked. Crap and dead-ends otherwise. She checked her phone again, made sure she hadn't silenced her notifications—again. And it literally pinged right then with a message from Mina.

-You're on Cal. I just left. Good luck hun. X

Cal breathed out hard. Flicked back a text.

-You're a gem. Enjoy your drive home, Be in touch. X

She could still be waiting some time.

Her fingers drummed a syncopated rhythm on the steering wheel. Her eyes ran across her rear-view and side mirror, back and forth, as she waited. The traffic was steady. Good, easier to disappear. What if the Range Rover owner had hung around town, gone to a café? Or if he took the opportunity to pay visits to anyone local, the whole timeframe opened. She'd bet on the guy just doing the favour for the salesman, no more.

The Range Rover should be plain to see with its distinctive styling and roof-racks. She sighed and glanced across the treetops beyond the carpark. A kookaburra was nutting off from a red-gum bough. Middle of the day. Probably being territorial. There'd be more of that, not just dawn and dusk, once spring arrived, she thought. Still a way off though.

The sky had become overcast, clouds folding into dark rolls as the moisture-laden air moved in from the coast and hit the escarpment. She reached for her water bottle, took a slug, and checked her mirror. A large white Pantech truck filled the view and blocked whatever was directly behind. Cal kept watching. As the truck passed she caught sight of the rear of a maroon SUV and the disappearing edges of the roof-racks on top. She'd nearly missed it.

She fired up the Ford and eased out into the traffic. The Range Rover, now some distance ahead, had pulled out to pass the white truck. Cal couldn't lose sight again around the hulk. But she needed traffic between them or a good distance. She caught sight of the SUV only when there was a bend in the road. Not ideal. She was sure they would be heading directly for Macquarie Pass and then Albion Park. But she didn't want the truck blocking her sight of the vehicle turning off left anywhere — or right for that matter.

As soon as she had some clear road and no oncoming traffic, she dropped a gear and overtook the Pantech. Now just three cars between her and the SUV, easily visible about 400 metres ahead. Too far away to get the rego which might have been useful.

The rest of the trip along Kangaloon Road was uneventful, and as she'd expected the Range Rover turned left near Robertson, then left again on the A48 towards Macquarie Pass.

Thirty minutes later, Cal expected the Range Rover to bear left and head for the M1 north to Wollongong. But the vehicle kept going towards the southern end of Lake Illawarra and then up Windang Peninsula. Cal held back to keep a pair of vehicles and distance between them. She followed along the road with the lakeshore suburbs on her left and the bushland and golf course on her right, the thin strip of land before Perkins Beach.

She flicked up a GPS map on her phone and tried to check that as well while still maintaining distance on the vehicles in front. Wished she had an off-sider and an extra set of eyes. Up ahead, the SUV turned left off the main road into Primbee, a lakeside suburb. The driver made several dog-legs that took him towards the Korrongulla Wetlands and bush. Cal slowed up and checked the map again as she held back. Was this character heading for home, visiting someone, or what?

On the satellite image a small industrial complex and a series of buildings backed onto the wetlands, accessed by a track that dead-ended several hundred metres into the bush. She could see a large shed in a clearing on the map.

She flicked her eyes up. The Range Rover had turned down the track. Cal couldn't follow.

Looking for cover, she drove on and turned into an industrial cul-de-sac 150 metres from the track entrance. A concrete repair business had several small mixer trucks in a rear yard ready for deliveries of wet-mix. Another mixer truck was parked in the entrance alley. Cal did a three-point turn and slotted behind it then walked out to the corner of the building where she could see the T-intersection where the track hit the street. She kept that in her peripheral vision as she studied the satellite map more closely.

What next? If the vehicle came out, did she follow again or go and check out the shed? She needed to decide before it happened. Shed could be promising.

Looking at the images on her phone, she confirmed there was only one major deviation off the track — to a substantial workshop or storage shed. There was a smaller layby midway along the main track with a pile of top-course for pot-hole maintenance. The main path terminated at the forest and scrubland, probably used by hikers and bird-watchers. Cal zoomed in on the access-way to the shed. In Street View she saw a locked gate barring entry and wire fencing that ran through the bush surrounding the building although the access track and immediately in front of the shed was cleared and mowed. She could make out the tall gate posts on either side of the entrance track. A small bulge suggested a CCTV camera was mounted three metres off the ground on one of the posts. A warning plaque advising against trespassing was also visible from the street-view image. The place definitely needed checking out. The driver who had gone to the shed would have to come back the same way. She'd wait for them, then go have a nosy round the lockup.

Fifteen minutes later the maroon Range Rover exited the track and headed back along Marsh Road towards the route in from the Primbee Bypass. Cal gave it another few minutes steered out around the rusting bowl of the mixer truck and headed into the trail towards the lockup. She didn't want her vehicle picked up by the CCTV, or her head for that matter. She parked in the layby beside the gravel pile several hundred metres back from the gated entrance. She took a pry-bar from her tool-bag in the trunk, slipped it down the side of her boot and stuck a torch in her back pocket.

It was mid-week; no one was around. The bush was mostly quiet except for the chirrup of honey-eaters and the distant passing of vehicles on the main road. Cal looked up and down the sandy track then crossed quickly into the scrub. She was too far away for the CCTV to capture her image and the brush growing on the side of the driveway and fence obscured that sightline as well. Using her arms to clear a path through the brush, she reached the six-strand wire fencing, jumped it and continued on a diagonal trajectory through the scrub on the other side. As she neared the clearing she slowed and crouched, scanning the surrounds.

A large, fat goanna was sunning itself in the open area in front of the shed; looked like an adult female with a narrower head than a male. The creature lifted her front higher on her forelegs at Cal's approach. Her tongue ran in and out of her mouth then she turned and scuttled for cover in the trees. Cal felt sorry to have disturbed her. Goanna should've been hibernating but it had been unseasonably warm for weeks, even if it was supposed to be winter.

The shed was one of those blind buildings — no windows, no natural light, a roller-door and a side-door beside it. Steel-frame with long-run metal cladding.

She skirted wide through the brush and headed towards the back to avoid the camera on the gate. Across the rear of the building, a concrete channel gutter carried the roof run-off around the sides and out to the sloping front area. As she'd suspected, there were no windows at the rear or on the sides of the building. They'd leave the structure too vulnerable to break-ins. No power lines ran in from the main track either. The CCTV must've been battery operated or solar. So, a blind work-shed with no power. Be pretty dark inside. Maybe there were skylights or transparent panels on the roof to light the interior? She needed to know what was in there. She craned back, checked the roof. The stud was about three metres, and with the sheer cladding there was nothing to climb up. She paced around the back again.

The site had been cleared out front but the bush grew close to the building from halfway down each side and across the back. She traversed it again, looking for a tree close enough and tall enough to get her near the roof. At the rear corner on the side closest the gate she found her best option—a young angophora with a trunk less than 20cm across. The sapling was easily six or seven metres high but was spindly near the top. There was nothing else. She shimmied from the base using the rough, furrowed bark and her strong grip to haul herself since there were no handy branches on the lower trunk. As she got to about two metres, the tree began to sway with her weight. She compensated by moving around the narrow trunk using curves and bumps in its shape to better absorb the extra gravitational pull of her body. As she got above the roofline she paused and caught her breath.

Just as she'd hoped, three sections on either side of the central roof-ridge had been clad with clear-span panels to allow light into the area below. Now she just had to get over there. Couldn't get much higher—the dwindling girth of the trunk would snap under her weight. And she wasn't close enough to jump across.

C'mon, get this done, you're nearly there she prodded herself. Just need to swing a little closer. Clinging on, her fingers grasping the thickest branch bases close to the tree trunk, she worked up a swaying momentum by throwing her weight back and forth out from the perpendicular centre, her legs flailing beyond. She hoped the return thrust of the trunk would fling her the extra distance like a lever. She hung back on her arms, the trunk returned beyond upright the opposite way. She leaned back further, pitching her weight as far as she could; the trunk bent back, then bounced the other way the same distance off vertical. One more, and hope to hell it doesn't break cos it's a long way down.

Again, like a child on a swing gaining height each time, she bounced herself away, and when the trunk whipped back she thrust her legs forward and let go her hands. As her legs tipped the pry-bar slid from her boot and clattered down the side of the building. Her feet hit the roof. She twisted her body to the side hoping her butt would land on the structure. It did, jamming the torch into her backside. Her feet began to slide on the steeply pitched roofing. She turned her sole and dug the side into the surface, catching the studded head of the last row of roofing screws.

She kept very still, gasping. A centimetre of rubber and an equally tiny alloy screw-head were holding her in position. Her other leg was crooked underneath her, and her hands were slippery with sweat. Even the motion of her breathing might be enough to break the hold of her boot-sole.

She held herself still, exhaled, and moved her hands to her body, wiping them slowly on the fabric. Her leg was cramping with the strain of holding her weight to that tiny spot. She looked behind her. Needed to move her trapped leg and get another toehold. She'd have to hang on by her fingertips as she turned, and quickly. She reached high to the nearest row of roof-screws above her, spread her fingers and dug them in as she flipped her crooked leg out, lost her original toehold, took all her weight through her fingers and scrabbled with both feet, now looking for a stop before her fingers gave out. Her right foot found the tiny bump, she missed first time with her left, and felt again across the surface with her boot then jammed that edge of her sole in. What a stupid fucking idea this had been. She was gonna slide off, break her leg, maybe both legs, or her back, or her neck. And no one would know.

She clung on, like a starfish spread-eagled, her cheek burning against the hot iron. She lifted her face away. She needed to get up to where she could safely straddle the ridge. Maybe she should've taken her boots off for better grip? No, then she'd likely burn her feet.

Just get up there. So, she did. She crawled and scraped and stuck and slipped her way to the top, and when she got there she lay on the ridge-capping with her arms and legs draped down either side of the roof-incline, resting a moment. Then she sat up. The tree-top skimming overview was heady. Climbing into or above a tree canopy always made her yearn for flight.

A black-faced monarch flitted nearby, catching insects on the wing, its rust-coloured chest flashing as it performed its feeding acrobatics. Cal breathed out heavily, her skin cooling in the air. She heard the cry of a duck overhead but didn't turn quickly enough to catch sight.

Work to do. She inched along the apex until she was over one of the clear sections of panelling. The floor-area below was probably equivalent to a three-bay garage. A third of it against one wall looked like storage, full of stacked cardboard boxes on shelving. The middle section was taken up with a dismantled dune-buggy, a fibre-glass bodied vehicle she hadn't seen the likes of since childhood. The remainder of the floor space was consumed by a large vehicle under a thin, nylon dust-cover. It was a pickup. And judging by the outline of the massive, smoothly curving fenders, a late model one.

Well, well. What now? Was it worth breaking in to further test her suspicions? Her pry-bar was now on the ground somewhere below. And what if she was wrong? At that moment, she heard the low hum of a vehicle. Not from the distant main road, but much closer. She dropped her body flat on the roof and stretched her neck. Through the scrub she caught a flash of maroon. He'd come back.

Chapter 19

THE DRIVER PARKED AT the gate. Cal kept still but couldn't make out his features through the heavy tint at the top of the vehicle's windscreen. When he got out and stood, looking over the property, Cal took a chance he'd be scanning down at eye-level and she took a quick peek at him before she ducked her head. He was about five eleven and thickset, strong looking. He walked over to the chain and padlock, checked them, then unlocked the gate and walked towards the shed. Cal could no longer see him. She clung on, her arms cramping and tense.

She heard his footsteps in the dry leaf duff and bark as he walked around the building. He walked the entire circumference of the shed. She heard him stop below where she'd dropped the pry-bar. Not good. But he couldn't know how long it had been there even if he saw it. Still, he was obviously twitchy and suspicious because her vehicle was nearby. She heard him return to the front and check the door was secure. She pressed her body into the roof ridges, her thigh muscles aching with fatigue and tension. He'd have to walk right back into the bush to see her on the roof. It might not even occur to him that anyone was up there.

Finally, he returned to the gate and re-locked it. When he drove away she heard him slow down where she'd parked. Would he simply think the vehicle belonged to a hiker? She didn't hear him get out. He could still have taken down her rego number. He could find her with that. Same as she would have tried to find him if she'd been able to read his. Had she just put herself right in the path of a possible killer? *Well, yeh, potentially. Whadda ya think you've been doing all this time Nyx? Playing Scrabble?*

So, what was that saying? May as well be hung for a sheep as for a lamb. Ugh. Not a pretty image. Who comes up with that shite? If this bloke was the guy Dif saw, he dumped a body. He may or may not have killed her, but it was suss whatever way he was involved. If she broke into the lockup and that vehicle was a Triton pickup with a Bidgee Boardriders sticker, she might have the doer. She had to try. What if the place was alarmed? *Just be quick. Get in, lift the cover, check. Piss off.* He'd seen her car. He might already be onto her. *Just do it, you're here now. Do it.*

She skidded her way down to the roof's edge, steadied herself then leapt across to the sapling. With the added momentum from her jump height the trunk snapped under her weight. Her body thumped into the ground. She landed on her side, with an acute, rasp of pain as a fallen branch snapped and tore through her shirt, jagging across the flesh over her ribs. She rolled and clasped at her side, moaning. Get up. Get up! Clutching the wound and wincing, she scuffled about in the debris, looking for the pry-bar she'd dropped earlier. Had he picked it up? Not seen it at all? She kicked through the leaves, using her toe as a probe. Her side was burning. She clinched her hand to the gash then looked at the blood filling her palm. The sight made her woozy. Her foot struck the weight of the tool. She picked it up and scuttled around to the front of the building.

Bypassing all caution now. She'd be caught on the security camera feed. Whatevs. She alternated jemmying the tip of the bar into the gap above and below the lock, throwing her weight into the thing for more leverage. Eventually the tongue of the lock sprang free. She ran in, lifted the edge of the vehicle cover, looked down at the licence plate holder. Empty. The plate had been removed. She pulled the cover further up and stepped towards the rear cab window, looked for the sticker.

Nothing.

'Fuck.' She touched the glass in disbelief. Her fingertips slid across the rear corner. She felt an outline, the thin residue of adhesive. Closed her eyes, followed the trace of a shield–shape. She pulled her phone from her front pocket, took a quick photo, dropped the nylon cover and sprinted for the door. Outside, a burly figure ran towards her from the gate.

Cal turned to the side of the building and took off into the scrub, still hunched, one hand clinging to the gash on her side, the other waving off branches in front of her. She ran and scrambled and slipped and all she could hear were her own gasps and yelps and the snapping branches behind her as her pursuer gave chase.

The ground was uneven, rising. She tried to remember what she'd seen on that map, how she could make the terrain work for her. How well did he know it? What else was hidden out there, beyond? She tried to focus as she negotiated the tree trunks and branches and fallen wood around her.

She'd heard a particular bird call on that roof. What was it? A chestnut teal duck. There must be water nearby. Of course—the coast wasn't distant. And that wetland.

An estuary. A swamp maybe. How would that help her? It would only slow her down. She needed cover, not exposure. Mangroves maybe. They were dense. Better than the sparse cover and rugged ground she was in now. She could visualise it, the outer part of the map she'd seen. She'd been focussed on the storage shed and the track. Now the area beyond was formulating from the recesses of her memory, the little tussock and water symbols on the map—they'd registered even though her focus had been closer in. Just keep going. Find the water. Outrun that bastard. You'll find your way.

She pictured the trajectory she'd just taken from the corner of the building as though from a bird's eye above her. She knew exactly which direction she needed to move in and tweaked her route accordingly. He was dropping behind. He couldn't keep up with her, even when she wasn't full-stretch with her torn side.

Now the terrain sloped downwards, like a shallow valley. This would lead her to the water. Even if she was losing her pursuer, she had to make her way back to her car somehow, probably via a long circuit if she wanted to be sure he hadn't set a trap for her. She lost concentration and her feet went from under her, then she was rolling through debris, the rough surface pounding and poking into her raw side. Still, she was getting away. And she was aware of more light above her. The water must be close. She scanned ahead and made for an opening, her boots already ploughing through marshy bog. At the edge of the estuary she looked left, mangroves and brush, and right, the open salt-flats and ocean beyond. She dove into the brackish water and stroked quickly towards the dark-green recesses of the saline woodland.

Her feet were heavy with her waterlogged boots. She'd lose them in the mud. She reached down and tugged them off, held the long uppers between her teeth. She stroked and kicked and waded onwards to cover. It was hard to know if she was still being followed with the splashing and sound of her own hoarse and ragged breathing but she wondered if he'd given up. And if he had, what was he going to do next?

Her jaw ached from clamping her boots in her mouth. She crouched into the lee of a mangrove clump and held them in her hand, catching her breath. Listened. No splashing. No cracking branches. Nothing but the subtle ripple of water through the tangled, damp vegetation.

She closed her eyes, pictured the map again, opened her eyes, looked for the sun and landmarks. The escarpment inland from the coast. The sun was to the left of absolute north, so maybe the time was about two o'clock. She had her bearings. She visualised the map again, the position of the lockup, and her estimation of where she currently was. How to skirt back to the car and still give herself some kind of advantage.

But she had no advantage. If he'd surmised that was her car, and not some random hiker, he had all the benefits of knowing she would be back there eventually. And he could choose to wait and ambush her. She needed to forget the car for now. That thought kicked her anxiety up a notch. Get to the nearest piece of urban real estate where she could hire something and get incognito pronto.

She waded further inland along the margin of the swamp and for three hundred metres fought her way through the aerial roots and branches, scrambling and sliding among the algae-clad morass. The air smelt of saline and decaying organic matter, the mud of the estuary, the silts that washed down from the escarpment. Smells she didn't find unpleasant as they were organic, but somewhat anaerobic and slightly sulphurous.

Eventually the ground rose away from the water. On all fours she emerged and sat among the tussocks, emptied the brackish water from her boots, dragged them on and was about to stand, but thought better of it. She squatted and gauged her surrounds again. She could hear traffic on the road she was aiming for, maybe a kilometre beyond across the scrubland. It wasn't forest but the small trees and brush gave a metre or two of cover. She sensed her pursuer wasn't watching, but even if he was, what was he going to do now? If he showed himself it was going to be as slow going for him as it was for her. And since she planned to hitch a ride with Joe Public, in full view, her pursuer would surely seek a hidden strategy.

As she stretched out her stride it occurred to her that she probably wasn't looking her sharpest just now. She felt her hair. It was tangled and spiked with twigs and debris. She put her hand to her face, felt the gritty, wet surface and put a matching image to that. Oh, well.

When she reached the edge of the roadway she ran her hands down the surface of her sodden, filthy jeans to clean them. She flapped her torn shirt to shake off the worst of the mess, combed her fingers through her hair, then crossed the road and stuck her thumb out for a ride north. She thought about her Ford and hated abandoning it back there but couldn't risk going back for it.

She must've looked horrendous. She held a shirt-tail and bent down to wipe it over her face. Was anyone going to risk picking up someone who looked like an escapee? Maybe she should start walking. The verge petered out at the overbridge, so, not an option. She needed to leave room for a potential good samaritan to pull over. She kept her thumb out and hoped. As she waited, it occurred to her that if something happened to Dif and to her as well, no one would know about the woman's body. She'd put a target on her own back. Well, she wasn't useless and she had access to people that the police didn't. She'd also sorted out some heavy situations up the Hawkesbury recently. Yeh, and managed to miss your aunt Zin's last moments in hospital. Shoved that niggle aside. You need to pass on what you know, just in case. How? Who? Scobie?

Eventually an old International tow-truck pulled in along from where Cal was standing. She hoisted herself up into the spartan, oily cabin. The metal floors had no mats or coverings.

'Where ya headed?' the gargantuan driver asked, barely looking at her, but his tone was friendly as he watched his rear-view mirror, ready to pull out again. He wore faded bib overalls on top of a grimy blue wife-beater. Black fur coated his shoulders and the tops of his arms, which had the girth of bolster cushions.

'Nearest servo with rentals,' Cal said.

The old bench seat was a thin two-inch rubber pad with cracked plastic covering that curled in rigid, gaping edges that looked dangerous. The front of the dashboard was decorated with empty Coke cans and twisted pie wrappers.

'Bit o' trouble with ya ride, eh?'

'Bit.'

'Gong then.'

'Sweet.' Cal looked out the side window as she pondered what the hell next.

The driver moved into the traffic and the engine noise in the cabin was like being inside a concrete-mixer twirling half-bricks. The lack of firewall insulation and floor matting did nothing to alleviate the racket. She wiggled her phone from her sodden pocket. Not surprisingly its face was black as the abyss. All her numbers there could be lost. Might be able to salvage the SIM-card. Anyway, she was just grateful to be heading away from the swamp and her chaser.

The towie dropped her on the southern industrial edge of Wollongong beside a rental outfit.

'Thanks, mate. Good of ya.' She climbed down from the tall cab and wandered over to the car yard.

What to get? Her ranger work truck was utilitarian and made sense to her. Ditto vans. She always felt like an alien in a traditional four-door sedan. If it was a hot-rod or custom she might find it bearable. But there was nothing like that in the yard and it wouldn't have served her if there was. She needed to disappear into ubiquity. She could see several basic old pickups on the lot. She chose a white Hilux with dark tints. Then she filled in the paperwork, ignoring the feeling that the staff might be considering calling the cops when she left.

At least she had her credit cards and licence with her dead phone. That was the next thing—get another phone. As she signed the papers, disregarding the horrified glances of the young woman staffer, she asked the way to the nearest market, convenience store or servo.

Less than half a kilometre along the thoroughfare, Cal zipped into a petrol station and bought a cheap handset and charger. While she was there, she used the bathroom and attempted to tidy up her appearance. She grabbed tissues from the dispenser by the pumps as she went back to the pickup. She leaned on the bonnet of the rental and extracted the SIM from her drowned phone. She wiped it down and laid it on the warm surface, turning it over in the sun every few seconds. Satisfied it was thoroughly dry she inserted it in the new phone, fired up the pickup, plugged the charger into the lighter socket and took off, ready to put some miles between herself and the South Coast.

Chapter 20

THE NEW PHONE PINGED with a text notification. Pirate had sent the engine and frame numbers regarding the Triton registration Dif had given her. The message ended with 'please delete'. At least she could confirm Brett Coswell's stolen numbers matched up if she needed to, though, like Dif, she figured his vehicle wasn't involved, only his plates. She needed to establish something regarding that.

Cal already had the address from Dif's prior search. South and inland from Greyridge, thirty minutes' drive. All she wanted was a long soak in a hot bath, clean clothes and her own bed. But with another question she needed answered, she wasn't going back to Sydney just yet. Her clothes had almost dried out. Might not be looking slick but she was ready to face someone.

She put the Stockton address into her GPS. It was a small service town with forestry and farming the main sources of local employment. It was after four thirty. Maybe this Coswell would've finished work, especially if he had an early start. She hoped to catch him at home.

Felt like she was dragging her body through molasses her energy levels were so low.

The house was in a recent subdivision with sterile-looking new-builds and plantings of inappropriate trees along the boundaries that would doubtless die or be ripped out in a year or two when the owners tired of them. The developers responsible for the plantings were long gone. Cal saw the silver Triton in the drive behind a red Kia hatchback. The roller door of the garage was up. A stringy young bloke with thinning blonde hair was tossing timber off-cuts into a firewood storage shed beside the fence.

'G'day. Looking for Brent Coswell,' Cal called as she approached.

The bloke looked up, a chunk of wood in his hand. Lifted his chin. 'That's me.'

'Sorry to bother you, mate. Friend of mine got caught up in some trouble, saw your pickup and got your rego. Just trying to help him sort it out.'

'Who are you?'

'Name's Cal Nyx. Just asking on behalf of my friend.'

'I reported my plates nicked to the registry and the coppers. Got replacements now.'

'So, someone stole them?'

'I've been through all this. What's it to you?' He chucked the wood against the back of the shed, picked up another.

'Long story, mate. My friend's in strife and we wanna get to the bottom of it. Your plates were put on another silver Triton. Cops don't know about this part of it so they've done nothing. Can you just tell me if you know where or when your plates were taken?'

Coswell tossed the wood, put his hands on his hips. 'Reckon it was at the mill. I was on arvy shift on the 18th. I hadn't noticed it before then.'

'That's back off the highway, north of here?'

'Yup.'

'They got CCTV, y'know?'

'Already asked. Front and back of my pickup were out of vision. If someone got in the driver's seat, they could've caught it on the cameras. But anyone could've scuttled along keeping low and hoiked ma plates.'

'Okay. Thanks, mate.'

'Hope this is the last of it,' Coswell mumbled, wondering how the innocuous theft of his plates had escalated to a matter of such interest.

Cal returned through the town and onto the highway where she pulled over onto the shoulder opposite the McCauliffe Mill. The sun had dropped, illuminating the treetop silhouettes of the hinterland in an orange glow. The mill car-park was fenced with two-metre-high chain-link that ran down both sides and across the front. On one side, a bulldozed clearing of sandstone rubble provided no cover, ditto the front entrance. The other side was clothed in patches of scrub. Possible for someone to hide there and maybe climb the fence. Had that been checked? Was it covered by CCTV? Another possibility was that whoever stole the plates also worked at the mill and used the car-park.

So, maybe someone had stolen plates off a silver Triton because they were using a silver Triton, one that could otherwise be traced to them. Local cops wouldn't have made a big deal about the stolen plates unless they'd got a hit about them later on some crime. And since what Dif had seen also hadn't been actioned, there'd been no follow-up. That in itself was suspicious. Dif's wariness about the senior cop, Tambor, down at Greyridge was looking increasingly well-founded.

Now what? She checked her phone.

She'd missed calls and texts from Scobie.

'Shit.' She was meant to get her from the airport.

Cal rang immediately.

Scobie answered, her tone cool. 'Get caught up?'

'I'm so sorry. Long story. I never would've made it on time. Guess you'll be wanting a quiet night?'

'Yeh, should do. Return to the maelstrom tomorrow. You okay?'

'Utterly rooted. Back to Sydney tonight, I'll stay at Zin's. Fill you in when I see you. Let me know when you're up for it.'

'Okay.'

'Glad Imogen's in the clear. You and the family must be relieved.'

'Absolutely. Not quite out of the woods but we'll take it. Drive safe. Talk soon.' Scobie rang off.

Cal had just put her phone down when it burred against her thigh. Pirate.

'How'd ya go, bud?'

'I ran through that footage. Swept it three times to be sure. No Mitsi Triton, no Range Rover.'

Cal clicked her tongue behind her teeth. 'Dammit.'

'I'm sorry, Cal. Really hoping I could've found something for you.'

'Nah. I'm grateful, must've been a tedious session. No worries, we move on. Be in touch, mate.'

Cal tapped her phone against the rim of the steering wheel. She'd convinced herself that someone had tried to fry Dif in that caravan. She'd seen the burn patterns, and the sink pipe removed. Maybe she was looking for the wrong vehicle. Someone not driving a Triton pickup or a Range Rover. Or perhaps they walked because they lived in the area. Maybe the person who did it lived in the actual caravan park. That would be too much of a coincidence surely.

So now what? Get a map of the area, decide on a reasonable walking distance, say, two and a half ks, see if any of the names on the Bidgee Boardrider's list lived within those parameters. But half the club members could live there—it was their local group. That wouldn't narrow things down. She needed something more concrete.

She ran her fingers through her hair, scratched her neck. Why wasn't she getting anywhere? What was she missing?

Make a decision. And don't trouble Scobie with some piece of unsubstantiated doodah that'll prove professionally humiliating and damaging.

But the further Cal went, the more convinced she was that Dif was in mortal danger because of what he'd seen. She had to weigh up protecting Dif, helping him, and not jeopardising Scobie's job if she asked her to help.

The sun had disappeared behind the ridgeline of bush beyond the mill. *Wonder if Coswell is done with his firewood? Save myself another trip back here and tick something off my list. Just be quick.*

She started the engine, pulled a U-turn and drove the short distance back to Coswell's house, parking beyond the light of a streetlamp half a dozen houses away. Coswell's drive was in darkness, lights on inside the rear windows of the dwelling. Cal pulled on a cap and jacket, grabbed her torch and phone, quietly closed the door and sauntered head-down to the end of Coswell's drive. There was no one on the street. She scooted up the drive, crouched beside the rear right wheel and moved her torchlight across the inner frame. *Praise Jah for massive tyre clearances on 4WD trucks.* There it was, the series of numbers. Just then an outside light came on at the back corner of the house. She took a quick snap of the frame number with her phone and took off back down the drive, reached the Hilux and drove off without her lights on.

She was panting as she made the Stockton highway turn-off. She clicked on her seatbelt. *Give that frame number to Pirate and if it matches his rego we can* eliminate this guy. Just ticking boxes. Back to Zin's, need a clean-up, grab a change of clothes.

Chapter 21

CAL THOUGHT ABOUT THE unknown house-guest. Had they returned meantime and what sort of mess or company might greet her inside Zin's cottage? She had a bit of a plan to flush them out.

It was after eight when she parked at one end of the alley behind Zin's house. She locked the car and walked quickly the hundred metres along the laneway to the back gate beside the garage doors. Slipped a key into the lock and passed into the yard and across to the back door of the cottage. She held her breath steady and inserted the key in the deadlock, making plenty of noise with the keys and stomping her boots on the floor. Then she scuttled quietly, reversing back out of the doorway and down the side path where she stood against the wall beside the broken window.

The plywood repair sheet bounced away from the window frame and hit the concrete as a foot kicked it out from inside. Cal waited for the figure to contact the ground before she scragged the character by the collar. 'Hey Little Ghost? What's happening?'

She couldn't tell the gender of the escapee. They were young, thin, wore baggy jeans, and an oversize hoodie, had shoulder-length dark-brown hair with random cotton-plaited rat-tails.

'Little Ghost? Ain't my name. Got the wrong dude.' A scratchy adolescent voice, gender still indeterminate.

'Yeh? What is your name then?'

Silence.

'You been staying in the rotunda over at the park?'

'Dunno.'

'Can't be very comfortable, 'specially now it's almost winter.'

''Pends what you're used to,' they mumbled.

'You got nowhere safe to go?'

Little Ghost shrugged.

'You got a swag?'

They pouted, shook their head.

Cal saw smooth, unblemished skin in the ambient light. 'You want some gear?'

'You a paedo?'

'Seriously?'

Little Ghost sneered, said nothing.

Cal gave the clothing in her grip a shake. 'Hey, I'm not trying to make things difficult for you. I can give you some camping gear. You can't keep busting in here.'

'Fuck you.'

The youth struggled in Cal's grasp, twisted out of her hold, took off down the side path and hurdled the front gate. Spiky little bastard. Better name than Little Ghost.

Cal wasn't going to give chase, but she followed and watched as they scarpered down towards the northern intersection. There was something familiar about the disappearing figure.

Cal crouched beside the front fence and set the timer on her phone. She swivelled around on her haunches and could see through the slats of the gate to the park on a diagonal sightline across the street. The far side of the park, which was probably less than quarter of an acre in size, was bordered by an alley that ran behind the houses on the other side of Collier Street. She figured that Spike would hit the intersection several hundred metres away, make a right and then another when they hit the alley and enter the park from the far side. It would take less than ten minutes.

Cal scanned the silhouetted shapes in the play area, the small rotunda with the domed green roof, the massive trunks of the Canary Island palms lining the path that bisected the lawns and led beyond to the shops and railway station.

It was getting late, quiet but for the low thrum of traffic on Parramatta Road a block away. No fruit bats in the trees—they'd headed north weeks ago for winter feeding grounds.

Cal glanced back and forth over the far edge of the park.

Then she saw the hunched shadow move from the light of the alley to the dark of the fence-line where houses neighboured the common. She lost sight as she had no angle on the boundary, but moments later, the crouched figure emerged, scooting from tree to tree across the open ground to the shelter of the dome.

Maybe the kid was homeless. Maybe that's why Cal had seen the light in the rotunda that recent night. They were sleeping there. And Zin's house was always dark. Cal only ever stayed in the sleepout and it wasn't visible from the front of the house, lights or no lights. Cal had never bothered with inside lights on a timer to deter burglars because Zin had always been home. It hadn't been necessary.

What to do? She felt for the kid. Was she too soft? What if they had a habit? Well, the home hadn't been ransacked. It was a warm, safe place to get some rest, or had been until Cal came back.

Cal showered and changed. She knew she had to speak with Scobie, sooner rather than later. Then her phone rang. Scobie.

'How's tricks, Inspector?'

Scobie's tone was sombre. 'Universe has been a bit heavy handed on my return. Got a child abduction in a mall. I'm going to be pretty tied up tomorrow. Just wanted to let you know.'

'Oh, that's nasty.'

'You had any joy on your travels?'

'Um, yes and no. Some stuff I might wanna run by you but sounds like you'll have your hands full.'

'Let's play it by ear. I miss you.'

'Me too.' Cal decided to bite the bullet. 'Hey, I know you're busy and the timing isn't ideal, but I need to talk with you, face-to-face. Can I come round?'

'I could do with some light relief,' Scobie said.

'Dunno if I can guarantee that. See you shortly.'

Guilt curled through Cal's guts. There was no way Scobie was going to be okay with what she was about to tell her. She knew that. But she'd put it off too long already.

A recent shower and easterly sea-breeze had dropped the temperature by five degrees. Streetlights reflected in the puddled road surface as Cal turned slowly into the Alexandria back lane. She parked and climbed the stairs carrying a bottle of pinot gris for Scobie and a six-pack of Peroni beer.

Scobie answered the door in a short white bathrobe. Her hair hung in damp strands. She smiled and planted a kiss as she ushered Cal in. 'Hey, stranger.'

Cal handed her the wine.

'Thank you. Am I gonna need this?'

Cal raised her eyebrows, her mouth formed an awkward grimace.

'Okay. Let's sit down.' Scobie grabbed a clean wineglass from the bench and handed Cal the bottle-opener. Classical music played quietly in the background. Cal knew nothing about it but suspected her aural faculties appreciated the variation in construction and tones from her own pick of tunes.

'Who's this?'

'Yo-yo Ma.'

'Oh yeh. She's good.'

'He.'

'Right.' Cal guffawed.

She sat on the couch, poured Scobie a wine, flipped off her bottle cap and clinked Scobie's glass.

'Speak up, Nyx.' Scobie said after a sip.

'Okay. There's more to tell you about Dif.' She took a deep breath and launched in. 'He saw a body dumped at the quarry. The guy saw him. That's why he took off.'

'Jesus.'

'He got evidence from the body—a piece of the blanket she was wrapped in and an earring. He couldn't retrieve her body. Next day some guy, maybe the same one who dumped the body, asked other rough sleepers about Dif and his camp. Dif had already taken off. It's possible this same guy found Dif at the Bidgee Caravan Park and tried to torch the van.' Cal took a long pull on her beer.

'Why didn't he go to the police?'

'He had warrants out. He couldn't go in person. He left an anonymous note at the local station, Greyridge.'

'But what he saw—the police would do something with that information. What about Crimestoppers, the tip-line?'

'No credit on his phone. He's on the margins, Scob. Plus, he was freaked out. He did what he could, leaving that note before he took off. He couldn't risk fronting them. He wouldn't survive inside. He just couldn't take that chance. It's kinda complicated.'

Cal's replacement phone rang. Luckily it vibrated as well since the ringtone was foreign to her.

'Cal Nyx.'

'Sergeant Trolley here. Southern Districts Highway Patrol. You the owner of a '64 Ford Futura?'

An iciness crawled across her chest. 'Yup,' she sighed.

'Sorry to inform you, we found it burnt out just off Marsh Rd earlier this evening.'

'Fuck me.'

'Insured, was it?'

'Yeh. But kinda irreplaceable.'

'Yeh. Well, sorry for that. The car's been towed to Wollongong impound. Guess your assessor will want to see it. Just contact our call centre to sort that.'

'Will do. Thanks,' she said flatly and ended the call.

'Fuck it.' She looked at Scobie. 'My fuckin car. Torched. I can't fuckin believe it.' She stood hands on hips. Stretched her arms, crossed them behind her head, puffed a long sigh from her nose, slumped down on the couch.

Scobie knew better than to speak platitudes. She shook her head, sat beside Cal, put an arm around her shoulders. 'I know how much it meant to you.' She pulled Cal into her side. 'There's anything I can do...?'

Cal took a slug of her beer. 'Shouldna left it there. That bastard torched it.'

'He could've waited for you, Cal. It was risky either way. You're in one piece. Sort of. I know you wouldn't agree but I'm glad to have you over your car.' She kept her tone light. 'Choice ride though it was,' she conceded.

Cal gave her a small, wry pout. 'Just got the thing sweet with the new engine, Jesus.' She emptied her beer.

Scobie scooted a new bottle along the table to her.

Cal flicked the top off. 'Guess I could start over with something else when they pay-out. Do something different.' She nodded thoughtfully.

'Just what you needed—a project.' Scobie made a silly grin, lifted her glass. 'So, where were we?' She raised her eyebrows.

'You were telling me about Dif. He didn't go to the police.' Scobie shook her head. 'I don't quite understand. And I'm a little nervous now you've revealed this to me I have to say.'

Cal paused, took a breath.

'It's not my place to say this, but it fills in the picture a bit. If Dif ended up in a cis-men's gaol they'd pulp him when they found out, and it's inevitable that they would, sooner or later. Even when they have that self-identification policy, how they decide which prison to send them to, it's still arbitrary. Or he could be put in solitary, permanently, for his own protection. Even if they were open to doing a deal on his warrants for his witness statement, they'd hold him on remand. He can't risk it. There's another thing too. The head cop at Greyridge is a turd. He had a go at Dif. Sexually I mean. He's bashed him as well. When Dif left that note he hoped the other staff there would find it. Obviously, they didn't. He was a mess, traumatised. I have to respect his wishes. He doesn't trust the cops and he's not coming out of hiding. Assuming he's still alive.'

'Jesus. I get all that—about Dif going inside. You know I do. But you have knowledge of a possible murder. If you absolutely trust that what Dif has told you is true. I can't have awareness of that and not take appropriate action. It's my job, Cal. I'm an officer of the law. You've put me in a really compromised position here.' Scobie put her glass down heavily.

Cal had never seen her upset. 'Look, I see that, and I'm sorry. But I need your help. It's awkward. I feel stuck too. He's my mate. He's asked me for help. And you're my … squeeze …' Cal looked up at Scobie with a hangdog tilt of her head.

Scobie was brusque. 'Don't.'

Cal put her hands up in surrender.

Scobie twiddled with her wine glass.

'I'm up to my neck here with the child abduction. Jesus, Cal.'

'Just give me a little time to see if I can touch base with him, explain to him. Try and bring him around. I have to assume he's still alive. Guess I can't take that for granted, based on what he's told me. I'm chasing stuff up too. Trying to get helpful leads.'

'You don't even know where he is. You said yourself, he could be dead, for God's sake. This should be left to the professionals. We know how to run an investigation. Fuck's sake, Cal. It's what we do.'

Scobie stood, went to the sliding doors and out onto the deck. A chilly breeze came in through the gap in the doorway. Cal could see Scobie breathing deeply, silhouetted by the city lights beyond.

Minutes later she came back in. 'Christ, I feel like a cigarette. Haven't craved one in years. You're a damn irritant, Nyx.' She turned and pulled the doors closed, shivering, holding her bathrobe tight.

Cal ploughed on. The water was over her head now anyway. 'Is there any way you can follow up on what he saw at the quarry? They must stockpile gravel and rock there for the road crews. If a body was dumped in the crusher there should be evidence or remnants somewhere, don't you reckon? It was only a couple of weeks back.'

'That could be a massive operation.'

'Yeh, I know. Couldn't they get the Dog Squad out there for starters? Just sweep the area?'

'You need to leave Cal. I have to clear my head. I'm not going to jeopardise my job.'

Chapter 22

Next morning at Richmond Command, Scobie got up from her desk and closed the door to her office. She dialled DI Troy Dunbar, head of Homicide in Wollongong.

Dunbar answered straight away. Scobie identified herself.

'How's tricks, Liz?'

Scobie blew a puff of exasperation. 'Child abduction, Troy. Wish I was on leave during this one.'

'Kids are the worst. Don't envy you. How can I help?'

'Not related to that, Troy, but bit of a sticky one. A witness to a possible homicide down your way is in hiding, scared for his safety. He claims he took evidence from a body dumped in a gravel chute at the Greyridge quarry several weeks ago. This evidence and knowledge has come to my notice via a friend of the witness. Bit unorthodox. Wondered if you could have a poke around?'

'Jeez. Okay. Why didn't he report it?'

'He's a rough sleeper. Has warrants out for minor stuff. Didn't want to risk being locked up. By all accounts he's pretty freaked out. Apparently, he tried to notify Greyridge anonymously.'

'Should be a record of that then.'

'Yes.' Scobie paused. 'Well, be that as it may, it doesn't appear anything has been followed up. I can get this alleged physical evidence to you. Just wondered if you could maybe get your Dog Squad to do a sweep?'

Dunbar bristled. 'Bit of a cheek.' He laughed but there was a hard edge to it. 'Not much to go on for a site of that dimension.'

'I can fine it down for you, Troy. I'll scan a map and highlight the chute. It was only weeks ago so a dog should pick up any scent if there's a body there.'

'We've got missing hikers in the bush at Fitzroy Falls and Search and Rescue on stand-by. They may need the dogs there.'

'Okay. I understand. Look, if you could just bear it in mind and ...' She drifted off. 'Sorry, Troy. Don't want to sound like I'm telling you what to do. Just thought I should run it by you—your patch 'n' all.'

'Sure. Has to be followed up, doesn't it? I'll get to it when I can. Good luck with the abduction.' Dunbar ended the call.

Scobie put her phone down, feeling chastised by her own conscience. Then Dunbar's final comment brought back the matter front and centre of her day. A missing child and a family hanging on. But she had one more call to make first.

She scrolled her contacts. Despite the knotty circumstances of their last contact, she hadn't deleted the number. She rang Sand Palotto.

'Liz. Long time.'

'It is indeed. Wondered if we could meet?'

Silence on the other end.

'It's not personal, Sand. I need a favour and I'd prefer not to ask over the phone. You name the place.'

'Oh, the effrontery.'

'Yeh, I know. What do you say?'

Palotto paused a moment then replied, 'I'm curious. Know the Blue Crab?'

'I'll find it.'

'Tonight, at eight then.'

Before leaving her office that evening, Scobie did a search for the Blue Crab on her phone. She didn't want anything relating to the matter on her work computer. The brasserie was on the South Coast, a renowned spot overlooking the waterway where whales and dolphins plied their way north and south, close to shore.

She went to her car. Helluva drive in peak hour but at least she'd be going against the flow for some of the way. Everything was crisscrossed and choked whichever direction she was heading. She reached across to the glove-box and grabbed her cologne, then decided against it, put the bottle back. She started the car and headed out.

An hour and a half later she dropped down the steep incline of the Bulli Pass to the old road and back-tracked several kilometres north up the coast. She turned into the car-park where the turquoise neon of a large-clawed crustacean confirmed her destination. The bar and brasserie were situated in a converted carriage-house on a rocky promontory overlooking the Tasman Sea. Coloured lights illuminated the main entrance under a gabled porch. The paintwork was distressed by the elements, obvious even at night. Scobie was fatigued but she pushed on. She reached into the bag and got her make-up out. She was halfway through touching up before wondering, why am I fussing? She was about to do her lipstick, decided against the red and applied a neutral instead, not wanting to give the wrong impression. She slipped the lid back on the lippy and headed into the bar.

Being a mid-week evening, the interior of the bar wasn't crowded but it was still noisy with general revelry. Scobie looked around at the scattered tables, couldn't see Palotto. Quiet music filtered through the background of loud conversations, reminiscent of millennium drum and bass with the edges filed off.

Scobie walked to the bar and ordered a sauv blanc from the bearded barman. Adjacent to the bar, a massive picture window gave an impressive view to the darkened ocean, streaked with broken rows of white-caps. The silhouettes of a pair of tankers jutted on the horizon, their decks stacked with containers like checker-boards catching the light of the setting sun as they waited to enter the southern port down the coast.

The barman served Scobie's drink and as she thanked him, she saw movement in the mirror behind his head.

Sand Palotto was still quite a sight. Tall and athletic, she had the broad shoulders of a swimmer. She carried herself in a powerful but elegant stride and held her chin with an upward tilt like a challenge. Scobie felt a discomfiting twinge of attraction and steeled herself as she turned, not wanting the other woman to come from behind her.

'Sand, thanks for this. What can I get you?'

Palotto reached for Scobie, bent slightly. Scobie left her cheek within reach, but her eyes moved away as Palotto kissed her.

'Heineken, thanks.' Palotto raised her eyebrows at the barman.

'Quite a view.' Scobie gestured at the window. 'Where shall we sit?'

'I'm happy at the bar. Quieter down that end.' Palotto indicated the curved section beyond the main length of the service area. When Palotto's drink arrived, they moved there and Palotto pulled out a stool for Scobie.

'You look well, Liz. Responsibilities of a DI must suit you.'

'Ha. Don't know about that.' Scobie felt skittish. 'How about yourself? Still palming off the higher-ups?'

'I'm a street D. This gig on the coast is temporary. Just keeping my path smooth and clear.' She tipped her bottle, kept her eyes on Scobie. There was a pause. They both left it.

Then Palotto spoke again. 'So, tell me, Liz, how can I help? You eaten, by the way? Seafood's terrific here.'

'I'm good thanks. Maybe later.' She took a breath. 'You knew someone in that voluntary search-dog's group. That still the case?'

'Mm. Rob's still with them as far as I know. Why?'

'This might sound dubious but just hear me out. Someone I know has a friend who saw a body dumped at Greyridge Quarry. That witness even went to the trouble of getting evidence from the body but couldn't move the body or do anything else.' Scobie could see Palotto pull her head back slightly with disbelief, but she carried on.

'Obviously, checking a site like that is an enormous financial undertaking for the department.'

Palotto held a hand up. 'Hang on. Why didn't this witness go to the police?'

'Seems they did. And it was Greyridge Police.'

Now Palotto shifted back on her stool, putting more distance between them. 'C'mon. When was this?'

'Just a few weeks ago.'

Palotto shook her head.

'The witness was a rough sleeper and has outstanding warrants. Knew he would likely not be believed. Some issue with the OIC there. But he left a note...'

'This sounds flimsy.'

'Look, Sand, I wouldn't come to you if I believed there was no substance here. The evidence this witness took can be delivered to Wollongong Command. But they're not going to set anything in motion on a whim. Here's the thing. Could your friend perhaps exercise their dog on one of the river walks beside the quarry? I mean, they have to give them regular workouts, don't they? Train them when they're not actually on the job? Say the handler happened to slip into the quarry site and have the dog run its snout around this particular area under the chute. If a body had been dumped there, would the dog react?

'Jesus, Liz. So, what if they agreed to that and did find something, how do they explain it to Southern Command? Because presumably that's your point—a positive hit from a cadaver dog and the full forensics works can kick-in, yeh?'

'I know it's a stretch. They could say they were running the dog by the river; the handler was relieving himself, the dog took off on the scent of something...' Scobie threw her hands out, then took a sip of wine. 'And when the handler retrieved the dog, it was doing the positive for a cadaver sign. Does it matter how it was achieved if they come up with something? I just thought with another fragment of possibility, albeit a fairly compelling one, it would give Southern the impetus to move on this claim.'

'It's gotta be tight if the case ends up in court.'

'Well, defence would be hard-pressed to dismiss cadaver evidence found by a specialist dog exercising nearby. Jury aren't going to quibble, are they?'

Palotto shook her head and emptied her beer. 'It's out there, Liz. N'other one?'

Scobie nodded. She looked out the window at the darkening view, the horizon barely visible as the heavy sky merged with the black ocean. She felt skinless, vulnerable. What had she done? She probably hadn't helped Cal's cause and she was stepping on the toes of her colleagues—first Dunbar's and now Palotto's. What the hell had she been thinking?

Palotto returned with drinks, sat down. 'Who's the friend of the witness? Old flame? New flame?'

Scobie sighed, blinked. 'New. She's solid and she's stand-up. I wouldn't be here asking you for help on an impulse. You know that. If a woman has been murdered and dumped, that's a crime.' Scobie looked steadily into Palotto's eyes.

Palotto held her gaze then shook her head, took a long draught on her beer.

Scobie spoke again. 'I should tell you: I spoke to Troy Dunbar at Wollongong earlier as a courtesy because the Police K9 Unit runs out of Southern Area. I told him what I've just told you, but he reckons the dog-squad will be tied up with an S&R at Fitzroy Falls. I just wondered if something could happen before the K9 Unit get pulled into that. Your friend was in Austimer, yeh? Not out of the realms of possibility they run their dog along the Kaiung tracks?'

'Thought this all through, huh? Seriously.' Palotto gave a small laugh, not unkindly. 'C'mon.' She pushed back her stool. 'Let's get some tucker. I'll call Rob while we wait for our order.'

Scobie felt her body loosen a little as some of the tension in her muscles released. It was after eight-thirty, she was tired and had a long drive back to Sydney but felt it rude not to share a meal considering the help she'd asked and was now being offered.

'My shout then.'

Chapter 23

Dif roused before first light, a cold breeze rolling along the riverbed, chilled above the water's flow. He wanted a fire and a hot drink but was more desperate to get moving. He tore the plastic from a snack-bar and took a bite before dressing his feet. Overnight his wounds had dried some. He wrapped his soles in the torn fabric then fitted his socks over the top and laced his boots. He'd be hobbling however he tried to walk, he'd just have to push through.

Gathering his meagre gear, he tied his bedroll, shook the water bottle and emptied it down his throat. He kicked sand over last night's fireplace and walked to the river to refill his bottle.

Pink light rimed the treetops on the eastern edge of the waterway. Kneeling to the water, the weight on the balls of his feet was already painful. *Whatev's. Move along mate.*

*

Feeling stymied and with only a few days left on her leave, Cal had to come up with something before time ran out, for Dif *and* for herself.

Back to the Primbee lockup and get an engine or frame number off that pickup, link the vehicle to the registered owner and their address, with or without licence plates. She'd finally have a name. And why hadn't he already destroyed the vehicle? Was she off track? It was late model, be worth a bit, but no big deal if he had insurance. Seemed risky hanging on to something that linked him to the body dumping, if indeed Cal had the right one.

She left Sydney and headed for the South Coast, not keen on returning to Primbee after her last epic visit, but it had to be done.

The rented Hilux was utilitarian, and she missed the ease of her Ford with its updated V8 engine, beefed up firewall and hood insulation to keep the interior quiet. She'd also fitted aftermarket bucket seats that provided better support and safety. This cabin was noisy and the bench seat tiring. All the miles she'd been putting in over the previous weeks were beginning to tell, especially now she didn't have her favourite ride. When all this was over, she'd get onto a new car project. A semi-trailer passed beside her, the ute rocking in its slipstream. She took a glug of water from her bottle, focussed on what lay ahead.

An hour and a half later, she approached Primbee on the northern end of Lake Illawarra.

This time she decided to walk in, and to do it under cover of night. She parked the Hilux on the concrete apron fronting a tyre shop on the main road. It meant she had a bit of a hike to the lockup but if the owner was alerted by the silent remote alarm, she could skedaddle back through the bush to the main road. She wouldn't lose another vehicle to arson.

As she made her way along the track beside the scrub margin, she could smell the residue of the fire as she approached the layby where her Ford was torched. She couldn't see the blackened area, could only imagine it beyond the brush and scrub that concealed the spot. She got off the track into the scrub, swallowing down her anger and sadness, steeled and more determined to get the lowlife responsible.

She'd never returned to the place where she'd left her car, certain that the individual who was after Dif would have their attention well and truly focussed on her as well. For the first time, she wondered if there was more than one person involved. Dif had only ever mentioned seeing one man that night at the quarry, which had fixed Cal's thinking along the singular offender track. But it did appear there were possibly two vehicles involved. That didn't necessarily mean a pair worked together, and until now she'd assumed one person had two vehicles. Not unusual. But for a moment, she thought that if someone was concentrating on her, they couldn't really be tracing Dif as well, could they? Especially since she guessed he was likely some good distance away. Two people involved in a crime could make some things easier, but it also increased the hazard for both. They'd really have to trust each other. It was certainly another angle to consider.

Cal avoided the gate cameras several hundred metres beyond and squeezed into the bush after climbing over the low wire fence. She made her way diagonally to where the shed stood beyond the clearing. The weak light from a new moon was lost behind a low bank of cloud blown in from the south. She used her pinpoint torch to find a clear route through the brush, walking carefully though she was almost certain she was alone out there. Through the twiggy maze she could make out three small pilot lights that shone from below the roofline of the building, illuminating the front. There was a solar-powered flood-light activated by a sensor also mounted midway along the front fascia. She didn't want to set that off.

She remained well within the bush close to the clearing and crept towards the side of the building. When she was adjacent to the side door she'd broken into last time, she stopped and checked her gear. She had the pry-bar, her torch and phone to photograph what she found. She would have to be quick because once she hit the door, the remote alarm would alert the owner or security firm.

The identifying numbers for the Triton would be stamped on the frame and the engine. Both would be linked to the registered owner despite the licence plates being removed. The problem was that getting to the engine bay would require releasing the bonnet catch which meant getting inside the cab which could be locked. The frame number should be inside the housing on the right rear behind the wheel. Easy peasy.

Presumably, the lockup door would have been repaired or replaced since her last break-in. The treetops above her swished and rattled in a gust from the coast. There was no other noise except traffic buzz from the distant main road that reached her when the wind blew.

She scuttled over to the doorway, pry-bar at the ready. Her torchlight picked up a bodgy repair. The metal frame housing the door had been hammered back into alignment and the same barrel lock was still in situ. Kinda slack with the security. Did the owner think the cameras and alarms were deterrent enough? No matter. She rammed the curved tip of the jemmy into the same spot as before and levered with all her weight behind it. The door popped first attempt, the metal obviously fatigued now from the previous stretching and beating. Cal shoved the tool down her boot and darted across the floor, her torch held between her teeth, her phone camera at the ready. But something in the space seemed different. The sounds of her movement seemed to bounce off the walls. She lifted her head, grasped the torch in her hand, ran it across the floor, then higher, a metre above the floor. She was looking at the old beach buggy and the shelving against the wall. No Triton pickup. The nylon dustcover was roughly rolled and left on the floor. She was too late.

'Fuck's sake.'

She looked around. There was no point dilly-dallying but she didn't want to leave with nothing. What else could be of help to her? Didn't have time to go through the all the boxes and shelves. She ran to the first shelf of cardboard boxes, pulled one down, flipped the top, shuffled through the papers. They appeared to be business records of some sort, print-outs. No help with the vehicle problem. Get out now, she told herself. She turned and was about to run for the door, then saw the dim form of the beach buggy again. Those vehicles weren't registered for on-road use. The top-frames and shells could be bought as kit sets. Engines were in the rear behind the seats and roll-bar, usually old, air-cooled Volkswagen motors. There'd be an engine number. She squatted at the rear of the machine.

The engines on beach-buggies had no boot-lid like the VW cars. They were exposed which probably aided the cooling. She ran the torch-beam across the engine block. It was clean but had a fine dust of oxidation on the alloy surfaces. She rubbed her fingers along trying to find a metal ledge where the number could be stamped. And it was right there in front of her, framed by the loop of the fan-belt and just above the dipstick. Impressed into the support block for the generator, a letter and seven numbers. Take a photo, you nong. How long had she been in here now? She'd totally lost her sense of time as she steadied her phone and torch. She clicked off a few quick shots then thought she could hear a vehicle, closer than the main road.

She ran to the door, pulled it to behind her but the catch no longer met up. She saw a sweep of lights illuminating the saplings and undergrowth beside the bush track. Couldn't tell what vehicle was behind the glare of the headlights and wasn't ready to have her retinas totally blasted and blinded if she waited for a front-on view. She needed her night vision. She took off into the vegetation, squeezing her eyes for a few seconds as she flailed with her arms in front of her, waiting for her night-sight to come on.

She heard the vehicle stop at the gate and the door open but she wanted to make more distance. She doubted anyone would follow her in the bush with the head-start she had. If she got back to the main road in good time, she could lie in wait and see who came driving out of the track. It's not like there were any other vehicles down there. Hopefully, her rented Hilux parked at the tyre shop would be passed over as a shop truck.

She waited, lying on the sandy surface a metre inside the margin of the scrub about fifty metres from the junction of the side-track and the main road. She could hear the sound of someone bashing at the metal door jamb, trying to re-secure the building. The noise travelled easily through the cool, quiet night. Five minutes later she heard the low thrum of a sedate V-eight engine moving along the track to the junction. Range Rover she thought. And sure enough, that's what pulled up at the T. Maybe she'd come away with another rego number to follow up, and she was poised, ready to read it off and memorise it. But she didn't get the opportunity. The wagon turned left, away from her and there was too much distance for her to make it out.

Hot-foot it to the Hilux and give chase? Too little traffic—she'd run the risk of being seen tailing him. Still, she wasn't empty-handed. She had an engine number off the VW engine to follow up, try to link into the geezer that way. She stood and slapped the grit from her jeans, jogged across the road and considered how quickly this bloke always got to the lockup. He must work and live really close-by. It didn't seem to matter if it was day or night, he got there within minutes of Cal breaking in each time. So, he can't have been coming from Bidgee or anywhere north up the coast.

Chapter 24

Scobie drained her morning coffee and was preparing to leave for work when her personal phone rang. Sand Palotto.

'Any luck?'

'You'll be a happy gal. Rob took his dog there early this morning before work. I described the area and showed him the map you gave me. Dog zigzagged and latched on under the chute just as you described. He was gonna inform Wollongong Command. Only difficulty now might be explaining how his dog escaped and then found human decomp sign in precisely the same area as a DI in Sydney had been informed of a body dumping. D's don't like those sort of coincidences, do they?'

'Luck, I say. Everyone needs a bit of that. You and your mate have gone out on a limb. I'm indebted to you both.'

'I'll call in my chit sometime.' Palotto said it neutrally.

'I can live with that. So, presumably Southern Area have to act on it, even if it was discovered unofficially? I mean, there's possible evidence of a serious crime, right?'

'For sure. Reasonable and probable grounds for a search. And police use the volunteer group on big pursuits anyway. They're legitimate and the dogs are well-trained. As you say, it's gotta be looked into and they have enough reason now. If there's been a murder then it's all to the good, I guess, even if the path there was a bit doubtful. Hopefully those things can be smoothed over. They'll be formally calling me in on this anyway. My gaff while I'm covering leave.'

'Hopefully Dunbar at Wollongong can kick things in motion now.'

'Reckon so. Anyway, glad I could help.'

'Nice one, Sand. Take care.'

After Palotto's call Scobie packed her tote, went down stairs to the carpark and headed out to Richmond.

An hour and fifteen later she was at her desk with a coffee. The O'Neill abduction had become a homicide. Her phone rang. Dunbar. She steeled herself.

'Troy, how are you?'

'Amazing thing happened down our way early this morning. Off-duty volunteer search dog and handler were exercising on the bush tracks by the Kaiung River. Dog slipped her lead, handler found her under a gravel descent in the quarry, giving a positive signal. Course, you might already know more about this than I do.'

'Not sure what you mean, Troy, but that's great news.'

'So, combined with the info you've already given me via your source, we need to take a look. You must be satisfied with your machinations.'

Scobie remained silent.

'I hope there won't be issues arising from why the handler was there at all. Probably fortuitous it wasn't one of ours,' Dunbar said with a veneer of sarcasm.

'All good then.'

'Dunno about that. Depending on what we find, I guess you'll feel that the ends justify the means. I don't like having my hand forced.'

'Fair enough. But you've got the go ahead that was needed.'

'You think you've done me a favour?' Dunbar's tone was incredulous.

Scobie gnawed the inside of her lower lip, remained silent.

'Anyway, I'll need those other items, the evidence your source retrieved.' Dunbar's ire was distracted. 'Another call coming in. Got to take it.'

'I'll get them to you ASAP and I'll be watching with interest, Troy.' Scobie ended the call.

*

After Cal left the Primbee lockup she drove back to Zin's place in Sydney. It was late when she'd parked in the Petersham back lane. Not up to dealing with Spike and in dire need of sleep, she went straight to her bedsit in the backyard and dozed on top of the covers.

Next morning, she tidied up, put clothing into a laundry bag and turned in circles, aware that there was little to do in this space but much more within the walls of Zin's cottage, and still she wasn't keen.

Her phone rang. Scobie. Oh boy. Was she gonna dropkick Cal to the curb? After first giving her a mouthful after the scene the other night? Front up and get it over with Nyx. She took a lungful of air, held it, then answered.

Scobie's tone all business.

'Wanted to let you know right away. Wollongong Dog Squad got a positive for cadaver yesterday afternoon at the quarry. So now the search begins. I've filled in their DIC Troy Dunbar with more background. He'll probably want to speak with you, Cal. I gave him your number. Hope that's okay.'

Cal was in shock. Mild, pleasant shock. Was the kick coming later?

'Course. That's great, though kinda sad too, the body, confirmed. I'm at Zin's. I should get this stuff to you, the bits Dif got. You in Richmond all day?'

'Yes. Now our abduction has sadly become a homicide.'

'Oh, that's awful. The poor parents. I'm sorry you have to deal with that.'

'Not looking forward to my day.'

'I'm gonna check in on Dee and Banjo, get some more clothes. Probs head south again tonight or in the morning. I'll have the stuff to you by mid-morning.'

'Okay. Chain of evidence is obviously compromised but we'll see it gets to Dunbar. You and Dif will need to sign declarations at some point.'

'Sure. Um. Thanks for this.'

'Gotta go. Talk later.'

Cal heard the click as Scobie ended the call. *Jeez, you've really fucked up Nyx. Isolating yourself more and more, just when shite is hotting up. Nice moves.*

Cal went immediately to the garage and retrieved the OTR package and put it under the front seat of the Hilux. She went back inside her sleepout, shoved gear in her overnight bag and left.

As she drove west, she considered what might happen next at the quarry. The cadaver dog got a positive hit. The detectives would still need to find actual evidence and it wouldn't be like sieving shovel-loads of dirt at a shallow gravesite. The gravel and rock piles she'd seen were enormous and probably contained tonnes of material. They'd be unstable as well she imagined. Not an easy quest.

Her phone rang. She put Dee on speaker.

'Hey, mate. Sorry to bother you but I might need a hand. Banjo's temp's up a little. I'm putting him on an antibiotic drip. I don't want to leave him but I've got a pregnant mare to check on near Richmond.'

'No worries. Not far away now. Just dropping something to Scobie then I'll be home. Less than ten minutes.'

'Thanks, Cal.'

'He gonna be okay?'

'Not sure. It's not a good sign.'

Cal put her foot down, called Scobie.

'Can you meet me in the car-park in five minutes? I'm needed at home, in a bit of a hurry.'

'Of course.'

Cal dropped a cog and floored the accelerator, hit the off-ramp three minutes later, ran an amber light, then lost some rubber doing a U-turn outside the locked car-park. She got out, retrieved the package from under the seat and took it to Scobie, who reached through the gate of the locked compound.

'Nothing like bringing attention to yourself,' Scobie said.

'Could say the same to you. S'pose a quickie's out of the question?'

Scobie rolled her eyes and returned to the side-entrance pathway. Cal was sure she detected a bit of extra swing in the sashay.

Cal drove quickly up the gravel drive at Kurrajong, didn't stop to greet the donkeys, parked directly outside Dee's cottage, grabbed her tote bag and hurried to the back door. Dee was in the kitchen. They had a quick hug.

'He's in the front room still. Didn't want to move him. I've set the drip up there. He's mildly sedated. If you could just sit with him until I get back.' Dee spoke quietly.

'No probs. You think the wound might be infected? Inside?' Cal whispered back.

'Maybe. There's no discharge. I just don't want to take any chances. I don't know how long I'll be.'

Cal put her hand on Dee's forearm. 'Take your time. I'm happy to wait with him, however long.'

After Dee had driven off, Cal walked over to the porch and nudged her boots off so she could approach

Banjo quietly along the polished wooden floor. Dee had positioned her patient in a large basket with layered blankets puffed around him. It was a cool day and the sunlight that came through the front windows fell in a broad swathe wouldn't have adversely affected his temperature. A drip tube was taped into one foreleg. Cal put her bag on the floor and lay on her side on the carpet beside Banjo. His eyes remained closed. She whispered a greeting and closed her eyes, concentrating on his breathing.

Having convinced herself that Banjo was relaxed and sleeping, Cal pulled her messenger satchel over and withdrew her laptop. Time to follow up the VW engine.

She began with a search of VW enthusiast clubs. Those beach buggies were mostly around in the sixties and seventies, and to her knowledge the one she'd seen looked like an original, the fibreglass bodywork faded and split in places—definitely not a recent attempt. She could be going a long way back. The air-cooled four-cylinder engines had been made since the mid-forties, wartime. Still, there were plenty of fanatics and clubs still around and she hoped that one of the nerds could help her out.

She began with online searches and wrote a form query, using the engine number she had from the lockup. She said in the email that she was trying to trace the engine's history as she was a curious novice. She hoped the engine had been sourced locally though there was no guarantee of that. One club had historic black and white photos of dune-buggies racing in the sand-hills edging the national park further north around Bundeena and Maianbar nearly five decades prior. Another photo had a line-up of the compact machines, with the drivers posing in front of them wearing nothing more than tans and Speedos. The cars had no racing safety harnesses either, just roll bars that wouldn't do much except save the vehicle from being crushed if the driver was thrown out.

She sent off the email to as many clubs as she could find in NSW. She might not get any response and it could take weeks. But she might get lucky, so she had to try. It was possible the engine originally came from interstate, but for now she focussed on NSW. Some of these boffins had an enormous depth of historic knowledge and were regularly online in chat groups. She might get a nibble.

When she was done, she dozed beside Banjo. She woke to her phone vibrating in her pocket. She propped herself up and checked. A text from Dee.

-All AOK here. See you shortly. X

Cal rubbed her eyes, looked at Banjo who slept, breathing steadily, and resisted an urge to smooch him. She rolled onto her back, gazed at the floral garlands and gumnuts on the pressed metal ceiling Dee had recently restored. She put her hands behind her head. Just keep still and wait until Dee arrives to appraise Banjo's status.

Fifteen minutes later she heard the approach of Dee's Suzuki 4WD.

Dee entered the room with a concerned frown as she put her medical bag on the couch and withdrew a digital thermometer. She knelt beside Cal and gently placed the probe inside Banjo's ear canal. Cal listened to the dog's steady breaths as she waited for the reading.

Dee withdrew the probe after a short wait. She smiled and gave Cal a thumbs up. 'He's dropped half a degree. Brilliant,' she whispered.

Cal gave a little sideways nod. 'I have that effect on people too.'

Dee knuckled her on the arm. Mouthed, "Coffee?"

Cal nodded and they both withdrew to the kitchen.

Dee spooned grounds into the stovetop espresso machine. She still kept her voice down. 'God, I'm so relieved. Another degree and I can relax a little. Thought I'd cleaned that wound thoroughly. Must've been some infection in his system.

His temp could still fluctuate a little but I'm happy with that drop. Thanks for sitting with him. You going back into town now?'

'Yeh, then on my way south again. Just some stuff to check on.'

'Planning on wearing your Ranger's uniform anytime soon?'

Cal raised her eyebrows. 'It does pull the ladies, it's true.'

'Pffftt,' Dee scoffed.

Cal called Scobie. 'Want a get-together before I go back down the coast?'

'Great minds.'

'Shall I grab some grub?'

'That's sweet of you. Already made you something.'

'Aww. You'll ruin me.'

'See you soon.'

Cal felt buoyed by a pleasant warmth. She wasn't used to being indulged since Zin had died. Her aunt had often pampered her with home-cooking and treats whenever Cal stayed in town.

She bounded up the back stairs to Scobie's Alexandria apartment. They embraced and went inside. The room smelt steamy with fenugreek and cardamom and toasted mustard seeds.

'Jeez, smells good.'

Scobie returned to the kitchen. 'Nearly ready. I've made you a curry.' She turned and smiled. 'My grandpop lived in Kerala.'

'Well, I'm happy to benefit from your geographically broad lineage. I'll just wash up.'

Scobie placed various dishes on the table—pickles and chutneys, and hot copper bowls with rich sauces and vegetables.

Cal sat, beaming. 'You've gone to so much trouble. I feel spoilt.'

'My pleasure.' Scobie kissed her on the temple.

They savoured the meal then retired to the couch to sprawl.

Cal wanted the easiness to go on. She was also desperate to fill Scobie in and find out if she'd come up with anything further herself. 'Can we talk shop?'

'Absolutely not.'

The doors to the balcony were open a crack and a light breeze kept the air pleasantly cool. In the background the city skyline glittered against the fading sunset.

Cal took a long swallow from her beer, clasped the bottle in both hands, leaned forward. 'Hey, something I've been meaning to ask about. Dif got a message to Greyridge cops before he took off. It could've meant the inquiry happened a lot sooner. Is that worth following up?'

Scobie was silent for a moment. 'Yeh. You did tell me that. I haven't had time to pursue it with everything else going on. Also, that sort of issue can be tricky.'

'You mean like jurisdictional politics or something.'

'Or something.'

Cal shook her head, frowned. 'Not really following.'

Scobie took a breath, put her hands on her knees.

'The DS at Greyridge, she's covering long service for the skipper there. I know her.'

Cal shook her head again, held her hands apart, open. 'I don't get the problem. You can't query a friend? It's off-limits?' Cal's tone bore a timbre of irritation.

'Oh, Christ, Cal. I was in a relationship with her. And you're right, it shouldn't be a big deal. It's ...awkward.' Now Scobie's tone was elevated.

Cal bit. 'So, what, I should be worried about it? You still have the hots for her?' Cal knew she sounded petulant.

'It's a bit fraught. If I'm seen to be questioning the integrity of her or anyone in her command, it looks shite.'

'Right. What's her name?' She noted Scobie hadn't answered her question.

'Sand Palotto.'

'Yeh, well, no worries. I just wanted to follow it up on Dif's behalf.'

Scobie replied quietly. 'I have a few other contacts down south. May not have any answers for a bit though. Have you heard from Dif today?

Distracted, Cal shook her head. 'Nothing for a day or so.'

Chapter 25

Stocky and muscular, DI Troy Dunbar exuded a quiet menace and energy. His dark hair was shorn in a Number One pelt without trendy fades. Mildly handsome in a brutish fashion, his bent nose and slightly undershot jaw gave him a pugilistic demeanour. With his arms at his sides, he often held his short fingers spread, primed.

He stood at the front of the Incident Room and briefed his team, outlining the information that had come via an alleged eyewitness and bolstered by an independent positive from a trained cadaver dog.

'Meantime, Media is putting their piece together and hoping we'll get some leads drawn via that announcement when we do make it. I'm bringing in all available officers as well as our core squad. Don't have to tell you how big this search area is.' Dunbar pointed a stubby finger at the aerial map on a visuals board.

'Foreman and manager at the site have gone through their inventory based on the last three weeks to help us with the grid search. We'll need to work in conjunction with their digger crews to move the gravel and rock. We've got two dog handlers on site as well to try and narrow things down. Greyridge are sending a few more bodies to help. I'll be liaising from here. DS Stuke is OIC at the quarry.

'Gate at the quarry wasn't broken into or cut. They used a key. I want someone working up a list of employees and former employees and anyone else who could have access to a key. Obviously it's not your usual dump site. Quarry foreman said some of these stockpiles can sit for years. The killer seemingly knew this—knew the body could be safely hidden for a very long time.

'But our first priority is finding evidence at the site and establishing our victim profile. The rest of you will be in here with all available uniforms taking calls from the public.'

When Dunbar returned to his office he got on the blower to Scobie in Richmond. He did the pleasantries and got down to business.

'We'll need a witness statement from this Dif Stangler. Currently dealing with hearsay. You know we require first-hand testimony.'

'Of course. But he's terrified, Troy—he's in hiding. He's not going to come anywhere near the South Coast. Greyridge Police apparently ignoring him reflects badly on us all. He won't go willingly to that jurisdiction. Assuming he's still in the land of the living. My contact hasn't had any communication from him in days. If he is still alive, perhaps we can do a recorded statement elsewhere? Can you speak with DPP and see what they say to that?'

'Likely to throw everything into reverse. We're trying to get some traction here and I'm not thrilled having to go through Richmond area command when I'm trying to run my own case.' Dunbar cleared his throat. 'What's your interest in this anyway? Your connection with this witness?'

'Look, I understand your annoyance, Troy. Really, I do. The witness first spoke to a personal friend of mine. This was after going into hiding and getting no action from the police at Greyridge. Anyway, the mutual friend brought it to me. I'm tied up with the O'Neill abduction/homicide. But we can work together and sort this. It's your case, Troy. I'll help where I can.'

'Can you tee things up your end for a statement if I get the go ahead from the DPP?' Dunbar said.

Scobie wiped sandwich crumbs from her desktop. 'I'll do my best. No promises. I'm certain he'll want watertight assurances regarding his safety, if he even agrees to it. I'll get back to you as soon as I have an answer. If worse comes to worst, DPP will just have to admit his evidence under the Hearsay Exceptions. There's provision in the law and Dif's situation would fulfil two of those requirements. He can't be found and reasonable steps have been taken to find him. And probably more pertinent, he's not giving oral evidence through fear. It's not ideal, I know.'

'Stronger for court if we have our eye-witness, but it is what it is.' Dunbar sighed.

Scobie outlined what Cal had told her about the Bidgee caravan and the possible attempt on Dif's life.

'Okay. Well, until we know different, let's plough on assuming he's safe. If we come up with enough evidence, the eyewitness account won't be crucial. Sorry to be brutal.'

'I understand. I'll update you when I have anything, Troy.'

After Dunbar had checked over the wording of the press release with the media officer, they both went to the media room and filmed the clip.

When he was done, Dunbar returned to the squad room where the crew waited in readiness for the calls.

*

Cal left Scobie's Alexandria apartment early the next morning and drove south to carry on with her search.

Parked near the coast and wondering how to tackle the silver Triton issue, an email notification buzzed on her phone.

She opened it and read.

Howdee. I may be able to help you. I'm club secretary and have been for some time now. We keep a lot of records because these old cars have been around for yonks and we old-timers are dropping off the perch. It's heartening that there's new interest and we're happy to share our combined knowledge. So, to your query. That engine has certainly been through the hands of this club. The engine was a Type

1 and an A code 1200 so it came out of an early Beetle. The original car was dismantled for parts because the body was badly corroded, beyond repair. The engine was used in a dune buggy belonging to another club member. This was back in 1971. Nils Larssen eventually became the owner of the dune bug and was going to restore it. Sadly, he passed away and the beach buggy was sold. That was our last record, 7 years ago. I believe his widow, Margurette Larssen, may still be alive. I've put her email address below. She may be able to assist.

Good luck with your research and restoration. We're here to help.

Kind regards,

Bill Toomey.

The excitement Cal had felt began to waver. What were the chances that this woman would still be alive or able to help? Still, she had to keep digging. She keyed off a quick email to Margurette Larssen and pondered where she could focus next.

Her phone burred. Scobie.

'Detective Inspector. How's tricks?'

'I think I need a holiday, frankly. OIC of the quarry case needs a witness statement from Dif. I know it's problematic and you haven't had a response for some time, but as Dif is the critical witness they need a statement from him. Can you just try and contact him? Ask him to do it?'

'He took off. He's not gonna come back here, is he? I can send him a message. Can't guarantee he'll get it, let alone respond.' She flicked her finger against the bottom of the steering wheel. 'If they find evidence of the body at the quarry, that's gonna prove something. They can go from there, surely?'

'It's about building a strong case. DPP need as many solid strands as they can put together and eye-witness testimony is a biggie, along with any compelling evidence. I'd really appreciate it if you could put it past Dif. And I fully get it's unlikely. I just have to ask for Dunbar.'

'I'll give it a go. Let you know.'

'You coming back up here any time soon?' Scobie's tone softened. The sultry burr threatened to turn Cal into a noodle.

'Yeh. Just following up a couple more things. Be in touch.'

She thumbed a text to Dif.

-Hope you get this mate. Cops need a witness statement. I know you won't return to Greyridge. Would you come to my place? Hole up there? No one really knows about it. I have a place I could stash you. Think about it. Hope you're OK.

She had no idea if her friend was still on the grid somewhere but she had to try. It was days since she'd heard anything from him. Maybe he couldn't get power because he was sleeping under a bridge somewhere. She was literally sending messages into the ether and hoping Dif was at the other end.

Cal had to wait on a reply to the email to Marguette Larsson, but she had several other possibilities to follow up while she was down the coast. One was the fact of Dif letting the Greyridge police know what he'd seen at the quarry and being ignored. If the police weren't going to follow it up, she was going to give matters there a nudge herself.

She drove to Greyridge and parked opposite the station, where a sapling lilli-pilli created a bubble of shade. She crossed the road and entered the building, a small, timber-clad structure, almost quaint compared to the standard Brutalist architecture of the stations in larger centres.

Beyond the reception counter—not glassed-in like some of the city offices—a male officer worked at a desk. A female plain-clothes leaned over his shoulder, discussing something on the computer monitor. They both looked up. Cal waited.

'Do for ya?' The standing officer spoke.

'G'day. Wondering if you can tell me the name of the officer dealing with the body at the quarry.' Cal attempted a friendly smile.

The officer pulled her head back, held her neck stiff. 'Who's asking?'

The sitting cop's hands rested on his keyboard.

'Cal Nyx.'

The standing officer came forward to the counter. Cal read her name tag. DS Sand Palotto. *Well, well, well.* She was about five foot ten, lithe, with short, glossy, chestnut-coloured hair that flopped over her forehead.

Her deep-amber eyes were steady and probing. She recognised something in Cal and vice versa.

'What's your interest in the quarry?' Palotto left it short, waiting for Cal to reveal what she knew.

'Friend of mine saw something. Made it known to this station. No one took any notice.' Cal's eyes swivelled between the pair. The guy at the keyboard looked uneasy.

'When was this then?' Palotto's hands rested on the counter-edge in a wide grip.

'Bout two weeks ago.'

'Ah. Meth-lab explosion up the line. Ds all busy with that. Could've slipped through the cracks. How was this information conveyed? Personally? A phone call?' Palotto asked.

'A note, I think. They wouldn't front here. Bit wary. Name's Dif Stangler.'

'A phone call or message would be logged. You have some ID?'

Cal lowered her head as she reached for her back pocket, flipped her wallet, flashed her driver's licence.

Palotto looked at it, handed it back. 'Want to leave a contact number? We'll check it out.'

Cal wasn't so easily fobbed off.

'So Dif wasn't known to you down here? No record?'

The seated officer did some cursory tapping at his keyboard, but was still listening, Cal sensed.

Palotto shook her head again. Changed stance, eyes going back to the desk behind.

The sitting officer looked up from his keyboard, nodded and spoke. His voice a higher rasp than Cal would have expected.

'DS Tambor was skipper then. He's on leave now. Dif Stangler was sleeping rough, wasn't he?'

'Yeh, he was.' Cal puffed out a small, frustrated sigh.

Palotto gave the officer a quick, hard look, then turned again to Cal.

Cal said, 'Okay. So, this DS Tambor, when is he due back?'

The seated officer remained quiet this time.

'Two weeks.' Palotto said. Cal saw the twitch of movement in her hands, the lift. Palotto had wanted to fold her arms but stopped herself.

Cal pulled a card from her wallet, slid it across the counter. 'Please give him this. I'd like to speak with him. Won't take much of his time.'

'Sure.' Palotto palmed the card and returned to the desk beyond the counter.

Cal went back to her car. They didn't give a fuck. Dif looked like a hobo, possibly had no family, or no one who might kick up a fuss if they couldn't be bothered investigating.

Back inside the station, DS Sand Palotto looked at the seated officer.

'Dif Stangler. I've seen that name. Something to do with the quarry search. Where's that briefing from last night?' She ran her hand through a tray of papers. 'You remember anyone leaving a note here, few weeks back?' she asked.

The sitting cop shook his head. 'No mention. Tambor doesn't have a lot of time for the roughies though. Thinks they're a blight.'

'Huh.' Palotto grunted, looked dubious. 'Anyway, carry on. I need to check something in here.' Palotto went into a side office, got online and pulled up Dif's record. Usual stuff for someone on the streets, or bush for that matter. Aside from the patina of rough-sleeping, he looked kinda harmless. Then she did a search on Cal Nyx.

Palotto read the record, sat back from her desk and raised her eyebrows. Nyx was a Kiwi, shot her stepfather when she was a minor, came to Australia and was fostered by an aunt, Zinnia Oslo.

Aha. So that's Liz Scobie's source. And true to type.

After Cal left the Greyridge station she knew she needed to move on. There was no more follow-up she could do with the police for now, and she was still waiting on a response to her email query about the VW, the frustration adding to her already strained and limited patience. Amidst all the vehicle leads she'd followed up, Pirate had found nothing on the CCTV searches.

Below her ragged synapses, a niggle scraped at the base of her brain. She thought over what Dif had described to her. He'd seen the body dumped at the chute late at night. How the hell had Dif gotten from Greyridge quarry to Bidgee, which was a good seven ks up the coast, in time to check in and get lodgings? It wasn't a 24/7 establishment.

He could've walked it but not quickly. Hitchhiking? He hadn't mentioned that, but it was a possibility. Still, surely it was after midnight by the time he got up the coast. Was it possible he just dossed down for the night somewhere near the quarry? That he didn't get to Bidgee until the next day?

He'd mentioned trying to notify the cops at Greyridge too. When had he done that? Could be she'd gotten her timings wrong on Dif's movements, and why wouldn't she? He'd said he was out of it and he'd not been that specific about his actions. Maybe Dif had scarpered up the hill to the top-site that night and dossed with others near Cobb's camp under the banyans. Before some numpty traveller gave him away next day to the Range Rover driver.

She needed to go back to Bidgee.

Chapter 26

CAL WALKED INTO THE office at the Bidgee Caravan Park and palmed five hundred dollars onto the counter.

'You want a cabin?' McHardie seemed confused.

'It doesn't fully cover the damage I know. It's an attempt at goodwill.'

McHardie left the notes on the countertop. Said nothing so Cal continued.

'Still tracking Dif. What's the latest time you'll take someone in?'

'Eleven pm.'

'Latecomers?'

'The No Vacancy sign comes on a timer at eleven pm.' McHardie huffed.

'Was Dif here more than one night?'

'Yes. He was more subdued the first night. I still had a rentable van.'

'Mind checking the dates again for me?'

McHardie flicked off the rubber page-holder with an irritated flourish and rolled the turning pages under the edge of his thumb. When he reached the appropriate week, he ran his finger down the page. The first entry for Dif Stangler was the last entry on the page.

'May 19th, like I told you last time.'

'Check over the page,' Cal said.

McHardie flopped the ledger pages around to face Cal who flicked over to the next page. She gazed down the first column.

'It's not a separate entry unless he paid out and then came back. Then it's re-registered.' McHardie turned back to the original page, ran across the columns instead of down. 'See, he stayed a second night, the 20th, which he paid for that afternoon. But he took off late that night and left me with the fire and the damage.'

'Okay. Gotcha, thanks.'

She went back to her car. She'd given Pirate the wrong date to check the CCTV. Dif hadn't been at Bidgee the night he saw the body dumped, the 18th. He was there the next two nights. He must've dossed elsewhere and gone to Bidgee the next day. That gave the Range Rover driver one night to scope out where exactly Dif was in the caravan park and the next night to incinerate the van. And that meant if she gave Pirate the new dates, maybe this time she'd find the Triton or the Range Rover on the footage. She immediately wrote Pirate a text with the new dates.

She tamped down her excitement, knowing she'd exhausted herself with little reward so far. Then again, though sore and frustrated, she hadn't come up completely empty at that storage shed. It was slow, but there were promising signs.

All the while in the back of her mind was Dif, the cipher. No contact for some time now. Was he safe? She had to plough on.

*

When the DNA lab test results came in for the items Dif had taken from the body, Troy Dunbar contacted Scobie as a professional courtesy since she and her contact had supplied the articles for testing. Scobie then rang Cal.

'The blanket, lock of hair and earring produced three DNA profiles—one male, three female. They'll need a sample from you and Dif to eliminate you both. Dunbar was surprised, expected two male profiles. Dif described that driver as heavyset. I explained Dif was trans. I'm sorry I had to divulge that without Dif's prior approval, but it saves complications.'

'I understand,' Cal said.

'They still need samples. You okay with that?'

'No probs.'

'And we still don't know where Dif is.'

'No.'

'Everything okay?' Scobie wasn't familiar with the terse version of Cal Nyx.

'Just a bit preoccupied.'

'Talk later then.' As Scobie ended the call she wondered if Cal's brevity had anything to do with their conversation the night before about her ex, Palotto. She had more than enough stacked in front of her without adding management of Cal Nyx's real or imagined slights.

*

As Cal returned to her vehicle she received an email notification from Margurette Larssen. She opened it, hoping it held good news—a lead, something.

Dear Cal,

I'm happy for you to come and look through Nils' garage. Everything to do with his cars was in there, and though most of his bits and pieces were cleared out, his paperwork was of no interest to anyone but him. In respect of that, I kept receipts of the sales of his tools etc. The tax department say for five years. (I should have had it all cleared out after last year's return.) You're welcome to come and see if you can find what you're looking for. I'm in a wheelchair and can't do it, I'm afraid.

Address and phone number below. I'm here most days but just check before you come in case I have an appointment in town.

Very best wishes,

M Larssen.

Cal had no time to waste. She rang and teed up a visit next morning. Another night sleeping in the ute. Getting too old for this. She bought a falafel roll and hot chips and parked by the point, watching surfers take the risky entry off the reef. She ate, walked to a nearby bin and dumped her rubbish. Did a few stretches. A cool southeast breeze crossed the grassy slope off the ocean. The horizon was broken by the outline of two freighters queuing for the port, their grey-green paintwork merging with the smokiness of the sky in an indistinct line. Whistling and peeping, three sooty oystercatchers skimmed the shore-break, heading south.

Cal walked back to the Hilux, got inside, pulled her jacket around her shoulders and closed her eyes. Her mind ran over the day. Sand Palotto, Scobie's ex.

*

Less than two kilometres along the coast to the north of where Cal was parked, the night-air thrummed with the growl of a massive diesel generator powering the array of floodlights at the quarry on the far side of the Kaiung River. The onshore wind carried the sound inland away from where Cal slept. Meanwhile, two teams of forensics techs worked several locations focussed on after consultation with the site foreman and management. Together with digger operators on overtime shifts, rock piles were laboriously scraped through for evidence. After the work of the clawed buckets, once the masses were stabilised, the cadaver dogs swept in and ran their noses over the area.

Scully, a liver-coloured German short-haired pointer zigzagged across her worksite in the damp gravel. She suddenly sat to attention.

Chapter 27

Hannah Griffith wiped the condensation from her refrigerated purchases before putting them away. She placed the tinned tomatoes and beans in the cupboard, snipped the bag of salad leaves, tossed them in clean water to freshen them up and poured herself a wine. She aimed the remote to the small screen and sat at the bench with a heavy exhale. It was good to be off her feet. News Hour.

Hannah took a sip of wine, scrolled through the notifications on her phone, pushed the phone aside, and turned up the volume. Special item from Crimestoppers. Police were looking for a possible Missing Person. Hannah took another sip, held the cool liquid on her tongue, swallowed. Then she froze, her eyes wide, staring at the TV.

The screen was filled by two images. A filigree earring with a garnet-like stone. *Simone. She wore one like that.* The blanket, an old 50s plaid. *Simone used to put it over the tear on her back seat.* No, couldn't be, don't be silly, she told herself. How long since she'd caught up with Simone? Had a girls' night? She sighed. Everyone just gets busy, huh. Strange though, both those things, so reminiscent of her old friend.

She tuned in to the item again.

The police announcer was emphatic on his final point. 'Anything—no matter how insignificant you may think it is—we want to hear from you.'

That gave her the impetus. They could decide if it was helpful information or not.

Hannah picked up her phone, dialled Crimestoppers.

Chapter 28

NEXT MORNING CAL WOKE early and peered through the windscreen. In the misty distance the far headland formed a soft curve, its definition lost in a haze of wave vapour and cloud. Gulls silhouetted in flattened M's floated above the waves. Closer in, a small tern raced along the unbroken face of a wave, its wingtips scything the glassy wall.

Cal felt a burr of excitement about her upcoming visit to Mrs Larssen, despite her less than restful night sleeping in the Hilux. Maybe today would bring a kernel of progress. It was barely 6.30am and Cal didn't want to arrive at an uncivilised time for an older woman in a wheelchair. Then again, it was possible Mrs Larssen was an early riser. Who knew? Cal hedged her bets and unkinked her body with a stroll along the headland. She planned to leave soon, grab a coffee and a bite before heading to Berry. Meantime, she drank in the surrounds and centred herself, perched on a low log fence facing the point.

Half a dozen riders were already out beyond the reef, waiting for waves, their dark, rubber-skinned bodies distinct against the leaden blue of the water and the pale grey sky. Though most people associated it with summer, surfing was a winter sport. The big swells came with the icy weather. Cal admired the dedication and toughness of those who pulled on a cold wetsuit and entered the chilled brine when there was barely light in the sky.

The Lexus she'd seen the first time with the Bidgee Boardriders' sticker eased into a nearby slot. She saw the surfer chick get out and watched as she unloaded her board from the roof-racks and set it down on the grass. Cal lifted her hand in a subtle acknowledgement as the woman walked back to her car. The woman lifted her chin and smiled. She was slight and sinewy, looked strong in an understated way.

Cal turned her body away from the woman so she could suit-up in private.

A few minutes later the surfer knelt on the grass beside her board and began scraping the surface with a wax comb.

'Tried it once or twice. Hopeless and too impatient.' Cal said.

'It's a bit of a thing.'

'And the balance, jeez. I love the water, but, nah, never got far. Stuck to body-surfing in the shallows.'

'That's fun too.'

The woman used two hands, rubbing the new wax block across the top of her ride.

'Must be peaceful, sitting out there, no noise, just rocking on the water,' Cal said.

The woman raised her eyebrows and nodded.

'The perfect escape.'

She stowed her gear in the boot of the Lexus, picked up her board and jogged for the rocks. 'Catch ya,' she called as she went past.

Before Cal left the car-park she wrote her phone number on a blank business card and stuck it under the wiper blade.

She signed herself "The Dog-paddler."

At the Greyridge shops Cal waited for her coffee and muffin. She knew Scobie would be up, getting ready to leave for work. She rang her.

'I met your ex.'

'Sorry?'

'Yesterday. I went to Greyridge to follow-up why Dif's message was ignored. Your ex was there, Palotto.'

'Right.'

'Is she responsible for the Dog Squad getting into action? If so, guess I can't be too testy about her involvement ay?'

'Oh, Cal. I don't want to get into this.'

'Yeh, right. Later then.'

Cal ended the call, took the proffered coffee from the barista and left.

Her phone vibed. Pirate.

'Okay. I trawled the footage for both of those cameras from 9.30 pm on the 19th and 20th. All black and white, obviously, so I can't give you anything on those vehicle colours. No sign of a Mitsi pickup at all. But I got a dark Range Rover on that intersection camera on the 20th. Going into the street to the holiday park 10.45 pm. Returned about 22 minutes later. I noticed on the first tracking the vehicle turning into that road—not from the main road but from the side road, the little layby from the play area. So I checked the CCTV from that camera on the changing sheds you mentioned and this bloke must've gone for a leak in there before he went to the caravan park. Like all CCTV it's grainy as hell but you could maybe estimate this bloke's height from the images.'

'Any joy with rego plate numbers?'

'I can't make out the numbers, Cal, but some of those techies the police use can enhance the buggery out of shit. It's a start though. If this is the vehicle you're looking for then this guy has to have some reason for driving down that road to the holiday-park and back. Sorry I couldn't give you more, mate.'

'Nah, that's great. I owe you one. Hey, unrelated, but some lowlife torched my Ford. I'm bloody gutted. Be looking for a new project.'

'Jeez. Scumbags.'

'Y'hear of anything, gimme a buzz.'

'For sure. Always got my ear to the ground.'

*

Constable Jesmin Follett put the call on hold and rushed to Dunbar's office, knocking beside the open door. 'Sir. Need to speak with you.'

Dunbar flapped his hand for his staffer to come in, his eyebrows raised.

'A woman, Hannah Griffith, says she recognises the earring and the blanket. Both items. Should we send someone or ask her to come in?'

'Where is she?'

'Hurstville.'

'Bit far right now. She give a name relating to the items she recognised?'

Follett flicked her eyes down at her notepad. 'Simone Pearce.'

'Get all the info and background you can get. Ask her if we can interview her later if necessary. Come back to me with everything you get when you finish the call.'

'Yes, sir.' Follett scuttled back to her desk.

Dunbar put the name Simone Pearce into the Misper database. No hits. He tried several different spellings of both names. Nothing. If Simone Pearce was the woman dumped at the quarry, it seemed she hadn't been reported missing.

*

Berry was about one hour's drive southwest through rolling countryside which made a change from the bland expressways Cal had been driving lately. Cops had DNA and a public plea for info. She had her own leads to follow up; maybe today's search would unearth gold. She thought of the call she'd made to Scobie and the crappy way she'd behaved, pulled at the seatbelt across her chest, tried to adjust out of her discomfort.

Early timber homes and commercial buildings, most well-maintained and restored, alongside street-plantings and mature trees gave the town of Berry a soft, nostalgic appearance. The Larssen address was inland of the town proper towards the foothills of the hinterland, in an area of grand old homes.

Cal found the large property, which had at least an acre of gardens surrounding a triple-storeyed colonial-style mansion. Traditional, white-painted clapboards, slated roofing and dark weather-shields beside the windows. Cal doubted they'd ever been shuttered; they belonged in the northern hemisphere.

She parked in the driveway under a trio of bare-limbed silver birch trees, their pale trunks stark against the deep green of camellia and rhododendron bushes planted behind them. The gardens were tidy and obviously regularly maintained, the sweeps of lawn closely mown. She crossed a pea-gravelled pathway to the front door atrium, rang the doorbell and waited. A large pair of potted cymbidium orchids stood in wrought-metal stands in the corners of the porch. Imagine keeping the dust and cobwebs off that lot she thought.

She turned as she heard the door open and was greeted by a woman in a neat woollen tweed skirt and crisp white shirt. She looked to be in her mid-sixties. Her short, curly grey hair was cut close, neat but unfussy.

She smiled. 'You must be Cal. Yes?'

Cal nodded and smiled back.

The woman delved into a discreet front pocket on her skirt and handed Cal a key on a tiny fob. 'I'm Jan, her assistant. Mrs Larssen says hello and good luck. The file boxes are in a cupboard in the kitchenette. The garages are round the side. Just drop the key through the slot there when you're done.' She nodded to a mail slot in the door.

'Thank you. Will do. Please give my regards to Mrs Larssen. I'm very grateful for her help.' Cal stepped back.

'I'll pass that on. Bye-bye.' Jan waited for Cal to turn away and closed the door.

Being introduced via a car-club contact seemed to greenlight any normal vetting process, Cal noted, happy for their trust in her. She followed the driveway around the side of the residence and found the large secondary building set back to one side at the rear of the house.

The triple garage was the size of a small house and probably better built and more salubrious than many dwellings Cal had known in Sydney. The white clapboard siding was dusty but sound, the paintwork well maintained. Shrub borders softened the corners of the structure. Cal went to the small side-door rather than the large front doors. There was a light switch to the right and the cavernous space was illuminated with a wattage that would've triple Cal's monthly electricity bill. What she would have given for such a workspace. Wooden benches ran along much of the rear wall and above several were tool shadow-boards like she remembered from her childhood, the silhouetted shapes of various tools painted on the pale green backboards so each piece was easy to replace when done with, and easy to find again. Cal walked across the space. Patches of darker concrete indicated where equipment and wheeled tool trolleys had stood in the past. A small partitioned-off anteroom at one end of the inner structure housed a compact bathroom behind a door and kitchenette. She could've moved in and happily lived there.

As Jan had suggested, three cardboard file boxes were stashed under the benchtop in a cupboard. Cal lugged the first one out and set the box beside her on the floor. She opened the lid and began her search. It was obvious as she riffled through the papers that this box was earlier records of parts and repairs. She was looking for post-2012, seven years ago, when Nils Larssen had died. She replaced the lid and turned the box around. One end had dates written in biro, "2007-2009". She put the box on the countertop and knelt down, swivelling the two remaining boxes so she could read the ends. The bottom box was the most recent, "2011-2013". She put the middle box on the bench and crouched to start on the third box.

Immediately she realised she was on track. The top two receipts were for a VW Transporter and a dual-cab Kombi he'd sold before he died. The guy had an impressive collection and both the vehicles had sold for close to twenty grand each. They'd probably fetch a lot more nearly a decade later. The receipts appeared to have been emptied from a hanger file and were no longer in chronological order. Sales made during his last years intermingled with the sell-off after he died. She had to read each one.

Not only did Nils Larssen have fully restored cars, he must have had a number of donor vehicles in other storage as many of the sold items were for separate engine and body parts. Collectors and restorers sometimes bought several vehicles in different states of neglect and made up one sound vehicle from the best of the combined pieces. The property seemed extensive and there were likely other sheds behind the house and garages.

Cal continued her scanning, putting aside the papers she'd checked on the bench beside the other boxes. She stretched the kinks out of her neck and shoulders and was three-quarters of the way through when she found what she was looking for.

It was a small, old-fashioned carbon-copy receipt book with a blue cover. All the dates inside were post-May 2012 when Nils Larssen had died. There were only a dozen or so receipts issued and the signature at the bottom was the same on each. It was a Larssen but Cal couldn't make out the first name. Possibly Mrs Larssen or maybe an adult child helping with divesting of the estate. Cal thumbed through the pages until she reached a receipt dated August 15th 2012. An orange beach buggy had been sold to a Sean Michalski for $3,800. His address was on the receipt: 54 Wallum Drive, Primbee.

Cal had seen that name before.

A current of excitement spiralled through her. Her fingers twitchy as she reached for her tote and unzipped a pocket at the rear, withdrawing the Bidgee Boardriders list Pirate had printed out for her. She ran a finger down the names and sure enough, there was Michalski. Her breath fluttered in her chest.

Chapter 29

Dunbar watched the interview with Hannah Griffith from an adjoining room. Simone Pearce still hadn't been reported missing by anyone.

DS Will Stuke and Detective Constable Mace Kivlin were conducting the interview. Stuke was a thin, pale individual with bony shoulders. His shirts looked like they were still on wire hangers. He was a calm and experienced detective. Like Stuke, Kivlin was in her mid-forties but had spent less time as a detective and often took the secondary role when they were interviewing. Kivlin was a trim, dark-haired woman with a neutral demeanour that gave little away and proved effective with suspects who were uncertain or anxious. Her dispassionate look seemed to draw out information from types who veered towards the wanting-to-please. Not so much with the hard-nuts.

DC Kivlin began with generalised questions.

'How well did you know Simone and how did you meet?'

'We've known each other for years. We both did an Ikebana night class and just hit it off, became pals. That was eight or nine years ago now.' Griffith's hands were clasped in her lap. Not surprisingly in the circumstances, she looked a little thrown-together. A woollen scarf and warm parka pulled hurriedly over her work clothes, strands of her chestnut hair caught between the collar and wrap.

'Where did she work?'

'In a florist's shop. Just her and another woman, Cherry Salas. She worked part-time. It meant they could both get alternate weekends off and keep their weekly hours manageable. Simone also worked as a translator. She did them online from home. She was fluent in Japanese. Did her OE in Hokkaido after high school.'

'Did she have a partner? Was she in a relationship?'

'She was married to George Billings.'

At the mention of this name, Dunbar in the Viewing Room indicated Officer Follett to do a records search. Back in the interview room, DC Kivlin carried on. DS Will Stuke had been taking notes as he sat beside her.

'Did you know George Billings?'

'Yes, I knew him. Can't say I ever really warmed to him. Simone behaved so differently when he was around. I'd meet her at cafés or at my own home. I'd only visit her place when I knew he wasn't there.'

'How was she different when George was around?'

'Just kind of ... cowed. He took up all the oxygen. She wasn't a submissive person at all usually. But when he was there it was like she disappeared. It was kinda disturbing to me, watching that happen to someone I cared about.

It made me wonder what it was like for her in private, y'know?'

'So, when did you last see or speak with Simone?'

'Probably about a month ago.'

'How did she seem? What did she talk about?'

'Well, she was pretty flat, I guess is how I'd describe her. It was sort of consistent with the way she was generally diminishing. I don't know how else to put it. I actually said something to her. I knew it was dicey. You don't bring up something like that lightly. Being indirectly critical of a partner or the marriage. It could cause a rift in your friendship. So I knew I was taking a risk. But I couldn't watch it any more. I know it kind of shocked her but I also saw that she recognised what I was saying. She got it. Someone outside of her saw what was happening. I think it brought us closer, despite my fears. She confided in me that she thought George might be having an affair.'

'What made her think that?'

'It wasn't a specific incident or anything—not that she mentioned to me anyway. She just sensed something had changed and that he seemed ... cagey was the term she used.'

'How did she feel about that?' Kivlin watched intently, moved her body slightly forward.

'Devastated. It's weird, isn't it, that someone could be so worn down by another person and then when their disloyalty and infidelity become apparent it's still utterly destabilising, even if—or especially if—it's a surprise.' Hannah shrugged.

'Had she ever talked about being unhappy in her relationship?'

'They had their problems like all couples. I know when she inherited that money George pressured her to put it into his business.'

'What money was that?'

'He had a building company but he was lazy and always spending money on himself. I suppose I shouldn't say that but it just seemed wrong. Simone was a hard worker. She'd inherited from her only relative, an aunt in the UK. George wanted her to sink it into his failing business. He was a handyman because he couldn't cut it in construction. The big jobs. Simone wouldn't budge. He couldn't stand that.'

'Would she leave him? Had she mentioned that?'

'Not specifically. I think she would've told me if she was planning that. It hadn't come to that point—well, not as far as I know.'

'What about an affair, if she was unhappy?'

Hannah Griffith sat back in her chair. 'You mean her? Simone?'

'Yes.' Kivlin nodded.

'If Simone wanted to be with someone else, she would have left George. It wasn't her style to do something behind someone's back like that.'

'Okay. So how often would you and Simone get together? I'm just trying to establish if it seems unusual to you, not hearing from her in a month.'

'Well, we saw each other regularly. Four weeks isn't anything odd. We're neither of us big on social media, but every six to eight weeks maybe we'd see each other in person. I wasn't concerned I hadn't heard from her...'

She shrugged and her face crumpled as her eyes teared up. 'Oh, God. What if something's happened to her?' Her hands went to her face and she hunched forward. 'It doesn't look good does it?' She tried to compose herself but a sob escaped from behind her hands.

Chapter 30

So now Cal had a name. Michalski. Was this who Dif saw that night at the quarry? Was she really equipped to front this person face-to-face? Maybe it was time to hand off to Scobie. But the moment she did that she would lose all control. If only she knew what Dif wanted her to do. It would be so much easier tackling this together.

Cal's phone burred. A text from an unknown number.

-Call me if you wanna leave the shallows. Or share a brew. Mieko.

Cal smiled, added Mieko to her contacts. She texted back.

-For sure. Cal.

So, there was a definite geographical logic becoming clear. Primbee was on the Windang Peninsula and it was close to Port Kembla. It was also the suburb where the lockup was. *Holy fuckin moly.* The nerves under her skin twitched into alert, like when a dog caught the scent of warm blood in the undergrowth.

She should she tell someone where she was going. She flicked off a text to Pirate.

-Mate, if I don't get back to you before 6pm, can you forward this message to a friend of mine?

She added Scobie's number and the address she was visiting.

Then she headed for the Windang Peninsula.

54 Wallum Drive, Primbee. It couldn't be coincidence that this address was so close to the lockup, surely? It was literally a matter of blocks away. She parked beside the curb outside the house. A concrete driveway ran beside the home to a garage set back from the rear corner of the building. She got out of the Hilux and walked towards the entrance. At the front of the house, the area beside the drive and front fence contained a small, dry lawn. A horseshoe of garden borders ran around its edges, containing succulents and hardy daisies. It was neat, if somewhat thirsty and neglected looking.

'He's not there, mate.'

Cal turned around, looking for where the voice came from. Across the street a tanned, middle-aged guy in a singlet was hosing out a portable concrete mixer on his driveway.

''E's away, 'nother week at least.'

'Can I get in touch with him?' Cal stepped towards the footpath.

'Overseas. Don't have a number. Just keep an eye on 'is place.'

'Oh.' She raised her chin. When did he leave? After the murder, maybe? 'Been gone long?' It was cheeky but she had to ask.

The guy paused. 'You a mate, are ya?'

Cal wasn't the best liar. 'Nah. Trying to trace an old vehicle he bought.'

She couldn't snoop around with Mr Neighbourly there. She went back to her car. Maybe she could leave a note for him to call her. Seemed like a wasted trip otherwise. She fossicked in her messenger tote and retrieved a notebook. She tore out a page and wrote down her name and number. She asked him to call her regarding a historic dune buggy project her club members were putting together. Hoped it sounded innocuous enough that he wouldn't be alerted to anything. She folded the note and pushed it through the slot in the letterbox. The guy across the road was still spraying out his mixer.

'I just put 'is bins out for 'im. Been gone three weeks now.'

Cal nodded. 'Thanks.'

She returned to her car.

As she drove away, she considered the information that Michalski was overseas. What if he'd lied to Mr Neighbourly back there? And was he coming back in a week as he'd told his neighbour? What if she found out he'd left before Dif's sighting at the quarry? Another dud lead and dead end. Well, that wasn't confirmed. It was the say-so of a neighbour. And if he was indeed still in the country at that time, he was still a prospect.

But if this bloke was out of the country when it happened, was someone else involved?

Could Pirate get into airline travel records and get proof of that?

Cal's eagerness wavered. She felt the current distance between herself and Scobie as a chasm. She was floundering, inexpert. Scobie had been right; she should've left it to the professionals. And now, after her ill-advised morning call to Scobie about meeting Palotto, she'd pretty much isolated herself behind a wall of pride. *You're on your own, Nyx. Well done.*

She grabbed a coffee and drove to the coast. She went over it all again until her brain fuzzed with static.

So, what was the thing she was missing? Who drove that Range Rover? Who'd make the risky trip back to the quarry camp to ask about Dif?

*

Dunbar tidied his desktop and turned off his computer. It was 8.15 pm. He was tired, hungry and irritable. A massive case, one good lead, no new evidence. Stasis. He pulled on a light sports coat. As he dropped his phone into an inside pocket it rang in his fingers. DS Stuke.

'Skip, we've got something.'

'Speak to me.'

'We've found bone pieces. Got some femur and other bits. Best thing, we got a section of jawbone.'

'Tell me there's teeth.'

'There's teeth Skip.'

'Yesss.'

'Forensics have asked for dental records of Simone Pearce.'

'I'll get someone on to it now. Great work, guys.'

Dunbar hung up. Thumped his fist on the desk. He felt the old conflict — elation that the team had made an important find and a dark sadness at what had led to that evidence.

He strode into the Incident Room. Constable Jesmin Follett was still working the phones from the Crimestoppers release. Dunbar lifted his chin to get her attention. When she'd finished the call, she waited.

'Get onto all the dentists on the coast. We're after Simone Pearce's records. Forensics need them ASAP. Ask them to be sent through first thing tomorrow. Get some help from the other probies if you need it. Then go home, get some rest.'

'Will do, sir.'

Chapter 31

CAL HAD DONE HER best and still couldn't put it together. Imposing herself mentally on the problem simply created circular runnels through her brain. It was one of those times she had to drop it and let her unconscious do the work. She stared over the water from the Windang Peninsula. The sun was dropping behind her and she could feel its warmth diminishing.

It wasn't just her frustration with trying to help Dif, and ostensibly failing. She was also shaken up by the whole Palotto thing. *You stupid nong. What's wrong with you? This shit doesn't bother you. Why now?* She wanted to retaliate and she wasn't willing to look at why, but she knew she should. She felt threatened. Palotto was from Scobie's world, an orbit that touched Cal only peripherally. Cal was the outsider. And those two had history. Something else Cal couldn't share. So what? She had her own history. She was no saint or aesthete. Why did it matter? *And you've pissed Scobie off. You're on shaky ground.*

She wrote a text to Mieko and hit the send button feeling a tremor of anticipation and anxiety and guilt all at once. Then she began rationalising why she might be setting up a meet with someone in a bar when she was fully conscious of how unsettling her response to Scobie's ex had been. A hot vortex of grit abraded the inside of her skull.

Back at the Hilux she drove to Warrawong and stopped at a strip mall, went to a bottle-shop and bought a hip-flask of Smirnoff. She went back to the pickup, spun off the lid of the flask and glugged a deep mouthful. The liquor seared the back of her throat as though the membrane was raw. Then the molten roll hit her stomach lining, numbing the nerve-endings as it passed. She puffed short, hard breaths from her nose, stared into the growing darkness until her vision blurred then took another slug. Her phone pinged with a reply from Mieko.

-I'm at The Whistler. Why not drop by?

Cal smiled, flicked back a text to Mieko, replaced the cap, put the bottle between her thighs and drove.

The carpark at the rear of The Whistler was half-full which suggested either it wasn't that popular or many of the punters lived nearby, in university accommodation. As Cal turned the engine off, she could hear the clamour from inside the bar which seemed to confirm the latter. She took another swig from the vodka flask and tossed the bottle into the glovebox. She chewed a half strip of gum and walked towards the rear entrance, spitting the gum into a bin as she passed. She opened the door and a wave of warm air heavy with beer fumes and countless lab-created scents fumed around her. The room was low-ceilinged, semi-dark and crowded with bodies three deep along the bar to the right.

On the left a row of small tables ran towards a platform stage at the other end of the room where band gear stood in a haze of coloured light, silent before the return of the musicians. Behind the tables, a long, narrow counter and high stools hugged the length of the wall. No empty seats. Cal saw a face turned her way. Mieko raised the bottle in her hand.

Cal made her way over. 'Hey. Get you another?'

'Sure.'

Cal returned to the phalanx of bodies at the bar and eventually secured a Heineken and a Peroni. She came back through the crush and clinked bottles with Mieko. Cal wasn't fond of crowds. Still, she could forgo her discomfort in pursuit of a distraction.

She asked, 'Who's playing?'

'Dog Snot and The Fat Staffies. Know them?'

Cal shook her head. 'Any good? Seem popular.'

'Retro noise.' Mieko took a pull on her beer. She was dressed in skate-wear—loose, layered gear, not the midriff-exposing stuff. Her long dreads were piled into a knitted cap. Her nose had a bump along the ridge and her warm, dark eyes glittered with mischief.

'You at the uni?' Cal asked.

Mieko nodded. 'Teaching and research. Marine ecology and biochemistry.'

'So, you're working when you're out on your board, huh?'

Mieko laughed. 'Hard to switch it off out there. But I've never seen it as anything but R and R.'

Twanging reverb and random snare drum hits alerted the punters that the band had returned to the stage.

Mieko indicated the far end of the service area, still as crowded as earlier. 'Smaller back bar if it's too much.'

'Let's do it.'

After 45 minutes in the other bar they retired to the back seat of the Lexus. Then to Mieko's flat in nearby Mt Ousley.

Next morning Cal woke to unfamiliar bed linen and surrounds. She could hear water running, a shower. The sun was coming through wooden blinds beyond the end of the bed and she could smell coffee and warm coconut oil. She looked up and saw steam coming from a mug on a small bamboo table. She reached for it as she heard the water stop then a shower-door opening. She sipped the coffee. It was good and strong.

Mieko appeared at the doorway wrapped in a towel. She smiled at Cal. 'Hey,' she said.

'Hey yourself. Thanks for the coffee.' Cal felt slightly bashful which was odd for her.

Mieko rubbed her dreads lightly with the towel, pointed to another on the end of the bed. 'Help yourself. I'm teaching this morning. I've left breakfast stuff out. If you eat breakfast.' She pouted at Cal.

'Thanks.' Cal drank her coffee while Mieko rubbed oil on her skin from a small ceramic bowl that caught the sunlight in the window.

'Guess the salt is hell on that baby-soft skin.' Cal laughed, heading for the shower before Mieko could strike back.

Mieko was on her way out the door when Cal returned from the bathroom.

Cal walked over and put an arm around Mieko, gave her a squeeze.

'That was fun last night. Thanks.'

'Yeh. Me too, Ranger Cal.' She kissed Cal. 'Take care.' She went down a short stairway to her Lexus.

Cal dressed, made herself a piece of toast and Vegemite, filled her water bottle then pulled the door shut. She tossed the key back through a slot in the door and went to the Hilux. As she drove away, she tried to focus her mind and somehow obliterate thoughts of Scobie. Anything to screen off the anxiety and confrontation scenarios. But she'd gone about as far as she could, following things up for Dif. She bit at a hangnail. It was probably time for her to just pass on what she had to the police. And probably best she do it via Scobie. She had to front the woman sometime. There was no getting away from it. She was heading back to Sydney.

With a small diversion to Pirate on the way.

Chapter 32

CAL STOPPED FOR PETROL at Heathcote and flicked Pirate a text.

-Mate could you use a Futura shell? It's straight as, no rust. Bit of smoke damage.

As she left the service centre her phone rang. Pirate.

Cal put her on speaker as she fanged up the freeway. The old Hilux didn't have Bluetooth.

'I'm suspicious,' Pirate said.

'You should be. Need another favour. Can't ask you to do it for nothing. Can I come to yours? I'm about forty minutes away.'

'Sure. You mind grabbing us some grub?'

'Burgers okay?'

'10-4.'

Cal stopped on the way and went through a drive-thru. Plant-based burgers for them both. See if she notices. As she waited, she checked her phone. Still nothing from Dif. Cal squeezed her anxiety down, thumbed a message.

-Hey mate, you okay? Be good to hear from you. Doing my best here. x

It was late afternoon when she knuckled Pirate's door and went in.

'Found your friend?' Pirate asked.

Cal shook her head. She handed Pirate a takeaway bag. 'I've done my dash. I've got a whole range of info, like spokes on a wheel, but I can't nail the hub it all hangs on. Driving me mental. I need your wondrous talents.'

Pirate made an expansive gesture with her arms. 'Here to help.' She opened her burger wrap and ate a handful of fries.

'The elusive Range Rover. I need the name and address of the owner. I've hit a wall.'

Pirate nodded, licked her fingers. 'You get this outta town?'

'Taste different?'

'Yeh, sorta.'

'You like?'

'Yeh. It's good. Texture's not the same.'

Cal finished her fries. Said nothing until Pirate was done. 'Veggie, mate.'

'Cheeky sod.' Pirate wiped her hands and turned to the keyboard, took a long draw on her drink-straw. 'No rego, right?'

'Nope. All I have is maroon paint, sports option, roof rails. Owner gets it serviced in Bowral.'

Pirate looked to the ceiling, which wasn't far above her, then she began to type.

While she worked Cal stood. 'Just gotta make a call.' She went outside and rang Scobie. The call went to her message service.

'I need to talk with you, and I need to apologise. Also need to give you what I have in this whole search for Dif, see if your colleagues can do anything with it. You home later?'

Cal returned inside, perched herself on a threadbare orange nylon 70s chair.

Pirate thumped the enter key repeatedly. Wrote something on a pad beside her. Knocked out more instructions through the keyboard.

Finally, she turned to Cal. 'Name Simone Pearce mean anything?'

Cal shook her head, her mouth bunched in a frown. She went and stood beside Pirate's seat.

'Registered to a business Cedarwoods Construction. I do a search on that, go through a maze and she's at the end of it. I'll do some more burrowing.'

Cal returned to her perch.

Several minutes later Pirate turned to Cal. 'How 'bout Billings, George? She's married to him.'

'Got an address?'

Tapping, thumping. How many keyboards did she annihilate with ruptured key springs Cal wondered?

'Primbee. 231 Loftus Drive.'

'Fucking ka-ching bingo! That's gotta be him.' Cal squeezed Pirate's shoulders in a bear hug. 'You're a legend.'

Cal scrawled the address on her hand, grabbed her messenger bag. 'Gotta fly, bud. I'll get the Futura towed up here when they release it.'

'Don't want your car, Cal. Forget it. Oh, and that's for you.' Pirate nodded towards an elegant bottle on a stand beside the door. Its contents glowed amber.

Cal turned back as she held the door.

'Rose-hip syrup. Good for you.'

'Aw, Pirate. You're too kind.' Cal held the bottle to her chest, blinked. Then she closed the door and ran for the Hilux.

She rang Scobie as she started the engine. Again, it went to message.

'On my way. Got some good info. See you soon.'

It was dark and the traffic on the Princes Highway would be chokka. She took back routes from Undercliff, heading for Alexandria.

Then her phone rang. Dee.

Chapter 33

Dee only called for emergencies.

'What is it, mate?'

Dee clicked her tongue in a pause of conflict. 'Hope I'm not wasting your time. But I just got home from a late callout, complications with a foaling. I saw a vehicle parked down the side road. Lights off. Dark coloured 4WD. Posh one by the looks. Could be nothing, I guess. But why would anyone be parked there? If they were lost, they'd go back to the main road, surely? If they wanted to make a call, they'd stop back under the lights on the main road, wouldn't they? Am I being silly?'

Cal felt a cold pond slowly freezing over her guts. 'You didn't go near? Check it out?'

'No. Not on my own. I just went up our drive, got inside and called you.'

'Can you see it now?'

'Not really. It's so dark out. Definitely no headlights. Might've gone now.'

'Lock the doors, ay. Banjo with you?'

'Yeh. Sorry, Cal. Might be nothing.'

'No. It's okay. I'm heading to you now.'

Cal ended the call. Shook her head. A dark-coloured 4WD. Maybe like a maroon Range Rover. And Dif might be there somewhere. Might not. Cal hadn't told Dee. Had promised Dif. Still acting like he was alive. She had to until she knew otherwise. Had to.

Cal texted Dif's number and hoped to fuck he got it.

-You need to get out. You know the other safe place. Rifle in the wash house above the cupboard.

She made another call, this time to Scobie. Once again, it went to her message service.

'Change of plan, sorry. Heading directly to Kurrajong. Be in touch.'

Cal looked at the gridlocked traffic, stuck the Hilux in low and jammed her boot to the floor, swerving into the bus lane and down a back alley in St Peter's. She needed to get onto a route west. She headed for Burwood in heavy traffic, took the M4 as far as Rose Hill then the A40 to Northmead. Finally, she got on the A2 west to Richmond forty minutes after leaving St Peters. She floored the Hilux. *Fuck the speed cameras.*

Cal didn't slow as she hit the gravel drive at the Kurrajong farm. She could see lights on at Dee's cottage. Her own quarters several hundred metres away were in darkness. If someone was there to get Dif they could've parked anywhere nearby. It wasn't hard to get across the paddocks on foot.

The rear of the pickup slewed and fish-tailed as she powered up the track, dust and stones airborne when she jumped on the brakes and put the vehicle sideways to her cabin. She wrenched on the handbrake and crouch-ran to the side of the small building. In the darkness on the leeside of the cabin, she made her way to the rear, grabbing a length of hardwood from the firewood stack as she passed.

Dif probably wouldn't be in there and hopefully got her message to leave the silo. But she had to be sure. She listened at the back door to her cabin then slowly turned the lever and pushed it open, keeping her body back. She listened again. Her fingers cramped with tension. She rubbed them along her thigh, reached around the door jamb and flicked the light switch on. The sudden illumination seemed doubly brilliant as her eyes sighted back and forth across the room. There were few places to hide. Her bed had storage drawers underneath, her clothes were on a rack behind a curtain against one wall. She made her way across there, the chunk of blue-gum raised high. She wrenched the cover back. No surprises. She breathed out long and slow. Her kitchenette bench and table looked untouched. Next, she went to her workshop, did the same routine. Nothing.

Finally, she crossed the fifty metres of ground to the silo. The sky was mostly clear but the moon was a thin lemon-rind casting little light. Pretty though, Cal thought, enjoying a split-second respite from her anxiety. She put her back against the corrugated inner wall of the re-purposed silo and crabbed slowly up the curving stairway, head turned to the mezzanine floor she'd built above.

She was looking the wrong way. He approached her from behind.

When she came to, she was sprawled at the base of the stairs, her head double-weight, faraway cicada-like noise in her ears. Her hand reached for her scalp in awkward orbits. She tried to remember where she was, what she'd been doing. It was so dark. She moved her hands around beside her body, felt grit. She stretched wider and her fingertips reached the vertical corrugated surface of the silo.

She'd been looking for Dif. Or an intruder. She scrabbled, using the wall as support, squeezed her eyes, tried to shake the blurriness from her vision. She pressed her hands into the wall and held herself upright as a queasy, swaying sensation floated through her. She wanted to throw up. Maybe she was concussed. Where was Dif? Then her stomach punched upwards and she vomited, gasping and spitting as she fell to her knees.

She needed a weapon. Remembered the chunk of blue-gum, found it beside the silo stairs. She staggered beyond the silo, got her bearings and headed for a copse of trees surrounding a massive old gum tree about two hundred metres away. Hurry up, she urged herself, despite wanting to curl up with heavy sedation.

Be quiet and find Dif. Some other stalker might be out there. Someone dangerous. Dif didn't hit you on the head. She made a circuitous stumbling recce, hiding in brush, getting herself closer to the big, central tree.

Crouching in the dust under an acacia, she closed her eyes, blinked them open and focussed through the gaunt branches to the upper reaches of the primeval eucalypt.

Then she heard something nearby. Delicate, in the sand of the ground, not above against a branch. A critter perhaps. She focussed again on the mass of the shadowed tree. Then she heard a more emphatic sound, guttural and vibrating through the air. A warning growl. A body hurtled past her and thudded into something to the right of her, metres away. A wild, bestial noise, savage and wet. Then the cries of a human in distress.

A light shone down from the tree onto a churning mass, dust plumes rising into the yellow beam. A man and a dog. An arm, rising and falling, a knife driving down.

'No!' Cal yelled, running with her club, smashing it into his shoulder and head again and again, avoiding his arm close to the dog. The man fell back with a roar of frustration. Now Banjo's jaws went at the man's throat.

'Hold, Banjo. Hold!' Cal yelled, with one almighty swing of the log against the momentarily stilled side of the man's head. And the thrashing stopped but not the throaty racket from Banjo's maw.

'Good dog. Leave.'

Banjo released, sat.

Another figure thumped onto the ground from the tree at Cal's side.

'Nice timing, Tarzan.' Cal panted, looking at Dif's lanky form. 'You okay?'

'Sweet as.' His voice croaky.

'Dee must've let him out to pee, or he broke out. Bloody Rin Tin Tin.' Cal ran her hands along the dog's flanks, felt warm stickiness. 'Gotta get you help, buddy,' she said to the dog.

She squinted as another pulse of nausea nudged her stomach and her headache thudded behind her eyes. 'You wearing a belt?' She asked Dif.

He nodded.

Cal held her hand out. 'Gimme.'

Dif unleashed it from his jeans' waist, handed it over.

Cal wrapped it around the prone figure's ankles, turned to Dif. 'Do it up tight. You be right with this prick for a minute?' She handed Dif the lump of firewood. 'Hit him again if you need to.' She lifted Banjo into her arms.

'Course,' Dif said.

Cal scooted back to Dee's. Banjo was a heavy for a dog who seemed compact.

Dee had heard the ruckus, raced down the steps to help Cal.

'Sorry to undo all your recent care. He's a bloody hero. Bastard had a knife. Hope you can sort it. You want me here? Dif's back with the low-life. I'll explain later,' she panted.

'Just help me get him sedated.'

They carried the dog to Dee's stand-by emergency set-up beyond the kitchen, laid him on the stainless table. He wasn't fighting them. His eyes were open, and he panted gently, flopped in their arms, benign. Blood drips indicated their path down the hall and into the room. Cal felt woozy. Dee looked and felt her way around Banjo's body, checked inside his gums. Once she'd injected a sedative into the scruff of his neck she turned to Cal.

'Go do what you need to. With any luck the injuries are muscular, repairable, not his vital organs. I may need a hand to get him into recovery.'

Cal stumbled back outside, pulled her phone, dialled triple one and asked for Police as she made her way back to where she'd left Dif.

She called as she approached. 'All good, mate? Cops are on their way. Maybe put your torch on so they can see us.'

There was no reply.

Dif was lying prone, his head against the tree trunk. He moaned quietly.

'Fuck. Fuck.' Cal knelt, slapped her friend's face gently. 'Dif, can you hear me?' She cradled his head.

Dif opened his eyes, squinted, closed them again. 'Sorry, Cal. He was playing possum.' Dif groaned with the effort of speaking. 'He kicked me down. Must've hit my head on the trunk.'

'We gotta get outta here. Can you walk?'

'Yeh. Give me a hand.' Dif reached for Cal's shoulder and they both struggled upright.

'C'mon. We're gonna get this maggot.'

The pair stumbled towards Cal's cabin and the Hilux. What a pair of crocks, Cal thought, fighting her blurred vision and sickness. She opened the passenger door for Dif, then ran to the driver's side and fired the ignition. She took off down the driveway and headed for the freeway south. As she powered up the main drag towards the motorway on-ramp she saw a pair of squad cars take the turn for Dee's, no doubt responding to her call. Well, she wasn't stopping.

'Where are we headed?' Dif rubbed at the side of his head. 'Man, I feel crook.'

'Should be some water under your seat.' Cal flicked her eyes at the speedo, kept it on 120 ks. 'Goin' south. Coast I guess. This prick thinks he's tidying up loose ends. We'll give him something new to worry about.'

Dif reached down and ran his hand across the floor, found the bottle. The blood going to his head raised another wave of wooziness. He scrabbled for the window winder and retched drily into the darkness.

'Far out,' he groaned. Opened the water bottle, rinsed, spat outside then drank. He offered the bottle to Cal, who shook her head, not keen on bile tainted mouthpieces, even from a mate.

'Sorry, mate. Not thinking.' Dif's sank back against the seat.

'Might be another one down there,' Cal said. 'Second thoughts.' She reached for the glovebox and retrieved the vodka bottle from the night with Mieko, took the lid off with her teeth and slugged. 'Want some?' She offered it to Dif who declined.

'What's the plan?' he asked.

Cal looked in the rear-view mirror. Traffic was light in both directions. 'Don't have one.'

They both chuckled.

'Wish I'd grabbed that rifle from the washhouse now. Sorry, mate,' Dif mumbled.

'Yeh, how come?'

'Wouldn't even know which way to hold it.'

'Fair enough. I'm not real keen either. Need 'em for injured animals sometimes though.'

Dif flicked his finger across the radio push-buttons, late-night talk-back. 'Got any music? Bit of a hike to the coast yeh?' He ran his hand across the lower parcel shelf.

'Coupla cassettes there.'

'Cassettes? Cal. Get hip.' He pulled two battered mix-tape cases, squinted at the scrawled lists, couldn't read them. Slotted one into the machine.

'You pick this vehicle because it matched your love of retro technology?'

'Piss off.'

'You heard of streaming?'

'Can't keep up with the inbuilt obsolescence, mate. I'm frozen in time, like something dug up from Pompeii.' She grinned, then winced as her jaw throbbed.

'You're shameless.' Dif wound up the volume as stomping 90s underground beats reverberated through the torn speaker cones. The pair began automatic head-banging.

'Fuck that hurts.' Cal laughed as the battered Hilux hummed its way through the darkness.

*

Scobie tried Cal but she must've turned her phone off, so she rang Richmond Command for an update from the night officer on the desk.

'Spoke to a Deena Mazzanti at the property. She was patching up a dog injured by an intruder. I asked if she'd made the 911 call. Said it must've been her tenant, Cal Nyx. Said she must've gone after the intruder as no one else was there and she'd heard Cal's vehicle leave.'

'Any idea what direction they were headed?'

'We're checking CCTV now. There was blood at the scene ...'

'Okay. Please update me with any developments.'

'Will do.'

Scobie ended the call, tried Cal again, left a voice message. "I'm worried for you. Please call when you can. Let me know if you need help.' She took a deep breath and held it before exhaling.

Chapter 34

CAL DESCENDED TOWARDS WOLLONGONG from the high escarpment and then headed for Port Kembla.

'There's a lockup. I've visited it a coupla times already. I've got a new address nearby. Might be where he lives. Think it's worth a look.'

'Okay. At least there's two of us now.'

'Exactly. The fuckin' A-team, mate.'

'Fuckin' A.'

'Too bad you rang the cops back there,' Dif said quietly.

Cal paused. 'Yeh. I panicked. Sorry. I get why you don't trust them.'

Dif looked out the window at the Port Kembla tower-lights and container cranes, lit up like a night football game. 'It's so ingrained that we should,' he said, his breath cooling into mist on the glass.

Cal drove along the Primbee Bypass and watched for the turnoff inland. She could smell the ocean through the air vents, the clean, cool air.

'How do you reckon he found your place?' Dif asked.

Cal slowed, made a right-hand turn into the suburb bordering the wetland she'd waded through. 'Probs same way I found him. Got a mate or himself into the Transport NSW site and got my address from my rego. I'm sure it was him who torched my Ford.'

She pulled over on a suburban street and turned off her lights, cranked her window down as she checked the address on an online map. She held it towards Dif then put it on satellite view and homed in.

'Just wondering if we can sneak in from the rear.' The aerial view showed a large outbuilding on the back corner of the property.

'We'll have to go through the neighbouring yard,' Dif said. 'Hope they don't have dogs.'

'Wonder what he's got in there,' Cal said.

'What are we looking for?'

'Not sure. Winging it. But there's still a missing Triton ute.'

Suddenly she looked up. 'Shhhh.' Her ears had picked up a vehicle accelerating nearby. At the end of the street, a T-intersection, a pickup drove through heading south. It was silver with a motocross bike on the back tray.

'Nooo.' Cal drawled.

'Like that one you mean?' Dif's hand clutched the dashboard as Cal pursued the other vehicle, her foot planted on the throttle and her lights still off. The suburban street-lighting was more than adequate.

'See if you can read the rego,' she said.

'Well, it's definitely not the plate I saw that night. That one ended in BB.'

'That was stolen. He would've put the original back on. No one's looking for that.'

Cal dragged the Hilux back into line as the back end lost grip on a corner. Dawn was still a way off and she couldn't keep driving with no lights—their proximity to the port meant there was truck traffic and port workers on the roads. Cal stopped before turning back onto the bypass to allow a small sedan to get between her and the pickup, then switched her lights back on. At the southern end of the peninsula the pickup was stopped at traffic lights and Cal was one car back.

'He doesn't know this vehicle. When I got to Kurrajong he was out stalking you and I parked behind my cabin. We should be incognito.'

'Wonder where he's going?' Dif said.

'We'll have an idea shortly.'

The lights changed and the traffic moved off inland. At Shellharbour the silver Triton took the M1 north. At Dapto it veered off inland onto the old Princes Highway. Then it turned left again towards Mt Kembla.

'Okay. Looks like we're going bush. Damn.' Cal said.

'What's up?'

'Gonna be hard to follow unseen out woop-woops.'

The Triton ahead of them accelerated up the escarpment. Cal no longer had a vehicle between them. She held back. A van passed her and dropped into her lane in front. As they climbed the steep incline the Triton suddenly took a deviation left along a gravel track into the bushland.

'What the fuck?' Cal muttered. She slowed as the van in front continued up the main road and kept her vehicle partially blocked. Cal quickly looked in her rear-vision mirror. No one behind her. She killed her lights and swerved left into the same track the Triton had taken. The red taillights ahead were already disappearing. She floored it.

Dif grabbed the handle above the door, his legs braced against the firewall.

'Do I risk my lights?' Cal said.

'No. It's straight for about three hundred metres. Then bend right. Who knows what's after that.'

Cal peered into the darkness, wound down her window, leaned her head out, slowed, slewed as she edged the curve.

'Can you hear him?'

Dif had wound down his window as well. 'Sort of.'

'Jesus, Dif, I can't fuckin' see.' Cal had slowed right down.

'I can hear him—sounds like he's going uphill again, pushing it. What's up here anyway? Aside from forest.'

'Think it used to be mining. Way back. Early settlers. 'Member we rode those old tracks one time?'

Dif squinted ahead, turned his ear beyond the window. 'Can't hear him. Maybe he's at the top or gone around the hill.'

Chapter 35

'THINK YOU'D BETTER STOP,' Dif hissed.

Cal slowed and gently braked. They both leaned out of their respective windows and listened.

'Anything?' Dif whispered.

'Can't tell over my fuckin' tinnitus,' Cal cursed.

'Let's run up on foot, have a look.'

They climbed out, closed the doors quietly and stoop-ran along the edge of the track to the corner of the ascent. Cal's nausea undiminished. She presumed Dif felt as seedy.

He was in front. He crouched and waved Cal down. 'I can see his lights through there.'

Among the tree trunks the headlights from the other vehicle were stationary, about two hundred metres away and shining into a clearing.

Several metallic knocks passed through the air. Cal recognised the sound of a tailgate dropping.

'Should we try and get closer?' Cal said.

'What if he leaves and drives down that way and sees our vehicle?'

'Can't remember if this road is a loop. Not like we can hide it anywhere.'

'Just take our chances, you think? Stay and watch?' Dif said.

'Yup. Let's get closer then.'

At that moment the distinctive sound of a two-stroke engine fired up. It revved then idled, remained stationary.

'He must've had a bike on the deck,' Cal whispered.

The headlights of the Triton moved further into the clearing and halted. The internal light went on as the driver's door opened, the driver exited. The vehicle moved forward then the light-beams curved downwards and they disappeared as a huge splash came through the darkness.

Mad sounds. A lake down there? Cal thought as the hiss and fizz of the hot engine bubbled and faded.

'He's gonna fuckin get away.'

Seconds later, the motorbike lights went on, the engine revved up and the machine sped away, not coming back the way they'd come but heading in the other direction.

'Back to the pickup. Run,' Cal yelled.

'We won't catch up now.' Dif stumbled and scrabbled after her as they skidded down the track to their vehicle.

Cal jumped in and fired it up, taking off as Dif was barely inside and closing his door. This time she flipped her lights on high-beam as they slithered into the darkness of the gravel road that topped out and began a winding descent.

'Must circle back, I reckon. Can't see him. You?' Cal squinted into the distance.

'No, nothing.'

'Okay. We've lost him. Back to that Primbee address? Reckon he'd return there or take off?'

'Who knows? What kind of logic does a murderer follow? Not getting caught. He's probably gone elsewhere.'

'We might find something at his place?'

'Why not tell your copper mate. You think she's kosher. Give her what you've got.'

Cal looked across at Dif without answering.

Dif mumbled, his head down. 'I'm wrung-out mate. With or without adrenalin. I'm so, so goddamn tired. And I feel like crap. Concussion maybe.'

'Not surprised. You done here Dif?'

'Reckon I am. I'm sorry, Cal.'

'Hey, forget it. You've been through hell. I feel pretty shite too. Want me to take you back to mine?'

'I'm just going to shut my eyes.' Which he did as his head lolled back on the headrest. 'But I know you're not done yet.'

'That tosser tried to barbecue you. Aside from everything else he did prior. You're right. I'm not quite done. You get some shuteye if you can. I've got one more thing to check.'

Cal dropped the Hilux down a gear and booted the throttle, no longer concerned with her lights being seen. Billings was probably well ahead anyway but Cal was primed for a confrontation. What had happened to

Banjo back at Kurrajong had melted away any remnant misgivings or hesitation.

As she drove through the heavily forested track, overhanging trees tunnelling both sides and above, she saw no glimpse of a taillight. Had Billings seen or heard them back there? Could be an ambush up ahead. Wouldn't be the first time. Why would he wait? But he might not have known he had a tail. Whatever, she was full-tilt back down the mountain. Dif was silent beside her, maybe even asleep. She frowned and squinted ahead as she pictured where she was headed. Her eyes burned, her headache bordered on migraine.

The sound under her wheels softened as she bumped across the transition onto sealed tarmac. Again, Cal dropped back a gear, screamed the engine to redline, changed up and blew towards Wollongong and the Windang Peninsula.

We followed him from Primbee, she thought. But it's near enough for him to have walked there from the lockup. Reckon he's parked the Range Rover there, out of sight. He got the ute out, drove to Primbee, picked up the trailbike and off he went. That's when we saw him. He's gotta go back there for the Rover if he wants to take off. Cal headed directly for the lockup near the wetland.

As she neared the approach and turnoff on Marsh Road, she slowed and veered across the driveway of the tyre shop where she'd parked once before.

'Sorry to wake you, mate.' Cal leaned across, opened the door. 'Outski, bro. Get in that doorway and stay there. Be back shortly.'

Dif shook his head, a groggy frown between his eyes.

'Go, bro.' Cal put her hand on his shoulder 'I gotta be quick.'

Dif climbed out, skulked to the shadowed doorway and sat down, pulling his knees up to his chin.

Cal yanked the door shut and drove onto the main road, taking the first left, the track to the lockup. As she passed the spot where she'd parked her Ford, she ground her teeth together so hard they squeaked inside her skull. She could see the security lights ahead over the front of the building. The gate was open.

She ran her hand under her seat and grabbed the wheel-brace, jammed it into the seat where Dif had been sitting.

'Not getting away this time, maggot.'

She drove into the gated entrance then backed up into the track at a 45-degree angle to the gateway, leaving a tempting gap. Probably wouldn't want to damage his bodywork going for the wire fence. Cal pulled out her phone and thumbed the address into a text message for Scobie.

Across the clearing, she watched the centre roller-door of the lockup ascend.

-Send the boys in blue. Now. Please.

Her engine idled as she gripped the steering wheel, watching.

The maroon Range Rover nosed out of the lockup and the door descended behind it. The driver had to be aware of her presence. No subterfuge. No hiding.

Cal revved the engine, dropped the pickup into first. She could hear the roar of the V8 as the Rover driver did the same. He was gonna go for the gap. The Rover's lights—now on high-beam—obliterated her vision like a nuclear blast. Cal dumped the clutch and floored the throttle. Her tyres churned sand. She aimed for where she imagined the front left fender of the other vehicle would be, timed for the line up to the gateway. Her tyres bit the compacted rubble beneath the sand. The Hilux launched, full noise. Cal threw her arms across her head at the last minute as she smashed into the corner of the Rover, skewing the opposite side of the vehicle into the steel gatepost where it embedded into the driver's side door, trapping Billings from exiting that way. So much for looking after the paintwork.

She shook herself, hauled the handbrake on, dropped the clutch to stall the engine and leapt from the cab with the wheel brace in her hand. Billings had undone his seat belt, fighting and flapping at the airbags that swathed his body. Cal swung the tyre-iron at the passenger side window, shattering glass across the seat.

Point made, she wrenched open the door and held the weapon high.

'Sit tight, Fuck-knuckle.'

Billings stared at her, his eyes bulged above the shining russet of his cheeks. He snicked the selector into Reverse and hit the gas. The open passenger door caught Cal as she tried to leap clear. She fell to the ground, rolled sideways, gasping, and grabbed at her back where the door had torn past.

Metal graunched against metal, a shrieking cacophony from the Range Rover's side panel folding back past the gatepost. On the nearside, the Rover dragged the nose of Cal's Hilux a metre before dislodging it, the passenger door flapping wide. Still holding the wheel-brace, Cal stumbled upright and threw herself into the pick-up. She dropped the tool, hit the gearstick to Neutral and twisted the ignition.

Meanwhile, Billings reversed back through the gateway, tearing the passenger-side-door back on its hinges.

He's gonna try for the fence. He's gonna get away.

The Hilux coughed but didn't fire.

'C'mon. Fuck ya.' She twisted the key again as Billings ploughed forward in the Range Rover aiming for the six-strand wire fence, clouds of dust pouring from the wheels.

No way they'll hold him. He's gone.

She planted her boot to the floor to open the throat of the carb. The Hilux sparked into life.

Hit him again. Do something.

The Rover bounced forward.

Cal slammed the gearstick into first and hit the gas. Steam gassed and billowed from the crumpled bonnet and surrounds. She pointed the truck towards where she thought Billings would exit.

But there was no impact. Just the high-pitched roiling of the Rover's engine and churning wheels. Billings had breached the wires, but the undercarriage of his SUV jammed on the lower bracing post for the gate. He'd not seen it in the dust, or forgotten it existed in his haste. No way that stump was gonna loose itself.

Cal watched through the open side as Billings shouldered the driver's door, but it was so damaged and crimped into the framing it wouldn't budge. He tried to crawl between the front seats. The passenger door hung open against the front fender, its bottom corner wedged in the ground and fence wires.

Cal left the Hilux positioned in front of the Rover, then grappled on the floor for the wheel brace. *Where's the coppers? How can I hold this prick?*

She got out, wielding the tool again.

'I'll fuckin use it,' she yelled as she held it high. Billings was struggling between the seats as he tried to make his way into the back. He reached for something on the floor behind the front seats. Cal could hear sirens in the distance.

Jesus. Has he got a gun? She couldn't see what he was scrabbling for. If he turned with a firearm she was done for. Chuck herself down behind the Hilux? That wasn't gonna do much if he was stood there with a weapon. *Do something. Now. You can't run.*

She threw herself into the Rover, the wheel brace in both hands, her fingers tight around the lugs on either end. Billings twisted back from the rear floor, his legs pinned between the front seats, left arm stuck under his body, his right-hand flailing with a bloodied knife as he squirmed to free himself. Cal's queasiness intensified at the sight. Made worse realising it was Banjo's blood on there. She lurched forward, pressing the bar of the brace into Billings forearm as her knees dug into his body. She made some unholy noise, her teeth ground together with the effort of plunging the tool downward as hard as her strength would allow. Billings squealed as the metal rod slid down to his wrist, levering it against the floor tunnel, snapping bones. The knife fell from his fingers. Cal released his arm and jammed the brace to his neck and jaw as he fell back. Her weight now sinking the bar deep into his throat as sirens blared along the track.

She pushed, pressed, squeezed, blurred red until they pulled her off him.

Chapter 36

SCOBIE HEADED BACK DOWN the hall towards her office then diverted along an adjoining hallway to the Interview Rooms. She opened a doorway into the Viewing Room where detectives could watch and, if needed, direct questioning through earpieces to personnel in the next room. Dif Stangler was sat at a table, his lanky frame hunched forwards, elbows on the table-top, his hands threaded into his hair as he held his forehead. Beside him an empty water bottle and coffee cup.

Scobie went out into the hall, knocked on the door and entered.

'Hello, Dif. I'm DI Scobie. Can I get you anything? Have you eaten?'

Stangler looked up; a tired smile shifted one side of his mouth. He shook his head. Scobie noticed the dark shadows beneath his eyes seemed more profound than in photos she'd seen, his cheeks pale and gaunt.

'Another coffee then?' Scobie said.

'Okay. Thanks.'

'I'll have it brought in. You did a good thing. Not turning away. You've helped bring justice for Simone Pearce.'

Dif gave a small nod. 'Simone Pearce. Now she has a name.' He dropped his eyes.

Scobie left the room then went up the hall to where Cal was being held. She knocked and went in. Cal was stretched back in a chair, her arms folded, her eyes closed.

'Hey.' Scobie smiled at her.

Cal opened her eyes. 'Hey, yourself.'

Scobie flicked her gaze up to the monitor indicating she had to maintain her professional demeanour.

'How're you doing? Must be exhausted.'

'I wanna collapse.'

'Get you anything?'

'No, thanks. Just wanna get home. See how Banjo is.'

'Of course. Shouldn't be too long now. They'll have follow-ups with you both another time. Get some rest. Call me when you're up for it.'

'Will do.'

Scobie nodded, left the room.

Cal and Dif were finally released after midday. In the back of a squad car heading to Kurrajong they had little to say due to fatigue and the presence of a police driver.

When they waved the police off Cal headed to her cabin and shot Dif a look to follow her.

'C'mon, you're safe here. Though you're welcome to stay in the silo if you prefer? I'm gonna check on Banjo then hit the hay.'

'Okay, I might go to the silo. Won't disturb you that way.'

'Come 'ere,' Cal said, approaching Dif with her arms open. She hugged him, held him. 'Bloody good to see ya, mate.' She let him go. 'Grab whatever you want from the fridge and cupboards. I'll get some supplies once we've slept. We'll have a big catch-up. Okay?'

'All good. Thanks for your help, Cal.'

'No worries, bud. We got there in the end, ay?'

Cal left and walked over to Dee's cottage. The day was one of those preludes of spring—clear sky, and warmth in the sun. She gave a gentle tap on the door and walked in, went to the pair of emergency rooms Dee had rigged up behind the kitchen. Her friend was leaning over a cage where Banjo lay on his side. His eyes were shut. Cal could see several shaved patches and stitched wounds along his flanks and upper thigh. She winced.

'How is he?' Cal whispered.

'Tough as teak. Still sedated.' Dee said quietly and motioned for Cal to move away with her. 'Think I got everything. Nasty, deep gashes at the back but they're muscular. He'll have to take it easy.'

'Good luck with that. Can I give him a smooch?'

'Leave him for now. He needs a lot of rest. You do too, by the look of it.'

'Yup. Going to bed now. So glad you were here for him. Buzz me if there's any change, yeh?'

'Course.'

Cal went back to her cabin, pulled the curtains, drank a huge glass of water and passed out on her bed.

Chapter 37

Late-afternoon, Dunbar called Scobie at her Richmond office.

'Towie and police divers pulled the Triton ute out of the abandoned tailing site at Mt Kembla an hour ago. On its way to impound now. They'll verify the engine and frame numbers. Water will bugger any forensic evidence.'

'Sounds promising though, Troy. Thanks for the update.'

'All good. Chalk this one up to Nyx and Stangler as well.'

'They certainly made their mark.'

'Unorthodox. You won't hear me encouraging Joe and Joanne Public to sort out criminal matters themselves,' Dunbar gruffed.

'Mm. Special circumstances here though. Dif was her friend and he had good reason to fear police involvement. Still, I take your point.'

'Lucky for us it didn't all go tits-up. And there'll be follow-up on Tambor I can assure you.'

'Talk soon then.' Scobie ended the call.

Cal slept for seven hours in her Kurrajong cabin. Woke around 9pm, showered and changed.

She rang Scobie. 'You up for a visit?'

'Sure.'

'See you in a bit.'

Cal wrote a note for Dif, pinned it on the door: "Let's have dinner and a few brews tonight."

She felt okay to leave, knowing Banjo was stable for the time being.

She borrowed Dee's Mazda runabout now the smashed up rental pickup was out of commission. That'll do wonders for my credit rating, she thought as she drove into the night, headed for Alexandria. Hopefully the police would help smooth things over with the hire company. *Time for some new wheels.* And no more trips to the south coast for a while. She was fine with that.

Then she thought of Mieko, followed by her impending convo with Scobie. She groaned and turned on the radio to drown out her brain-fuzz.

Just over an hour later she climbed the stairs and knocked on Scobie's door.

Scobie answered, held the door back, a wan smile on her lips.

'C'mon in.'

They didn't hug or kiss. Cal stood in the lounge, felt awkward.

Scobie indicated the sofa. 'Drink? I'm having a wine.'

'Beer, thanks.' Cal sat, feeling a dull heaviness from her shoulders down through her body. She cleared her throat as Scobie passed her a Peroni and sat in a chair opposite.

'Feeling rested?'

'Yeh. Look, I've been an idiot. I behaved like a prat. You didn't deserve that.'

Scobie sipped her wine, remained quiet.

'It gets worse.' Cal puffed out a full sigh, looked away then brought her gaze back on Scobie. 'I fucked someone. I felt threatened and I did it with someone else.' She looked away again, her face and chest hot with shame.

Finally, she took a drink of her beer. Her thumbnail picked at the label as she brought her eyes back to Scobie.

'Well, thanks for the apology. You are a bloody idiot.' Scobie paused. 'But we never set up some kind of exclusive thing, Cal. We can have that conversation. If you want to fuck around, be up front. I guess what concerns me is your motivation. If you did it to hurt me or prove something to yourself then you're harming others. Surely you see that?'

Cal dropped her eyes again. Wanted to lash out but knew she felt defensive because Scobie was right, and, *fuck's sake*, Scobie was being very reasonable. Cal brought her eyes back up to Scobie's face.

'I've got a lot on my plate and so do you,' Scobie continued. 'I don't expect being with someone to be without difficulty at times. But I do expect grown-up behaviour. I need transparency.'

Cal nodded silently. She didn't dare open her mouth.

'Maybe we'll talk about this more later.' Scobie put a hand out to Cal who almost leapt across the space - but managed several decorous steps - into the other woman's embrace.

Chapter 38

Next morning, in Alexandria, Cal checked a text from Pirate.

-Got something to show ya. Drop by when you're in the 'hood.

Cal rolled back over and pressed herself against Scobie's body, hugging her tightly.

'I wanna mess you up.'

'Be my guest.'

Later that morning, in Scobie's kitchen.

'You ready to hear what they've put together?' Scobie said.

'Fire away.' Cal gestured with the plunger. Scobie shook her head as Cal refilled her own coffee cup.

'Billings lived in Primbee, as did Michalski, his nephew. At this stage we don't think Michalski is involved. They both grew up in the south coast area and Billings was familiar with the Greyridge quarry from his youth. Sean Michalski does plant maintenance on the conveyors and the trucks. He's on a regular maintenance rotation there, as well as at the Port Kembla Container Terminal. He often works nightshift so they don't lose daylight workhours with stationary machinery. Currently he's out of the country and has been for some weeks.

'It seems Billings wanted to get rid of his partner, Simone Pearce. He was having an online affair and didn't want to pay out on a property settlement, so he decided to get rid of her. The planning he did will go to premeditation.'

'Lowlife,' Cal muttered.

'They think Billings wanted to use a key at the quarry because a break-in would draw attention. He got a key cut using Michalski's set. If he'd simply taken his nephew's key on the nominated night, he would've had to return it by the next morning after dumping the body. Too risky. Plus, it would've left Billings at the mercy of any plans Michalski might have had on the chosen night. Remember, we think Michalski was unaware of any of this. Getting the key cut in advance gave Billings time to prepare and take the opportunity to kill Simone Pearce when he had other things ready to go. Michalski's trip overseas also gave Billings an opening. Billings must've thought it was all perfect and untraceable.'

Cal scowled and shook her head.

'They think his original plan was to "borrow" and return the Triton pickup to Michalski's home garage. Michalski's vehicle was more ubiquitous than his fancy Range Rover. He'd stolen plates so Michalski wouldn't be caught up in his shenanigans. Billings sneaked in at night and got Michalski's Triton out of the garage. He would've replaced it later with the original plates back on and no one would have been any the wiser. Billings thought he'd be safe dumping a body at night in the quarry. That strategy got derailed when Dif saw him. Billings had to come up with new tactics on the fly because he was seen.'

Cal added her own take. 'So, Billings knew there was now a possibility that a link could be made between someone who worked at the quarry and a silver Triton. His nephew would be implicated and therefore it could lead back to Billings. If Billings hadn't been seen, it would all be sweet.'

Scobie nodded. 'He had to make it look like the pickup was stolen. But how could he make that appear random? Especially if it was garaged. Could that point to a workmate of Michalski's, someone who knew he was away, rather than at Billings? Billings had to avoid connection to anything to do with the body because he had an obvious link to the victim. The Triton wasn't ever reported stolen because Michalski was overseas and still is.'

'Interesting homecoming awaits,' Cal said.

'Michalski's neighbour was hunting the weekend Billings took the Triton. So he didn't hear or see anything. And even if he'd been home, he was across the street so he wouldn't necessarily have heard anything. He never physically checked inside the garage anyway. Just kept himself a visible presence and put Michalski's bins out each week so it looked like someone was home. When everything went pear-shaped, and knowing you were onto him, Billings moved the Triton from the Primbee lockup where he'd stashed it. He dumped it in the dam hoping it wouldn't be found, or not for a good long time. Those tailing dams are very deep. And the water would thwart forensics, which hadn't been a huge issue in his original plan. It was supposed to fix his problem, but he got caught out. Again. Thanks to you two.'

Scobie nodded deferentially, then leaned over and kissed Cal before continuing.

'He'd thought about all this for some time—planned everything. He never would have expected to be seen from the river in the dead of night by a rough sleeper. The other roughies were all at the compound by the estuary. Nowhere near the quarry. If it hadn't been for Dif seeing him dump the body, he probably would've gotten away with it.

'And your good work linked the two vehicles. The only leads were the silver Triton Dif saw and the maroon Range Rover seen by the other rough sleepers. Billings bought that Range Rover with Simone Pearce's inheritance money before he'd even gotten rid of her. But you tracked that down, figuring the driver must have been the killer. Plus, you linked his Range Rover with the lockup where he'd stashed the Triton. You tied it all up. You witnessed the Triton there before it was dumped, and saw that shield-shaped sticker identifying the vehicle as Michalski's, even though it had been removed from the rear window.'

Cal held her hands apart in an expansive gesture.

'What can I say? I'm a fuckin' genius.'

'You're a galah. Billings had a key to the lockup. He'd copied that as well from Michalski's keys. The damage to the door-lock was done by you, but it wasn't damaged before then, according to you, so it was opened with a key. Billings had to have been the one who put the Triton there because Michalski was out of the country and couldn't have done it. You observed the Triton there and then later saw that it was gone. So, both you and Dif are critical witnesses for the prosecution case.'

'That might be satisfying. What's for brekkie?' Cal asked.

'What do you feel like? You want to go out?'

'Nah, I want to stay in one place for a bit.'

'You need something grounding.' Scobie went behind the counter.

'You put your feet up. I'll do it.' Cal stood, nudged her away to the other side of the bench.

'Settle down,' Scobie jibed, then carried on with the story. 'Billings made up some story about Simone taking off with a bloke on a yacht. Saying she took off just made things convenient. They had a joint account for the business. They both also had separate accounts. She hasn't touched hers, obviously.'

'How 'bout an omelette?'

'Yummo.'

Cal gathered eggs, parmesan, tomatoes from the fridge. A bunch of parsley stood in a glass of water on the counter. She wrenched off a small handful, rinsed it under the tap, shook it and knifed through it on the chopping board. Then looked up from what she was doing.

'Even if Billings' DNA was found on the items Dif took from the body that night, the defence can still argue that of course his DNA was there—they were in a relationship. But if that blanket doesn't show any other DNA except Simone's and George Billings' and Dif's, then you have another strong pointer to Billings as the killer. Even if it's not 'clean' evidence in the manner it was collected and by whom, won't it have legal relevance in court?'

'Defence could try and lay it on Dif,' Scobie said.

'What motive would a rough sleeper have for murdering a stranger? How are they going to connect Dif to Simone? It's ridiculous,' Cal said.

'Defence can go for broke.' Scobie raised her hands, tapped off the points. 'We can link Billings to the site and the evidence, and we have a motive. It's pretty compelling. The impound boys found two keys on the key ring in the ignition of the Triton—one for the quarry and one for the lockup. Billings must've had a brain-fade. Forensics are checking the machining on the keys. It's looking like he made his own copies using blanks and a Dremel tool. They found a Dremel at the workshop so techies will be comparing the tool-marks. It's looking good. More evidence of premeditation. Plus, there's no reason for George Billings to have a key to the Greyridge quarry. He doesn't work there.'

'Dif witnessed that as well—Billings using the key at the quarry,' Cal said. 'And at the dam, he had the engine running when he guided the truck off the lip. So, the keys were in the ignition. If he'd pushed it in, he could've kept his keys. But then his steering lock would've stymied him I guess.'

'The last piece may be tying Billings to those stolen plates. The closeness between him and his nephew may not be enough. Dunbar's squad is trawling CCTV footage for the MacCauliffe Mill roadway for the 18th May when the plates were stolen. Something you pointed out a while back. Billings probably drove the Range Rover. As for motive, I don't think it's in question. He benefits financially if he gets rid of Simone and he can carry on with his new relationship unhindered. They're going through his computer and phone now. Affair started through an online dating site. Should have a timeline shortly.'

'Cynical prick.' Cal felt hollow. There was little triumph in nailing Billings. Sure, he'd likely end up behind bars, but so what? Simone's potential and future had been taken from her. Nothing counterbalanced that into any form of cosmic equilibrium.

Midmorning, Cal made a quick diversion to Petersham before she went to Pirate's place. She parked in the back lane and unlocked the gate, went to Zin's rear porch and unlocked the door.

'Hello?' she called out. 'Anyone home?'

She walked up to the first bedroom door, looked in. The bedding was neatly rolled on the floor beside the bed. Spike's still not using the comfy option, she thought. Probably feels safer down there.

She went back to the kitchen and opened a drawer, took out some notepaper and a pencil.

Hey, Spike, let's have a chat. I think we can work something out. Maybe along the lines of—you get a safe, warm sleeping pod, use of a bathroom and kitchen and I get a part-time caretaker and watch-person. Think on it.

She signed the note and left it on the table under the sugar bowl, then locked up and left.

When Cal arrived at Undercliff, Pirate lumbered down the long rear lawn to a pair of old garages adjoining the back lane.

She turned to Cal before they went in.

'Now, I know this isn't your usual. It's not Aussie and it's not Yank but keep an open mind.' Pirate undid the Master padlock and opened the door. It was dark inside, but Cal could see something under a heavy cover. Smaller, lower than what she was used to. She frowned slightly.

Pirate waited until she was in the room. 'Ready?'

Cal nodded.

Pirate flipped a light switch on the wall then tugged off the cover.

A roadster, mid-sixties, Datsun. Cal was familiar with the car—a popular, tough little convertible. Nice lines; squat, slightly flared guards. The body was patchy, half rubbed down, half in grey primer. Much of the trim was piled on the small rear parcel space behind the front seats.

'What's the story?' Cal inched around the vehicle.

'I'm never going to get to it. The Galaxie is way off being finished and that's my pride and joy. This is going to waste. I was planning to do some classic races in it, but I have to be realistic.' She shrugged her heavy shoulders.

'Jeez. It's outa left field. Okay if I pop the hood?'

'Course.'

Cal leant down into the driver's side, found the lever, and released the catch. 'This the two litre?' she asked.

Pirate nodded. 'Bores have been re-sleeved. Not even run in. Compressions all good. New headers. Carbs need doing. Minor stuff and cosmetics.'

'Probs need to re-do all the brake seals and lines,' Cal said as she looked over the engine. A simple pushrod four cylinder but the Japanese designers had gotten a lot of oomph from the small power-plant. And with the minimal weight of the convertible body, the little cars could fly. Handled well too if they had decent tyres on them. Cal smiled. Felt covetous of the compact speedster. Not a good sign.

'You've got my interest mate. I was thinking of a "sleeper" after what happened to the Ford. Something that doesn't bring any attention but under the hood has a really bad-ass donk. I need something to get my blood moving, y'know? If I'm giving up a rod, then I need a car that I wanna drive.'

Pirate nodded. 'Maybe you could tackle both?'

Cal high-fived her. 'Now ya talkin.'

When Cal left Pirate's place, she flicked a text to Dif.

-Gotta coupla car projects in the offing, might need some help. You want in?

*

Lying on a sun-lounge on the seventh floor of the Gold Coast apartment, DS Lyle Tambor flipped his sunglasses down and drained the last of his Bloody Mary. Bit decadent but, hey, it could pass for brunch, and he was on holiday after all. The vodka warmed his insides, an easy glow running through his shoulders and torso. He picked up his iPad and briefly scanned the weekend edition of *The Press* from NSW. He spotted and read a small item, his eyes drawn to the word Greyridge, then quarry. What?

Body? Husband charged by police. This isn't how the story's s'posed to go.

Tambor's blood chilled.

He dropped the iPad on the glass-topped table, stood shakily and grabbed the balcony rail for support. A sound ricocheted around his brain as the sun-lounger toppled and clattered to the tiles.

'You right out there, darl?' A nasal, feminine voice from inside the apartment.

If the body at the quarry wasn't Vic Lasprilla's work, what the hell had that shiny bastard been referring to?

Anything odd happens in the next fortnight, don't dig too deep, huh?

Lasprilla had paid him to take care of something. But it wasn't the body in the quarry. So, what the fuck had he missed?

And just how far was Lasprilla's reach?

Acknowledgments

A writer faces the blank screen or page alone, but a manuscript does not become a novel without the precious input of others.

I thank the following peeps for helping to get this book over the mountain: Renée for walking beside me through the early drafts. Marian Evans for her patient reads, tireless funding endeavours, endless optimism and for being a third of this Spiral Collective. Lesley Marshall for her generous and stellar editing. Alex Adsett and Nadine Rubin Nathan for their interest and editorial suggestions. Biz Hayman for her top-notch dark and moody cover design. Tracey Savage for coffee, moral support, lolly cigarettes and proof-reading that went beyond proofing.

Thanks also to Julie Macken, Renée and Marian Evans for letters of funding support when you were all stacked with your own projects. Your efforts mean so much to me.

About Author

Kim writes from the wild coastal solitude of Aotearoa (New Zealand), the vast expanses of Australia and any big city that'll have her. She makes stuff. Her hands are ingrained with engine oil.

Also by Kim Hunt:

The Beautiful Dead, the first Cal Nyx novel, published February 2020.

The Corrector, an Evin Hart crime novel set in Aotearoa (NZ), coming late 2023.

The Freezer, the third Cal Nyx novel, scheduled to land in 2024.

www.kimhuntauthor.com